Someone Else's Baby

D0610725

Someone Else's Baby

Ruby Speechley

hera

First published in Great Britain in 2019 by Hera

This edition published in 2020 by

Hera Books
28b Cricketfield Road
London, E5 8NS
United Kingdom

Copyright © Ruby Speechley, 2019

The moral right of Ruby Speechley to be identified as the author of this work has been asserted in accordance with the Copyright, Designs and Patents Act, 1988.

All rights reserved. No part of this publication may be reproduced or transmitted in any form or by any means, electronic or mechanical, including photocopy, recording, or any information storage and retrieval system, without permission in writing from the publisher.

A CIP catalogue record for this book is available from the British Library.

Print ISBN 978 1 78863 777 0
Ebook ISBN 978 1 912973 13 2

This book is a work of fiction. Names, characters, businesses, organizations, places and events are either the product of the author's imagination or are used fictitiously. Any resemblance to actual persons, living or dead, events or locales is entirely coincidental.

Printed and bound in Great Britain by Clays Ltd, Elcograf S.p.A.

For Isa.
My little sunshine.

Helena Luisa Teixeira Lopes
19 March 1977 – 16 August 2017

Prologue

She's running as hard as she can on this cold blustery night, gasping and coughing, straining to breathe. No coat or jumper, only a torn summer dress and canvas shoes with not enough grip so she slips and stumbles towards the edge of the cliff. The black water shimmers hungrily, thundering over the pebbles as the sea comes in, rattling them like a thousand bones as it draws out again.

You call to her over and over, but she doesn't stop, doesn't look back because she knows you're catching her up. And when you do, you thrust your fist into her back. She falls into the night, her screams echoing around you. The thud of her landing on cold, solid rocks makes you shut your eyes for a second.

A light illuminates the tiny sun-room of a cottage down on the beach. Someone is standing at the window, watching you run away.

Chapter One

I'd made up my mind, this was the last time.

It was ten to three on a dreary Saturday. I'd normally be pushing Alice on a swing at the park by now. But I wanted this, I really did.

'You ready, hun?' Steve rubbed his hands down his faded black jeans, then opened his laptop and signed into Skype.

I paced up and down our studio flat, barely twelve strides in either direction. He switched on the TV in the corner and sat Alice in front of it. The rusk in her hand had gone soft from gnawing with her new tooth, poor mite. She'd smeared it all over her face and in her angel hair, which was beginning to smell. I opened the kitchenette window and breathed in fresh January rain.

'It's time,' Steve called, adjusting the webcam.

A jolt shot through me. I smoothed down my hair for the millionth time and plonked myself next to him in the old wicker chair, the one we sneaked out of a skip after the pub one night. That was before Alice came along and made us all sensible. It creaked its complaint as I sat down.

'Hey, how are you guys?' Brenda tickled the air with her finger wave. 'You look well, honey.' Her lips matched her poppy print dress.

I smiled back, wishing I could reach through the screen and hug her. She slid the beads of her crimson necklace up and down. So much about her reminded me of Mum when she was at her most fragile.

'Good Christmas?' Malcolm cleared his throat and said it again. He was a spindly man who wore smart V-neck jumpers. His black hair fascinated me; I tried to spot evidence of dye because his beard was mostly white.

Both Brenda and Malcolm were in their late forties, twice my twenty-four years.

'Alice isn't that aware of Christmas or Santa yet.' Mum's old fibre-optic tree balanced on the windowsill did the trick, but Alice had cried when the musical snowman couldn't dance any more.

'No Santa here.' Brenda exaggerated a sad face. They were cuddled up together on a cream leather sofa in the glass-roofed extension of their kitchen.

As though she understood every word, Alice gave a gurgling laugh. Her chubby little fingers jangled a plastic tambourine.

'Aw, did you hear that, Malcolm?' Brenda tipped her head so her blonde fringe fell across her eye.

'Thank you so much for the Christmas food hamper and the gorgeous pack of toiletries. It's really kind of you and was such a lovely surprise. I thought the delivery guy had got the wrong house! And Alice is besotted with her new teddy, aren't you, sweetheart?' I held it up to the screen before passing it to her outstretched hands.

'It's our pleasure,' Brenda said, turning her face up to Malcolm's. He smiled warmly.

'Yeah, thanks guys, really good of you. Right, are we all ready?' Steve patted my leg. We exchanged a glance. Everyone nodded in silence.

I reached down for my handbag and took out a long box. Brenda began half-crying, half-laughing. Malcolm brushed the tears from her cheeks with his thumb.

'I'll be back in a minute.' I waved the slim box at the screen and slunk away to the bathroom.

My fingers trembled as I ripped open the packet. I took a deep breath and sat on the toilet, pointing the stick downwards into the bowl. What if it was negative a third time? How would I tell Brenda this was the last time? The thought of failure dragged my whole body down. I hadn't realised this would be so hard. Each disappointment was like living through Mum's losses all over again. I shut my eyes, but my mind opened the image of Mum crying, curled up on the bathroom floor, her flowery dress pulled up, blood between her legs, on her fingers. She hadn't noticed ten-year-old me standing at the door, not knowing what to do, whether to tell her the chips were burning.

I pressed my knuckles against my forehead. My face was as pale as my hair in the shower door reflection. I thought it would be so easy. I'd fallen pregnant straight away with Alice.

When I finished, I sat on the lid, staring at the blank little window. One solid blue line emerged. Slowly another paler line appeared next to it. My heart skipped. I blinked several times, but it didn't change. This was it. Tears pricked my eyes picturing Brenda's face. If only someone could have done this for Mum years ago, we might still be a proper family.

Back in the living area, I kept the plastic stick hidden behind my back and did my best to keep a straight face. Steve stopped his conversation midway. Malcolm's chest heaved up and down.

'I can't look.' Brenda covered her eyes with her childlike hands.

'Keeping our fingers crossed,' Malcolm said.

'Surprise!' I whipped it out for them all to see.

'Oh my god.' Steve grabbed my wrist and peered closer.

'Brenda, look, look!' Malcolm shook her arm. Brenda peeped through her fingers, but he pulled her hands away.

'It can't be, it can't possibly be,' Brenda whispered.

My heart bloomed.

'Charlotte's pregnant. It's really happening.' Malcolm cupped Brenda's face.

'It certainly looks like it.' Steve beamed. He stood up and gave me a hug.

'It's such good news.' I held my smile.

'You all right?' Steve tried to catch my eye.

I nodded, my hand covering my mouth. Tears filled my eyes.

'Oh my god!' Brenda cried as it hit her.

'We can't thank you enough.' Malcolm leaned towards the screen, beaming.

My stomach tightened. I'd thought about being a surrogate for so long it was hard to believe it was finally *real*.

There was no going back.

Chapter Two

Steve shut his laptop. 'That's it then, we're on our way.'

I flopped out on the sofa bed and gazed at the soft cloud shapes and blue sky we'd painted on the ceiling. All I had to do was get on with my life for the next eight months and deliver this baby safely to its new parents. I touched my stomach and wondered at the new life growing there. But I kept seeing an image of Malcolm's sperm invading me, finding my egg. I shuddered. Too intimate, even though we hadn't touched. Steve had been the one who'd made me comfortable in the hotel room, carefully injecting the fresh sample inside me using one of those syringes from a kids' medicine bottle. Still, it would be worth it to see Brenda's face when I finally handed her the baby.

From the first moment I held Alice in my arms, I knew how lucky I was, how easy it had been for me. Carrying a baby to full term had been so hard for Mum, it made me think about doing this for someone like her. Make a real difference to their lives. As a kid, I remembered hearing a story on the news about a middle-aged woman having a baby for her twenty-something daughter. I'd only been about fourteen but I'd wished I was older so I could help Mum like that.

'No regrets?' Steve reached for my hand.

I shook my head. Meeting Kelly at prenatal class had been the turning point. Her baby had been due about two weeks before Alice. At first I didn't understand who the man and woman were that she brought along every week, but we got talking and I found out they were her brother and sister-in-law. Kelly had offered to have their baby. It was such a lovely thing to do. She said she couldn't watch them suffer any longer. They'd already lost two babies at around twenty weeks. Both of Kelly's previous pregnancies had been straightforward, so she thought why not do this one thing that could change their lives, make them happy? Hearing her story cemented it in my mind – I wanted to be a surrogate.

'How about you?' I looked at Steve.

'Nah, not at all. For starters, you really want to do this, and now it turns out I need to buy Jack out, poor bloody sod.'

'I know.' I kissed his cheek. 'That will be our priority as soon as the first payment comes. And I promise we'll be there for him, Janet and the kids.'

'Hell yeah.' His eyes reddened. 'I still can't get my head round it. One minute we're down the pub having a laugh, and the next he's telling me he's got cancer in his balls.'

'But he'll get through it. There's a good survival rate.'

'I know. Makes you think though, doesn't it?'

I nodded. When we signed up for surrogacy, we hadn't banked on his business partner falling ill. After surgery, Jack would have to start chemo, and he needed that money ASAP to pay the mortgage, support his family. Steve would have to take over his side of the business, or we'd lose everything he'd worked so hard for, and our future along with it. It'd taken him months to do up the clapped-out Subaru while finishing his apprenticeship. Selling his precious Scooby to start a business with Jack had been a big gamble.

'Malcolm said they'll send a cheque next week.' He lay down next to me.

'And after we've given half to Jack, we can pay our rent arrears and credit card.' I hoped we'd be able to put something by for Alice's future, once we got the rest of the money. I wanted her to have everything I didn't. Maybe I could afford to go to college and uni, train to be a teacher. I could see myself sitting at a desk stacked with books, rows of eager-faced children in front of me.

'We can go up town and have a slap-up meal.' He pulled me close.

'We need to be careful or the money will be gone in no time. Let's hope you do well at the garage once you're the sole owner. I might be able to increase my hours at the deli.'

'We need a new car too, a decent one with a bigger boot.' He kissed my hair.

'I want us to start saving for Alice as well though, so she can go to uni one day.'

'Do you think she'll want to?' Steve wrinkled his nose.

'Why not? I want her to have a better start in life than I did.' I rolled on my side and cuddled up to him. 'Everything will go smoothly, won't it? I mean there's nothing we haven't planned for, is there?'

'It's gonna be easy, you wait and see.' He nuzzled my neck.

'Easy for you maybe.' I nudged him in the ribs and he pretended to be wounded, half hanging off the bed. 'You don't think we'll feel like one's missing, do you?'

'It won't be ours, hun. All the websites say you need to start off in the right frame of mind. You've got to remember, you're just the incubator.'

'I'm the biological mum.' I sat up. It was hard to admit that I wouldn't find it easy giving a baby away. I'd read about a woman who'd changed her mind. Would I have a last-minute panic?

One woman advised trying to distance yourself emotionally. I didn't know if that was possible.

'You said you're okay with it.' He sat up and tipped my chin so I had to look at him.

'I am. I'll be fine.'

I grabbed my notebook from the pile of books on the carpet and flicked through the pages. I'd made a note of every single website and forum I'd been on in the last six months and written down a list of advice from each. Most said it would be harder the traditional way, because the baby was biologically mine, I was much more likely to become attached to it. But I didn't fancy hormone treatments or having an embryo implanted.

The first place I'd looked for advice was one of the mums' websites. I'd always checked there for parenting tips. I found a thread on their forum about surrogacy. I knew from what Kelly had told me that it was illegal to advertise yourself as a surrogate or intended parents, what the couple you have the baby for are called.

I scanned through some of the quotes I'd jotted down.

Lots of us prefer independent matching. There are some great private groups on Facebook.

The best way to get into the surro world is to chat to both surrogates and IPs.

Agencies offer you no more protection than indie routes.

Be aware that no surrogacy agreement is legally binding, so it doesn't matter what agency you choose, they offer nothing more than guidance and advice.

It is totally possible to do indie surrogacy, that way you avoid agency fees which can be very high.

We'd taken the advice and not gone to an agency. Not all charged the surrogate but you had to fit their strict list of requirements – some wanted to see a report from your GP, others were only interested in helping host surrogates – where they implanted an embryo in your womb – just the thought of it made me queasy. I'd spoken to lots of surrogates and intended parents before I got chatting to Brenda on a forum. There was one piece of advice I'd circled in my notebook that still made me smile: *You'll know when you've found the right match*. And I had known with Brenda, straight away. She said she'd been hoping to find that special woman to carry her baby and felt certain that person was me.

Steve plumped up his pillow. 'Sad getting to that age and not having a family, isn't it? I mean, they'll pretty much be pensioners when the kid's a teenager.'

'Lots of people have them later.'

'S'pose.'

'Not their fault, is it? Shows how lucky we are.' I picked Alice up, kissed her warm doughy cheek and squeezed her tight. She giggled softly in my ear, her blonde curls tickling my face.

'We should make a list of all the things you need, like vitamins and antenatal classes. They can pay for all that.'

'I think they'll expect those things to be included in the expenses.' It was weird to even be discussing money to do with having a baby. But thinking about it, it was reasonable for them to pay for certain things. As long as they didn't give us a ridiculously high amount, which could be seen as buying a baby. Giving us three cheques over the nine months was a good way of doing it, so we were in control of what we spent the money on.

Steve took Alice from me. I dragged my laptop towards me and logged on to one of the forums. I'd posted a question about whether the intended parents were legally obliged to let the surrogate stay in touch after the parental transfer had gone through. I clicked on the thread and several replies came up. I read them out to Steve.

'I take it this is in the agreement? As you probably know, agreements aren't covered by law, but in my experience, as long as both sides are happy with future contact, and are clear about each other's expectations, it's a reasonable thing to request/expect.

'I think you need to take into account that the IPs may want to go their own way at some point, so even if they say now that you can be part of the child's life, they could change their minds. I don't think you can do anything about that as they'd be the legal parents by then and aren't obliged to stay in touch with you.

'This is why it's so important to build a good relationship with your intended parents from the start. I feel I've become part of my IPs' extended family. I get to see their beautiful daughter at least twice a year.'

'I don't see why you're so worried when it's your name on the birth certificate,' Steve said, 'you hold all the power until you consent to transfer parental rights to them.'

'But it's afterwards that I'm worried about.'

'If you think about it, they're probably more nervous than you are.' He opened a picture book for Alice.

'But there's no reason why I wouldn't go ahead as agreed.'

'I know, but from their point of view they have to hope that *you* don't change your mind and want to keep it. It's a give and take situation.'

'I suppose so, but I think it's almost unheard of for a surrogate to go back on her word and decide to keep the baby.'

'All the forums say it's about mutual trust and respect. Haven't you written that down a million times?' He pointed to a picture of a cat and meowed. Alice copied him. We all laughed.

'Yeah, I know. Just feels so much more real now I'm actually pregnant. I wanted to check over everything again.'

Malcolm and Brenda *had* agreed to keep in touch after the transfer of parental rights, although he'd not been so keen. I hoped they wouldn't have any reason to change their minds because being able to see the child grow up was going to be the best part of it for me.

'You need to relax. Shall I see if Dan and Carly are about for a takeaway?' Steve clapped Alice's hands together.

'Yeah, why not?'

He texted them and by nine o'clock we were all sitting round the TV, watching *Big Brother* turned down low and eating Chinese.

'So, you're really going through with it?' Carly tied up her purple hair before stuffing her face with chicken noodles.

'Yeah, think so.' I glanced at Steve and gave him a sideways grin.

'Are you…?' Carly pointed to my stomach.

I nodded, smiling.

'Oh my god. Congrats!' She wrapped me in a Parma violets-scented hug.

'Nice one.' Dan prised the top off a bottle of Tiger beer and handed it to Carly. Flashing lights and cheers from *Big Brother* made us all look at the screen.

I dragged myself over to the sink and poured a glass of tap water. What if I did find it too hard giving up the baby? I stared down at my non-existent bump.

'You're missing it.' Carly waved me over.

'I'm feeling a bit queasy.' The stench of the takeaway filled my nose.

'Do you want water?' Steve pushed himself up from the beanbag.

'I've got some, thanks.' I pulled back the sliding door to the bathroom and leaned over the toilet. I could only be about four weeks. I'd not been sick once with Alice.

When I came out, all I wanted to do was lie down, but Carly and Dan were sitting on the sofa bed. I wished we had a little bedroom I could slip away to.

'You look as white as snow.' Carly elbowed Dan and stood up. 'We'll go, darling, leave you in peace.'

'Yeah, we can watch this next door.' Dan cleared up their plates and Steve dumped them in the sink.

'See you in a minute, mate.' Dan picked up the rest of their beers. 'I hope you feel better.'

Steve flattened down the sofa bed and pulled out the ready made up duvet from the space underneath. I watched for any movement from Alice, fast asleep in her cot. She could sleep through pretty much any noise.

'I won't stay long.' Steve took his car washing bucket out from under the kitchen sink, removing the sponge and various bottles of shampoo and polish. 'I'll leave this here for you.'

'Makes me icky just looking at it.'

'Text me if you need anything.' He pecked me on the forehead and left. I could hear him rap his knuckles on next door, and the slam of it closing behind him. For a split second I wished I wasn't pregnant. I hoped this sickness would pass. Eight long months stretched ahead, but I thought of Brenda's happy tears and despite all their shiny ornaments and plush carpets, they didn't have the one treasure they really wanted, that *I* could provide for them. If only Mum would see it that way. Tomorrow I'd have to break the news to her.

Chapter Three

I was sick at various times during the night. It all blurred into one big mess that seemed to go on for hours and hours. When I woke up in the morning, I reached for the ginger biscuit I'd left by the side of the bed. I'd read in *Baby* magazine that if you nibbled one before sitting up, you were less likely to actually vomit. My stomach wobbled. I wasn't convinced.

'Want some tea with that?' Steve sat up, rubbing his hand through his hair. 'I heard you getting up. Lost count how many times. Are you okay?'

I shook my head and dashed to the bathroom.

Afterwards, I sat on the toilet seat. How could this pregnancy be so different? What if I was sick up until the end? My hands trembled. I needed to eat, but I wasn't sure I'd be able to keep anything down.

I made it to the kitchenette and steadied myself against the wall. Steve took one look at me, scooped me up and gently laid me down on the bed.

'I can't go to work like this.' I snuggled under the duvet.

'Do you want me to call in for you?' He brought over a mug of ginger tea and a piece of near burnt toast.

'Would you?' I sat up. There was no way I could face talking to Tash.

'Thing is, how long do you think this will carry on? I mean, Tash relies on you, doesn't she?'

'But she can't have someone around food who might throw up any second.'

'So what do I tell her?'

'Say I'll be back in a couple of days, most likely. Then we'll just have to wait and see.' I had no idea if this was going to carry on or not. I reached to the floor for my mobile and showed him Tash's number.

'I'm guessing you don't want me to tell her the real reason?' Steve touched the call button.

'God no. She'd probably have a breakdown.'

I cringed at every word of him telling her I had a sickness bug. I could picture her wondering how the hell she was going to get all those lunch orders ready in time.

'How'd she take it?' I squinted. Wouldn't I have to tell people the truth when I started showing?

'She hopes you feel better, agreed it would be pointless you going in.' He sat on the bed.

I hated lying, but sometimes there was no other way.

'I'm going to call Mum.' Phoning would be easier right now. I couldn't face seeing her disappointment.

'You're kidding?' He rested his hand on my back and looked right into my eyes so I couldn't hide my anxiety.

'I need to tell her. I just want her to support me.'

'You know what she'll say.' He passed me the phone. 'Anyway, won't she be busy cutting someone's hair?'

I glanced at the clock, then tapped in the number. 'It's me,' I said in a bright voice.

'What's the matter, Charlotte? You know I'm working.'

'Sorry, I thought you started later on a Friday.' For a second, the words I wanted to say were trapped in my mouth. 'I've made a decision… I'm going to be a surrogate.'

Mum was silent.

‘Charlotte, we’ve talked about this.’

‘I’m going to do it,’ I sat up, ‘you can’t change my mind.’

‘Look, I know you think you’re doing this for me, but I don’t want you to.’ The line became muffled, as though she’d put her hand over the receiver.

‘I want to help a woman who can’t hold a baby till the end of a pregnancy, like you.’ I was gripping the phone so hard, my hand hurt. I held back the gathering tears. Something shifted down the line.

‘I want you to think hard about this. It affects me too, especially as you said it’ll be half yours. You’ll be giving away my grandchild.’

‘But it won’t be yours.’ I sighed. Why couldn’t she at least try and get her head around it?

‘You’ll be the mother.’

I stood up. ‘But Steve’s not the dad. It won’t be *our* baby.’ The silence stretched until I thought it would snap. ‘Anyway, it’s too late.’

‘What?’

‘I’m already pregnant.’

‘But you’ve not thought it through properly. You need to give yourself longer than a few weeks.’ The pitch of her voice went up.

’I’ve been thinking about it for years, Mum, I just hadn’t told anyone. You of all people know how it feels to desperately want a baby with every cell in your body. Why can’t you understand?’ I felt my face heat up.

‘Why can’t she adopt?’

‘Because surrogacy’s an option now.’ Of all people, I thought she would totally get it. I’d lived through three of her five stillbirths. She knew how badly it had affected me.

‘But how well do you know these people?’

'Really well. We've become friends over the last four, almost five months. They've been married for twenty years, Mum. They run their own property business from home in Orkney. What else is there to know? They're decent people.' I tipped my face up to the heavens. Steve slowly shook his head with a 'told you so' expression.

'You might think you do, but only yesterday I read in a magazine at the doctors about a surrogate who had a baby for a couple she was convinced she knew. But a month after they took the baby home, she paid them an unexpected visit. The poor thing had barely been fed or washed and was dressed in a grubby babygro that was far too small.'

'That's horrible, but, Mum, there's bound to be the odd bad experience. I've told you not to read those magazines, they're full of scare stories.'

'How did you do it anyway, with a turkey baster?' The pitch of her voice became almost comically squeaky.

'No, Mum, a special syringe.' I was not about to go into detail.

'It's not right though, is it?'

'Why not?' How did she always manage to turn me into a whiny child?

'It's not natural.'

'Mu-um!' I clenched my teeth.

'I don't know what else to say.' Mum's voice became faint, a sure sign she was about to cry. 'I hope and pray you change your mind.'

'I'm sorry—' The phone cut off. I took it away from my ear and stared at the receiver.

Mum's upset fluttered in my chest like a scorched moth.

'Don't even say it.' I chucked the phone on the bed.

'I'm not saying anything,' Steve kissed the top of my head, 'I'm off to work. Got to get some flyers printed to bring in some new customers.' He shoved the unused bucket closer to the bed. 'Call me if you need anything.'

Alice woke up as soon as the front door clicked shut. She'd normally lie quiet for a few minutes, but she started to grizzle. Her third new tooth in as many months. And now she'd probably slept too long and was starving.

I changed her nappy and put her bottle of milk in the microwave to warm. While I was waiting, I pushed the window open. The restless sun was trying hard to squeeze bright rays into the gloom. My mood lifted at the thought of spring coming. A couple of kids in school uniform were kicking a ball about on the communal green. Bedford may not be the greatest place on earth to live, but to us it was home.

Across the road, a woman with short curly dark hair looked out of place wearing oversized sunglasses at this time of year. She was standing stock-still, dressed in a smart grey trouser suit and cream stilettos. Probably an estate agent waiting for a client.

The microwave beeped. Damn. The milk was too hot now. I filled a plastic jug with cold water and sat the bottle in it. Alice started to cry.

'Come on, sweetheart.' I picked her up, kissed her hot cheek and gently jogged her up and down. On breakfast TV a woman was sitting opposite the presenters, breastfeeding her baby while discussing people complaining about women doing it in public, as though it was something dirty. Mum had never breastfed me, said it made her shudder at the thought. I hadn't found it easy and stopped at three months.

While I was feeding Alice her bottle, Brenda messaged me.

How are you? I still can't believe this is finally happening. I didn't think I was ever going to be a mom!

I blinked at the message. Here was proof that I was doing the right thing. I was giving this woman the gift of becoming a mum. I started to tap out a reply saying I was fine, feeling great, then immediately deleted it. I needed to be honest with Brenda. Share the good and bad, or this relationship wasn't going to work.

Not great, had to miss work today. Morning sickness has kicked in, so if you're in any doubt, there's your proof!

Oooh no! Poor you. Hope you're coping okay?

I'll be fine, honestly, it's all going to be worth it, I typed, holding Alice over my shoulder, waiting for a big burp. I sat Alice back in her high chair and gave her half a rusk while I chopped up a banana.

My phone pinged.

Aw, thank you. I'm so grateful. I just wish I could share your suffering.

I kissed Alice's biscuit-smelling hair. I'd get through this rough patch whatever it took.

I've been getting a strong craving for lemons, the smell and the taste!

Ha ha, how strange! I've been drinking nothing but lemon tea for the past three days. Now I know why!

How weird is that?

I know, isn't it? Hey, I was thinking, why don't we go shopping together when we next come down, when you feel a bit better?

Yeah, that would be fun.

I've been buying already, couldn't help myself. What do you think?

A photo popped up on my phone. A beautiful crib they'd bought that morning. It had a floating canopy tied at the sides. I imagined its gentle rocking motion, soothing a newborn Sleeping Beauty. I'd dreamed of having something like it while I was pregnant with Alice, but we'd ended up with a second-hand Moses basket that cost a fiver from a neighbour.

Lovely! I replied, my stomach twisting into an ugly knot. Maybe we'd be able to afford something like it for our next baby. I groaned at another wave of nausea. I dashed to the bathroom, reaching the toilet just in time.

I put Alice back in her cot and had a quick shower. I couldn't face eating anything, so I poured a glass of water and opened my laptop. I clicked to open the minimised window of Malcolm and Brenda's website: *Premier Properties*, their faces in the professionally taken photos on the About page smiled back at me. In their profiles it said they'd both started out working for the same estate agents but quickly moved on to form a partnership, renovating flats and houses. *We provide an all-round service you can trust.* The photos of the houses they'd sold were incredible, pure luxury. I copied and pasted their address into Streetmap. Their home was more of a mansion, Victorian-looking on its own plot of land, with a wide driveway surrounded by mature trees and bushes. I'd be happy with one or two bedrooms and a little garden for Alice to play in.

I clicked on the surrogacy forum window and scanned through the new threads. Nothing caught my eye, so I opened my messages and scrolled back to the beginning. It was five months since I'd first posted about wanting to be a surrogate.

I'd specifically said I wanted to help an older couple who'd almost given up hope of ever having a child. I honestly didn't know if anyone would reply but Brenda had messaged me almost straight away. My hand was shaking as I'd opened her reply.

I've been waiting for a post from someone just like you! Thank you so much for your generous offer to be a surrogate for a desperate couple like us. My husband Malcolm and I have suffered eleven miscarriages. We can't go on trying but don't know where else to turn. Our ages are against us now but we're in a privileged position of being comfortable financially and we're aching to give a loving home to our baby. Please, please would you consider helping us? Brenda x

The crushing heartache had left me sitting there for several minutes as fragments of my mum's losses played out in my mind: her sobbing, curled up on the bed for days, then standing in front of the full-length mirror, rubbing the empty, shrinking bump, and the silence in the house when there should have been a baby crying. And me hiding under my bed reading, not daring to make a sound, knowing that my very existence was a cruel reminder.

These were the exact kind of couple I'd dreamed of helping. I'd typed my reply with tears in my eyes.

I'm so desperately sorry for all you and your husband have been through. I can only imagine how much heartbreak you've endured. I imagine you've considered all options, such as adoption? If you're sure surrogacy is for you, I would very much like to get to know you both, perhaps we can meet up? Charlotte x

Brenda's reply was instant. Her desperation reverberated through every word.

That would be wonderful, thank you! We live in Orkney but are in London the week after next, if that would suit you? I would happily have considered adoption, but Malcolm so wants to have a child that is truly his own. For me, sadly, I don't have any eggs to donate, so the fact that you're happy to be a traditional surrogate works perfectly for us and is another reason why we were so attracted to your kind and heartfelt offer. We're excited to have found you, Charlotte! Brenda x

We'd got to know them more through texts and emails. Then we met them in London face-to-face two weeks later, to see if we all got on. I'd known instantly that they were the right couple. Three weeks after that, we had our first try. Two failed attempts with Malcolm and I'd begun to wonder if he was firing blanks. Obviously not. Third time lucky.

And at last I was pregnant. Yet the responsibility weighed heavily in my chest.

I touched my flat belly. What could possibly go wrong?

Chapter Four

'Finished those salads yet?' Tash called from the front counter. The elaborate bun on the top of her head wobbled every time she spoke. The deli was beginning to fill with a queue winding round the tables. Rain dripped off people's coats and umbrellas, leaving tiny puddles on the tiled floor. I'd mop that up as soon as the lunchtime rush died down.

Tash had been off with me ever since I'd been back. No surprise there. She couldn't bring me down though, I was too pleased to be feeling well again. When I woke up this morning, the rush of excitement at being pregnant had really kicked in. I'd not stopped smiling since. Five weeks already.

'Coming,' I shouted. I finished labelling the orders and stacked them in a box ready for collection. I couldn't wait for Shell to turn up. Someone understanding to share every twinge with. As I leaned down to pick up a second box, a searing heat sliced through my groin. I clamped my legs shut. 'Nooo,' I whispered, squeezing my hands into fists.

'Salads, Charlotte?' Tash glanced over her shoulder at me. 'What have you gone and done now?'

'Sorry, give me a minute,' I groaned.

'Probably cut her finger,' she said to the next suit in the queue, then she turned back to me and hissed, 'What's wrong with you today?'

'I've got this shooting pain, down there,' I whispered, pointing.

Tash tutted and helped me sit down. 'Will you be all right a minute? Where's Shell when you need her?'

I groaned as another wave of pain wrenched through me. I knew exactly what it meant. It was far more intense than any period I'd had. There could only be one reason. My chest deflated at the loss of the life that would never be.

'Now then, what's up with you?' Tash asked. 'Off a week then back with this? What's going on?'

'I think I'm miscarrying.' I pressed my fist to my mouth. Was it because I hadn't loved it completely, as though it were my own? Could the baby sense this on a cellular level?

'You never said you were pregnant.' Tash put her arm around me. I breathed in her fragrant aroma of freshly chopped mint and cucumber, but it didn't even make me feel nauseous.

'I'm only a few weeks. I was going to tell you.'

'For these people again?' She tilted her head at me in that 'told you so' way of hers.

I nodded.

'Charlotte, love.' She held me at arm's length and raised one side of her mouth in a half-hearted smile. 'Isn't it your third go at this?'

'Yes, but the first time I've got pregnant.'

'But now you're losing an actual baby. What further signs do you need?' She gently patted my arm.

A deep sadness swept through me. I wished I could do something to stop it. 'You know about Mum. I didn't want to just give up.' Sometimes working for Tash was like having another mother, always telling me what to do. It was as if they knew each other. Maybe they were both right. But I couldn't bear the thought of letting Brenda down.

I felt a tug in my chest like the twang of a double bass string. Tash couldn't have kids. Didn't like me having one for someone older, like her. I'd thought that as long as I kept in touch with the child, what would there be to regret? But now there was no child to watch grow up.

The bell above the door tinkled. Shell walked in. I let out a long, grateful sigh.

'At last. You're late,' Tash said, 'right let's get you home, Charlotte.'

I stood up to go but my legs wobbled. Tash grabbed hold of me round the shoulders and walked me to her car. It felt as though my energy and strength had drained away along with this baby's life. All I wanted to do was curl up in bed with a hot-water bottle. My heart ached for Brenda. How would I break the news? It would destroy her.

Chapter Five

After Tash had dropped me off, I texted Steve to see if he could pick Alice up from Mum's on his way back from work.

I took two paracetamol and lay on the bed with a hot-water bottle. I'd given Brenda hope of having her own baby, but now I'd be adding to her pain. Had it been that half glass of wine before the morning sickness had kicked in? I couldn't tell them about that. Or it might have been the spoonful of Stilton and walnut sandwich filler. A soft, mouldy cheese, on the banned list.

Steve texted me back.

What's wrong?

I tried to sit up. *Call me*, I typed. My mobile rang.

'You okay?' Steve asked, out of breath. I imagined him hauling himself up from underneath a car.

'I'm losing the baby.' I started to cry.

'Oh no, hun, are you sure?'

'I'm bleeding like fuck.'

'Jeez.'

I pictured him scraping back his gelled hair.

'Tash had to bring me home.'

'Do you want me to call the doc?'

'It's okay, I'll call them in a minute.' I wiped my eyes on the back of my hand. 'How do I tell Brenda?'

'Dunno. Won't hurt to wait though, will it? We seriously need that cash.'

'*What*? I'm not going to lie to them. How can you even be thinking about money right now?'

Silence.

'I've lost my baby— their baby!' Each word struck a back-hand across my face. For a second, I forgot it wasn't mine but it hurt just as much as if it was.

'I've promised Jack. He had his op last week.' His voice was quiet, barely audible.

'I know, I'm sorry, but what can I do?'

'Look, I knock off in an hour. We can have a chat, over a glass or two if you like?'

'I don't want wine! Let's speak later.' I put the phone down. My temples throbbed. This poor little thing, not quite a fully formed human but still loved, still longed for. I had loved it too, of course I had. Stupid to think I could breeze through a pregnancy without having feelings for the new little person growing inside me.

I called the doctor and made an appointment. As the call ended, a shooting pain ripped through my insides. I stumbled back to the bathroom, my legs wobbly, and pulled another thick pad from the packet by the bath. I sat on the toilet. An image flicked across my mind of me as a child peeking around our old bathroom door that first time I'd heard Mum's sobs. The shock of seeing her slumped on the floor, blood soaked through her cream dress, smeared on her bare legs and pooling at her feet. When she'd seen me standing there, she'd screeched at me to fetch my dad. I'd never forgotten the desolate look in her eyes.

Back in the kitchen, I topped up the hot-water bottle and sipped my glass of water. There was a light tap tap on the front door. I opened it to Jean from the flat upstairs, wearing old denim dungarees, her orange hair scraped up in a messy bun, showing a fan of white.

'I saw you being dropped off earlier...' Her voice trailed off when she saw the hot-water bottle clutched to my chest. 'Are you okay?'

'Not really,' I pulled a tissue out from my sleeve. 'I'm losing the baby.' I wiped my nose. It only seemed five minutes ago that I was telling her about Brenda and how excited we all were at my pregnancy news.

'Oh, Charlotte, I'm so sorry, do you want me to go?'

'No, stay for a few minutes, please.'

She followed me in.

I sat on the bed, the hot-water bottle pressed across my groin. 'I know what you're going to say, but I really believed it would be easier than this.'

'I'm not judging you, Charlotte. I admire you for what you're doing.'

'Do you?' I looked up at her anguished face, the flash of red in her cheeks. 'My pregnancy with Alice was so straightforward. Do you think it could be stress from the responsibility? Or maybe it happened because I wasn't strict enough following their rules of not drinking or eating certain foods?' In our agreement, Malcolm had insisted on writing a list of food and drink they didn't want me to have. It wasn't necessary because it was similar to advice given to all pregnant women by medical experts, about not drinking alcohol, not smoking, avoiding caffeine, soft cheese, pât*é*, etc. And the choice was down to the individual woman.

'It's hard to know for sure but you can't blame yourself.' She sat near me on the wicker chair. 'Every pregnancy is different. Jacob was six weeks early. Biggest shock of my life.'

'But I feel like I've let them down, especially Brenda.'

'You have not. This was a kind thing of you to do for people you barely know.'

'It feels like I'm living through Mum's losses again, except this time it's me.' Jean had only met Mum briefly, but I'd confided in her about how losing my brothers and sisters had affected me, why I was so determined to be a surrogate.

'Charlotte, love, you're too kind-hearted for your own good.' She came over and hugged me. I sobbed into her shoulder. After a few minutes, she grabbed a couple of tissues from the box on the table and sat with her arm around me.

'I feel so bad for Brenda. When I found out I was pregnant with Alice, I was nervous about telling Steve because I knew he'd worry about our lack of space and money. We'd only been married a year. I'd longed for a baby so much it hurt. I'd like us to have more children of our own one day. I'm lucky to have that choice.'

'You've got years ahead of you to have more of your own babies and this loss doesn't mean it will happen again, I promise you.'

'I hope you're right. I loved being pregnant with Alice. I didn't mind people reaching out to touch my bump as though it was their good luck Buddha. And I was able to carry on as normal right up until the birth. Steve said my bump looked like a large football strapped to my belly and that from behind you'd never have even known I was pregnant. I was so lucky I didn't suffer from any tiredness or swollen ankles like some of the mums at playgroup.'

'And you're a fantastic mum to Alice. She's always a joy to look after. Talking of which, I've got twins to collect from pre-school, then my own school run.' She checked her watch. 'Do you want me to pick Alice up for you?'

'It's okay, Steve's going.'

'If there's anything I can do to help, you know where I am.' She gave me a hug and stood up.

I followed her out to the hall and thanked her as she went out of the main door. I unlocked our postbox and stuck my hand in. The postman must have been by now. I felt around. It seemed empty at first, but my fingertips brushed over a corner of paper. A single envelope lay at the bottom. I reached in and took it out. It was addressed to me in neat capital letters.

Back in the flat, I eased open the gummed flap with a knife and took out a cheque in my name. I blinked a few times at all the zeros, trying to make them stay still. Ten thousand pounds. I'd never seen a cheque for so much money. I thought of Jack and his family and how this golden ticket would be enough to help them and save the business. But how could we keep this now there was no baby?

Chapter Six

Once we'd settled Alice in her cot that evening, Steve and I sat on the sofa bed holding hands, the TV on low. He poured me another cup of tea and topped up his glass of wine, a cheap bottle from the offie.

'Sorry I couldn't come with you to the docs.'

'There's nothing you could have done.' I pressed a creased-up tissue to my eyes as another round of tears spilled out.

'But you've lost a baby and I promised to be there for you every step.' He kissed my hand.

'I know this is hard on you because it's not technically mine, but I still feel like shit.' The oven beeped.

Steve hugged me. 'I'll get that.'

I sat up and put a cushion on my lap. He handed me a plate of burgers, chips and beans and squirted tomato ketchup all over his food. As soon as I saw it, I couldn't face eating. Steve scoffed his down in no time.

'I'll get that cheque in the bank first thing, let it clear then we'll see about calling them,' he said.

'We can't take their money and not produce a baby. What if Brenda texts me or wants to Skype?'

'Tell her you're still sick, that it's not a good time?'

'She'll know something's up, I know she will.' Brenda didn't deserve to be lied to.

'Tell her you've got it bad, can't keep a thing down.'

'I won't lie to her.' I couldn't mess Brenda about.

After Steve had finished and I'd eaten all I could, he took the plates out to the kitchenette and came back with the rest of the bottle.

'I'm just trying to support you. Look what you've been through for them already. We need that money to pay our debts. What would I tell Jack?'

'I know.' I snuggled up to him and he wrapped his arm around me, pulling me closer.

'You know it's entirely up to you.' He turned the TV over to *Million Pound Drop*. The couple lost three hundred grand on the first question. 'Be easier to go on there to get some cash wouldn't it?' Steve said.

'Maybe, but the number of people that go home with nothing…'

'True.'

'I just wanted to make a difference to someone's life. Give them the chance of having a baby.'

'I know, hun.'

The painkillers were beginning to wear off. The doctor had told me to go home and rest but to call her if the pain or bleeding got worse. I groaned as I pushed myself up from the sofa and took two more paracetamol with a glass of water. My phone beeped.

How are you?

My heart stopped. 'It's Brenda,' I whispered, as if she could hear us.

Steve crossed his arms.

Not too bad, thanks, I replied.

Good to hear. We're down your way on Saturday. Okay to call in and say hello?

My eyes widened. I held the phone up to show Steve.

'Hang on.' He held my arm away. The couple on TV had lost another £100k. 'The answer was Man City, you knob!' Steve shouted.

I showed him the message again. He smiled and shrugged.

'Let's say yes, so we can tell them face-to-face.'

He nodded.

'The cheque will have cleared by the weekend.'

'Are you going to tell them you lost the baby the night before they arrive? Won't that look a bit of a coincidence?'

'No. I'll say we wanted to tell them in person.' I stared at the phone. 'It would be horrible for them to find out by text.'

I texted back: *Yeah, of course. Look forward to seeing you both.* I touched my stomach. My eyes filled up again at the thought of telling Brenda there was no longer a baby. I'd failed.

A few moments later my phone beeped again.

I want to ask your advice about car seats for newborns and these buggy systems. Would love to get an old-fashioned pram, a big old Silver Cross, but they're not practical, are they? Maybe we could go to the shops and check some out, if you're feeling up to it?

I glanced out of the window at a flurry of snow lit up by the winter sunshine, melting as soon as the flakes touched the ground. I remembered the sparks of excitement when I was pregnant with Alice. But I also couldn't shift the memory of Mum's nervous joy at yet another pregnancy, her arms almost permanently cupped around her bump, as though she had the power to prevent it from dying.

I don't think I am yet, but we can go through all the different types of prams online if you like? I can show you what I used for Alice.

I paused before I pressed send. Maybe I should tell her now? No. It would be too cruel. I wanted to be able to give her a hug, console her. Guilt sank its teeth into me.

Thank you, that'll be so helpful! It's probably far too early to buy one anyway. We'll be at yours mid-afternoon, okay?

Ouch. Yes, way too early.

That'll be great. Alice should have had her nap by then. See you Saturday xx

Can't wait! Xx

'So, they're coming then?' Steve's eyes stayed fixed on the TV. The couple were coming to the end of their game.

'Yeah. It would be too awful seeing Brenda upset over Skype and not being able to comfort her.'

'Get in there!' Steve roared at the TV. The couple had won £40,000.

He took my hands in his, shifted round so he was facing me. 'Look, I know you don't care about the cash and I love you for just wanting to help someone like Brenda, but think about trying for them again?' He looked into my eyes. 'I really want to help my best mate and his family, because they desperately need the money back he put into the business. God knows if the chemo will even work. I just know I wouldn't be able to live with myself if I didn't help him.' He glanced down. I kissed his open palm. He looked up again with tears in his hangdog eyes. 'And I want to do my best to carry on building the business – it's our future at stake here too – you, me and Alice. And when you're ready, you'll be able to apply for a teacher training course and put some away for Alice.'

I nodded and stared down at our hands entwined; his ingrained with oil and dirt around the nails, next to my tiny pale fingers. 'Okay, if they want me to try one final time, I promise I'll seriously think about it.'

Chapter Seven

As Saturday approached, I couldn't keep still. My mind going over and over everything they might say, asking why I hadn't told them straight away. The thought of them thinking I was a liar left me feeling nauseous. The bleeding was relentless, and the sadness wouldn't shift, I couldn't seem to bring myself to smile about anything. By the end of Wednesday, I told Steve I'd have to call Brenda, prepare them for the bad news.

After the lunchtime rush, I stood in the back yard of the deli and dialled. The answerphone kicked in.

'Hi Brenda, it's Charlotte, I'm really sorry, but I should have said… there's something important I need to tell you both on Saturday. Hope you're okay. Bye!' As soon as I hung up, I wanted to kick myself for sounding so cheerful.

Tash called out to me. 'See that woman over there, in front of the laundrette? Been there all morning.' She stood at the counter, pulling on a fresh pair of transparent hygiene gloves. They made me shudder and think of hospital.

'So?' I stood with my hand on my hip, peering out of the window. The woman had dark curly hair and sunglasses. I frowned. She looked a lot like the woman I saw outside our flat.

'What do you think she's doing?'

'I don't know.'

'I've got a good mind to go over there and ask her. Might be from the social, keeping tabs on someone. Not claiming anything illegally are you?'

'Of course not!' Maybe it's someone famous. She looks a bit like that singer from The Saturdays.'

'Really, do you think so?' She checked her face in the tiny love-heart mirror stuck to the top of the till. 'Do you think she'll pop in for a sandwich?'

I smiled to myself as I cleared up the remaining tables of all the lunchtime debris. I sprayed pink disinfectant and wiped them down with a hot cloth. I paused at the window. Maybe she was a businesswoman looking to buy up empty properties. Wouldn't bother round here.

I rinsed the cloth and hung it up to dry in the room out the back, then checked my phone. No new message from Brenda.

'Is it okay to pop down the garage now?' I asked.

'Oh god, yeah. Poor Steve will be half starved.'

'Well, he could have walked up. Must be having a busy morning.' I didn't bother taking my apron off. I wrapped his sandwich in foil and took a bottle of Coke out of the fridge. One of the few perks of working here.

It was an overcast, blustery day that threatened rain. As I stepped out of the shop, I glanced across at the woman. Her eyes were fixed on something. I trotted along the high street, putting my head down against the wind.

Steve was half under a car when I called out to him.

'Lifesaver,' he said, letting his spanner clang to the ground. He slid out from under the Beamer and wiped his oily fingers on his overalls. 'You all right then?' He took a glug of Coke, then ripped into the foil, biting off almost half the cheese and pickle sandwich in one go.

'I've not heard back from Brenda. She normally answers straight away.' I laced my fingers together. 'Do you think she's guessed and is upset with me?'

'They'll understand, they're decent people.' Steve rolled the foil up in a ball and chucked it at one of the other mechanics.

'Oi!' a bald-headed man shouted over the car bonnet.

'I'll try calling her again a bit later.'

As I turned to go, I noticed the woman was across the road now. My stomach dropped with a thud. 'That's strange.'

'What is?' Steve stood behind me, his arms around my waist, kissing my neck.

'That woman in a suit across the road. She was outside the deli, now she's moved up here.'

'Yeah, and?' Steve laughed. 'You've been watching too many episodes of *Vera*.'

'Do you think she's an estate agent?' At that moment, the woman hotfooted it away. It couldn't be the same person, I must be overthinking it.

Back at the deli, I tried Brenda again several times, but it kept ringing. Not even the answerphone kicked in.

Chapter Eight

When I got home, I sat Alice in her chair and fed her a boiled egg and bread soldiers. Afterwards, we played 'Round and Round the Garden' on each other until we were both flushed from giggling and being tickled.

'Come and play with Daisy.' I sat Alice on the playmat with her favourite cloth doll and looked up Malcolm's number. I'd never rung him before. I'd always gone through Brenda. Hopefully he wouldn't be annoyed at me for calling him out of the blue. The phone gave a click. The line went dead. I tried again, but the line was definitely not in use. There were still no messages from Brenda and no answer when I tried to call her again. Strange. I thought back to the message I'd left. Perhaps they *were* upset with me.

When Steve arrived home two hours later, I was pacing up and down the flat, phone in hand. Alice had gone to sleep. The lights were dimmed. A pile of ironing sat on the end of the bed. I'd normally have ploughed through it by now.

'What if they've changed their minds and don't want to be contacted?' I opened the fridge, took our dinner out and slammed the door shut.

'Hello to you too.' He gave me a kiss on the lips.

I stabbed a fork in the cellophane of two spaghetti Bolognese ready meals.

'That would be a bit odd, wouldn't it? It's Malcolm's baby.'

'I know, but why haven't they replied? What if I was still pregnant and they decided they didn't want it any more? We'd be left with a baby that wasn't yours.' I shoved one of the meals in the microwave and pulled a face as though I'd caught a whiff of mouldy cheese.

'You worry too much.' He put his arms around me. 'They've got no reason to do that. They want a baby more than anything.'

I burrowed my head into the warmth of his chest.

'They'll be in touch soon, then we can break it to them and say that even though this one's gone, you'll try for them again.' He crouched in front of me and took my hands in his.

'It's meant to be my decision,' I said, trying not to be drawn into his puppy dog eyes.

'I know, but we both have a say in it, don't we? I mean, you might not be able to work if you get sick again and I'll have to pick up the slack.'

'Thanks a lot.' I pulled my hands out of his and turned away as though he'd slapped me.

'Come here, you daft mare. I didn't mean it like that.' He grabbed my wrist and gently pulled me round to face him. 'What I meant was, it would be totally understandable. You'd need to take it easy. I'm happy to do anything and everything for you and Alice, you know that.'

I traced down his face with my fingertips, from the smooth skin to the line of stubble. I loved every inch of him and I wanted to believe he was right, but I couldn't shift the thought that Malcolm and Brenda had changed their minds. What if I did go ahead and get pregnant once more? They could do this again. We'd be completely stuck. I scanned round the flat trying to think what could be moved to create more room but there was nowhere to fit another cot. The clothes horse filled the small gap between the TV and the door to the cupboard-sized hall, and when the sofa bed was out, there was just enough room to walk around it.

The microwave beeped. Steve pulled on an oven glove and lifted out the box of food. I tipped his dinner onto a plate while he put mine in and switched it on. He sat down to eat while I watched mine spin slowly round and round.

Why would she change her mind? They longed to be parents. I was worrying too much. When I pictured Brenda's empty arms, she immediately morphed into Mum. I needed to do this for so many reasons. Jack was relying on us. And Steve's business. Our whole future was in their hands.

Chapter Nine

On Saturday morning, I checked my phone every few minutes. Still nothing from Brenda. The same worry swam around and around my mind. I'd lost their precious baby,

We kept busy by cleaning the flat and washing clothes. I wished we were going down the snooker club with Carly and Dan as usual instead. But I was still bleeding, a heavier period than usual and a strong metallic smell.

'What if they've had an accident? Who would know to tell us?'

'Unlikely.' Steve swung Alice up in the air, making her gurgle. 'I checked our account this morning and their cheque's cleared.' A thread of saliva fell from Alice's lips. 'Yuk, little lady. I think I see another new tooth.'

After lunch, my phone beeped. 'It's Brenda, thank god! She says she's just got my message. They're only two hours away.' I let out a big breath.

'What did I tell you?'

'Don't you think that's odd though? I mean, she's been texting me every day, then suddenly she's not looked at her phone for ages?'

'They must have been somewhere with no coverage.' He sat Alice on his knee and wiped her glistening chin with a muslin cloth, then the dribble on his T-shirt.

'Yeah, I suppose.'

–

When Brenda and Malcolm arrived, Steve carried Alice in his arms and let them in the main door. I checked my pasty, no-make-up face in the mirror. I heard them chatting as they approached. My stomach clenched. This was going to be harder than I'd imagined.

'Lovely to see you,' I said, giving Brenda a hug, arranging my face into a weak smile. She handed me an enormous bunch of dark red roses with sprays of white baby's breath. 'They're beautiful, thank you.' I closed my eyes and inhaled their scent. I hugged her again.

'These are for you too,' Malcolm handed me a box of Swiss chocolates.

'Thank you.' I kissed his cheek. He smiled as he checked me up and down, lingering on my non-existent bump. He'd not guessed, surely? He shrugged off his leather jacket and draped it over the back of the wicker chair. Springy white chest hair crept over the seam of his V-neck jumper, making him look older.

'You look so pale.' Brenda cupped my face with icy fingers.

'This is for you, little lady.' Malcolm knelt down and handed Alice a small package. Her tiny fingers curled around it. She grinned and gurgled at him, showing the dot of white emerging from her pink gums. Malcolm's face lit up with wonder. He helped her tear off the paper and take out a soft toy bunny. Alice gave an excited squeal. Brenda's hand sprung to her mouth, instant tears in her eyes. I exchanged a glance with Steve. In a few moments I'd be breaking their hearts.

Steve took the flowers from me and laid them in the kitchen sink in water.

Brenda seemed tense as she chatted and fussed over Alice and her new tooth, as though she didn't want anyone else to speak. Perhaps she sensed something was wrong.

The first time we'd met them was for lunch in Côte Brasserie, Covent Garden. They were visiting London for a few days, doing touristy things, seeing *Les Misérables*, the V&A, shopping in Oxford Street and Harrods.

When we arrived, they were already there, half a bottle of wine down, huddled together in a corner. Brenda's face had flushed at seeing us. She wore an elegant flowing skirt and blouse, and Malcolm came across as chirpy and friendly, smartly dressed. Both stood to greet us. Malcolm shook our hands, placing his other hand on top, looking us each in the eye. Brenda hugged us as though we were old friends. I remember a shine in her eyes had made me wonder if she'd been crying. From what I'd gathered in our little chats on the forum, having a child was a huge deal to her.

The American accent had surprised me; I'd assumed she was British, she'd never said otherwise. She told me much later, she'd been brought up in New York and left there as a teen to travel around Europe, which diluted her accent. Although sometimes it slipped away completely, and I'd pretend not to notice.

'Tell us about you. What makes you want to be a surrogate?' Malcolm had asked, filling up our wine glasses. He wore a sharp suit with a plain navy V-neck underneath and an expensive watch. Steve held my hand while I told them about Mum's stillbirths, that I'd wished a surrogate could have helped my parents; it might have saved their marriage. Brenda had started to cry. She leaned over and hugged me. When I pulled back, I saw my mum's tormented face in hers.

'Ever since I was a little girl,' Brenda had begun, dabbing at her eyes, 'I dreamed of becoming a mom. I came from a big family, six of us, and I'm the eldest so I was used to looking after the others. I just assumed I'd go on to have kids. But all my brothers and sisters overtook me, having families of their own while I got to the point where I couldn't bear to tell them I'd miscarried yet again. After the eleventh time, I had a breakdown. I didn't want to carry on living. My body had failed me. *I* felt a failure. I told Malcolm to go and find someone who could give him a child, but he wouldn't hear of it. He's stuck with me through it all.' She'd reached for his hand and for a few moments they were lost in each other's gaze.

'Why didn't you adopt or use a surrogate years ago?' I'd asked.

'Like I said, Malcolm wasn't keen on adoption and we never thought surrogacy was for people like us. It seemed so alien. But as the years went on we had to look at other options.'

'And the baby not being genetically yours doesn't worry you?'

'Not at all.' Brenda's lips had lifted in a brief smile.

'So you're happy with half its genes coming from me?'

'We have similar colour hair, complexion. I think it's a good match.'

We had all nodded in agreement.

'A colleague at work used a surrogate,' Malcolm had said, clearing his throat, 'it was the first time the idea seemed viable, so I mentioned it to Brenda. We talked it over, agreed that our surrogate had to be someone special that we both connected with and, well, here we are.' He'd kissed Brenda's cheek, teasing out a stray length of hair from around her neck. She'd given a not-quite-there nod and instantly I'd recognised the ragged look in her eyes; images that couldn't be unseen, ghosts of the unborn, barely a flicker of light or hope left.

I drew in a sharp breath, transported back to our kitchen on Bridge Street, aged fourteen: Mum standing in front of me in her flowery nightdress, a pendulum of blood dripping between her legs, a teacup smashed to pieces on the floor.

I pushed the memories away.

Brenda reached out for my stomach, but I flinched. Shit.

'We need to talk,' I said. All of them became quiet. My face burned.

'You said in your message that you had something to tell us. Is the sickness still bad?' Brenda sat in the corner of the sofa, Malcolm's arm around her. Steve switched on the kettle.

'Not exactly.'

'That's good, isn't it?' Brenda rested her hand on Malcolm's knee.

I perched on the edge of the wicker chair. The boiling kettle punctuated the silence. There was no kind way of breaking this to them.

'I'm sorry, but I've got some bad news.' I crossed and uncrossed my legs. 'I've miscarried.' The words sounded to me like it was my fault.

Brenda blinked and blinked. Her mouth fell open and stayed like it. Malcolm swallowed a couple of times and tried to clear his throat.

'We're so sorry.' I knitted my fingers together, pressing the bones until they hurt. Steve came up behind me and gently touched my shoulder to let me know he was right there with me.

Brenda picked up the teddy that Alice had chucked at her feet. She pressed it to her chest and started to cry. I knelt in front of her and took her hand. Malcolm put his arm around her shoulders and pulled her towards him.

'When did this happen?' Malcolm asked.

I glanced at Steve. 'A few days ago. I started bleeding and it hasn't stopped. I didn't know how to tell you. I didn't want to do it by text or over the phone.'

'You've seen a doctor?' he asked.

'Yes. There was nothing they could do, it was so early on.'

Malcolm shut his eyes and nodded.

'How are you feeling?' Brenda wiped her eyes.

'Physically I'm okay, a bit weak but mainly I'm just gutted for you both. I really thought this was the one.'

'So did we.' Malcolm kissed Brenda's hair, his fingers pressing into her arm.

'I'm so sorry.' My heart ached for them.

None of us spoke while Steve finished making the tea.

'Sugar anyone?' he called, squeezing out a teabag with a spoon.

'One each for us,' Malcolm said.

'Not for me.' Brenda's frown quickly changed into a smile.

'Silly me. She's always giving up the bad stuff. I can't keep up with her.' Malcolm darted a look from me to Steve and back again.

Brenda gave a hollow laugh.

'Where were you anyway? Charlotte tried to call you.' Steve brought the tea over.

'Madeira. On business. Dreadful coverage.' Malcolm took the mug with the milk still spinning.

'You didn't say. I was getting worried.' I sat back on my heels and passed a stacking cup to Alice. She put it straight to her mouth. Steve came and sat next to me. He stacked three plastic cups and Alice knocked them straight over, giggling and flapping her sausage arms.

Brenda stared down at us, head tilted.

'As you know, we travel around for work, so it's not always easy to get a good signal.' Malcolm fixed his eyes on me and blew the steam from his drink.

'Sorry, we should have contacted you.' Brenda's puffy eyes flickered. Her hands gripped her bag tight.

'It's okay though, because Charlotte and I have decided to give it another go for you.'

I shot Steve a look. 'If you'd like us to, of course,' I added.

'Oh, would you? Really? That's wonderful.' Brenda smiled as she wiped her tears away.

'That's very good of you.' Malcolm pulled out his hanky and passed it to her. His eyes darted about the room, landing on our vintage poster of *The Godfather*, one corner hanging off the wall. Was he changing his mind about our suitability? They could easily decide to use a different couple.

'Charlotte's been through a lot. We all have, as a family. There are potential dangers to her health, loss of earnings and all that,' Steve said.

Malcolm's eyes narrowed. 'Of course. We understand.' He put down his mug. The corner of his mouth twitched. 'I can go to twenty-five.'

Steve's eyebrows shot up. 'How about thirty?' He gave one of his excitable grins.

My eyes popped wide. This was bonkers, they were bargaining the price of a baby. What about Brenda? Didn't she have any say in it? I stared at her, willing her to speak but she looked away and stayed silent.

'Stop! Please stop this.' I held up my hands. 'Twenty-five is plenty. It's only for expenses remember? We're not selling a person here.' Surely Brenda was as annoyed as me? But her face was blank. Why didn't she say something?

'Okay, okay.' Steve's face dropped.

'This will include the ten you've already had. You'll get another five at the six-month point and ten when we take the baby.' Malcolm drank the last of his tea down in one go. A warm smile spread across his face like butter.

'Yeah, sounds good to me, what do you think, hun?'

Now he was asking! I nodded. The extra money would be handy. I'd be able to afford fresh fruit for Alice rather than that syrupy muck out of a tin. But what if I miscarried again? Would we have to pay it back? I couldn't even bear to ask.

'As soon as I've had a normal period, we'll be ready to try again.' I picked Alice up and wiped rusk off her face. Her nappy stank.

'We could meet at the same hotel.' Brenda blew her nose.

'Fine with us.' Steve stood up. 'More tea anyone?'

'Please.' Brenda gently elbowed Malcolm, who nodded. She passed Steve their mugs.

'Didn't drink any alcohol did you?' Malcolm asked.

Did he really just ask that? 'Of course not,' I said.

'Or soft cheese, coffee?'

'No!' I wasn't going to admit to anything.

'Would you consider giving up work for the whole nine months?'

'Look, I'm sorry, I'm not being funny, but even if you wrap me up in cotton wool, these things just happen.' I lifted Alice up and kissed her forehead.

'Are you suggesting Charlotte wasn't careful?' Steve topped up the teas and clonked them on the coffee table a bit too loudly.

'It's okay, Steve, they're entitled to ask.'

Everyone stayed silent for several moments. The air was thick with the words we all wanted to say.

'These factors come into it. It's too easy to become complacent,' Malcolm said.

'Charlotte was as careful as it's possible to be. I mean she loves a bit of Brie and all the rest of it. She's sacrificing a lot.'

'Can we set a date now?' Brenda asked me as though it was just the two of us. She took her diary out.

'Okay, give us a sec and I'll have a look.' I passed Alice to Steve.

'Three weeks from now or is that too soon?' Brenda pressed open the pocket-sized pages.

I took the calendar down from the wall and checked my period dates. 'How about four, maybe five weeks? I'll let you know for certain nearer the time. Make sure I'm all back to normal.'

Malcolm nodded. 'Good. We want you to be in the best of health. Are you still taking supplements?'

'Yes and I promise I'll carry on with them.' I would be much more careful with everything this time.

'We're just so grateful, aren't we, Malcolm?'

He nodded at his wife and his eyes misted over. Poor bloke. All he wanted was to be a dad.

He pushed himself up. 'Where's your bathroom?'

'He worries about every little thing,' Brenda whispered when he'd gone, 'and he doesn't like to show how hard this is for him, how much he's hurting.'

I sat next to her and touched her arm with my fingertips. 'Brenda, I have to be really honest, if this one doesn't take, I'm not sure I can do it again.' I didn't want to upset her even more, but the words slipped out.

Brenda looked down at the hanky she was twisting in her lap. The muffled sound of Malcolm speaking on his mobile drifted in.

'You do understand this is really stressful for me too?' I said.

'It must be, I'm sorry. I hope this next one is our miracle baby.' Brenda appealed to me with her eyes. I felt bad for coming out with it, but I had to be honest.

'Sorry to cut this short, but we need to get going.' Malcolm stood at the door frowning, his face drawn and pale. Losing the baby must have really knocked him sideways.

Brenda glared at him.

'Wave bye, bye,' I said to Alice, holding her hand up and gently waving it.

Brenda kissed the top of Alice's downy head. 'Hope to see you both in a few weeks. Let's all pray that this time luck shines on us.' She gave me a hug, and then Steve. Malcolm shook my hand firmly. I searched his face for what he might be feeling, but he wouldn't look directly at me. My dad had been the same, holding it all in until the weight of loss, the built-up emotion, broke him in two. I hoped this didn't happen to Brenda and Malcolm.

Steve saw them to the main door while I watched from the kitchenette window with Alice. They drove off in their brand new Jag.

'You were supposed to let me say about trying again,' I told Steve when he came back in.

'Saved you the trouble.' He grinned.

'No. You should have left it to me. What if I'd decided not to do it?' I sat Alice on her playmat and handed her a teething ring.

'Oh come on. You wanted this, remember?' He opened the fridge, took out a cold beer and rolled it up and down his cheek.

'Yes all right.' I play-slapped his arm.

'Now I can transfer the money to Jack and pay off our bills.' He opened his laptop.

'I'm just worried something will go wrong again.'

'Why would it?'

'We must be sensible with the rest of the money.'

'I know.' He drank a mouthful of beer and logged in to our joint bank account. 'Don't you think it was a bit weird him not knowing if his wife takes sugar or not?'

'Yeah, maybe. She probably told him she's on a no-sugar diet and he didn't take any notice. I don't think I'd want to do it.' I wrinkled my nose.

'Why would you? You're giving up plenty for them already. Right, all done. Six grand to Jack. Now for our rent arrears.'

Twenty-five thousand pounds. More than most surrogates got for expenses. I should be grateful, but a sense of unease had burrowed under my skin.

Chapter Ten

We arrived at the Holiday Inn Hotel in Peterborough late on Monday afternoon, almost a month after Brenda and Malcolm had come to our flat.

Steve parked up. I took a deep breath and blew the freezing air in a white stream from my lips. This was the part I hated the most. I hoped to god that after tonight I'd never have to go through it again. I shuddered just thinking about it.

'Looks like they're already here,' I said. Their Jag was on the far side of the car park. Snow was forecast. I pictured us trapped in the hotel for days with Malcolm and Brenda, having to be rescued by a snow plough. 'Do you think I should call Mum, see if she's fed Alice yet?' I'd told her to get her to bed by seven at the latest and have a nap herself because she was bound to be up in the night.

'She'll be fine.' Steve lifted our overnight bag from the boot.

The woman behind the desk smiled. 'Can I take a name please?'

'Charlotte Morgan.'

At that moment, Malcolm clattered through the door. He'd grown a moustache and was seesawing his pursed lips from side to side as though trying to shift this thing that had appeared on his top lip. I pulled on Steve's arm, trying not to giggle.

'Ah good, you're here.' Malcolm shook Steve's hand, then clasped mine. His skin was dry and rough. 'Settle yourselves in, go for a swim or a sauna, then give us a buzz later when you're ready.'

The woman's thick painted brows rose up. Great, now she thought we were swingers.

'Will do, thanks,' I said.

Malcolm rubbed his sandpaper hands together and trotted off.

'Here we are, Room 19, our best Deluxe double.' The receptionist handed me the key.

'And payment?' I asked. I guessed Malcolm had paid again but we didn't want to take it for granted.

'All been settled by your gentleman friend.' A smile slid up her face.

'Nice one.' Steve nodded at me.

'Breakfast is served between eight and ten. You're welcome to use all the facilities. There's a pool, spa, sauna room, hot tub and gym. The restaurant opens at seven p.m. I hope you enjoy your stay.'

Our room was bigger than before, modern and clean with a double wardrobe, sofa, and en-suite shower cubicle and bath.

'Ooh look at this.' There was a bouquet of roses arranged in a vase on the coffee table.

Steve fell back on the enormous bed. I opened the window. In the distance a lorry on the A1 hooted and another replied in a little tune.

If only there was a more glamorous way of doing this. We'd agreed at the start to do it our own way, on our own terms. This was a private arrangement between four sensible adults. Lots of people on the forum had done it before us. A few minutes of being uncomfortable would be worth it. Surrogates posted their photos up all the time. That special moment an intended mother holds her baby for the first time; that's what it was all about for me. I needed to push the worry away and focus on that. Think about Brenda and the bigger picture.

Steve took out a small towel we'd brought from home and put the plastic syringe on top, ready for later.

My phone buzzed, giving me a start.

'Oh god, it's Mum.'

'You'd better answer in case it's about Alice.'

I waved at him to turn the TV down. 'Everything okay, Mum?' I put the call on loudspeaker.

'Alice is fine. She's being a treasure.'

'Thank god, you had me worried.' I pressed my palm to my chest, rolled my eyes at Steve.

'I just wanted to ask you to think really hard about what you're doing.'

'Mu-um. We've been over this.'

'That's not the point. I don't want you getting hurt. What about the risks to your health? Anything could go wrong.'

'It's not going to.' I did not need this right now. Steve raised his eyes to the ceiling.

'Will the baby have a chance to know where it came from?'

'Yes, we've agreed those things. You don't need to worry.' I clenched my teeth.

'But what if they change their minds and you're left with another man's baby?'

'I can't think why they would do that.' After the scare of not being able to get hold of them, I was trying hard not to worry about this. I couldn't think of one logical reason why they would back out.

'They could feel threatened having the birth mum around. Some women can get very possessive. And what if the child decides to live with you when it's older? They might be afraid of losing it to you. Have you thought about that?'

'Mum, please. Enough,' I shouted, 'I've just told you, they're happy for me to stay in touch after they become the legal parents.' I shook my head at Steve. He lay on the bed, his arm across his face.

Silence.

'I'm just looking out for you, that's all.'

'I know, Mum, I'm sorry, I didn't mean to snap, but I'm going to go now. I'll talk to you in the morning.' I didn't wait for her reply. Tears pricked my eyes. All those years of heartache. I'd felt it too. 'Why can't she accept this? Be pleased with what I've decided.'

'Come here.' Steve reached out to me.

I sat next to him and he curled his fingers between mine.

'She'll get used to it, I promise. She's trying to protect you because you're her only child. It would be strange if she wasn't like this.'

'I suppose.' I wiped my eyes. I knew from Mum how it felt, that deep-seated longing for a baby, the hunger gnawing at you down to the bone, turning to a fever, sending you out of your mind.

Steve put his arms around me. 'Are you sure you're okay with this? Do you want to have a bit longer to think?'

'No, I'm fine. I've never been more ready for anything in my life.' And in that moment, saying it aloud, I really meant it.

–

After a swim and a shower, we met Malcolm and Brenda in the restaurant. He was wearing another V-neck jumper, this time slate grey. Brenda wore a wrap-over dress, hair tied up, sensible court shoes and navy tights. They leaned into each other, shoulders touching, chatting quietly. I hoped me and Steve would grow that comfortable so I didn't have to worry about wearing matching underwear or straightening the frizz out of my hair every morning. One day, if we both worked hard and used the expenses money wisely, we might be able to afford elegant clothes and weekends away in country hotels. If Mum was across the room right now, it would be easy to pair her and Brenda up as friends. The similarities between them made it easier for me to do this. Two peas in a pod, Nan would have said.

'You all right mate?' Steve patted Malcolm's shoulder. They shook hands.

I gave Brenda a hug, holding her a bit longer than usual as I squeezed my eyes shut and silently prayed for it to work this time. When she pulled away, there were tears in her eyes.

'It's going to happen this time. I have such a strong feeling in my bones,' Brenda blurted out. Malcolm and Steve were quiet, watching us.

'I feel it too.' I held her hands gently. A strong aura wrapped around us. If the lights were switched off, I was certain we'd be able to see it. God moves in mysterious ways, Nan used to say.

We ordered from the à la carte menu and Malcolm chose a bottle of Moët. The waiter popped it open, filling four champagne flutes.

'Here's to our success.' Malcolm raised his glass, then clinked it with each of ours. 'I want you to have this now, whatever the outcome tonight.' He stuffed a wad of fifty-pound notes in my hand and looked me directly in the eye. 'I want you to know how much we appreciate this. It's not been easy for you, has it?'

I held the heavy bundle tight, not sure whether to hand it back. The weight of responsibility pressed down on me.

'Best to put it away,' Brenda whispered.

I mouthed thank you to them and stuffed it in my handbag.

'Here's to you both, let's hope it's a success this time.' I drained my glass. Malcolm immediately topped it up. I stopped him halfway. 'Best not to have too much, eh?'

Steve was unusually quiet. For once he seemed unfazed by the money. He reached over and laid his hand on top of mine. If only we could guarantee it would work this time. The familiar mixture of yearning and dread every time Mum fell pregnant, churned around my stomach. I'd coped by ticking the days off on a calendar, praying that this was the one who would survive and be born alive. But it was never to be, and I'd ended up marking the day each of them died, with a big black cross.

Chapter Eleven

Back in our room, I sat at the small round table by the window and took out the wad of notes. I flicked the crisp edges.

'Do you want me to count it?' Steve switched on the TV and stretched out on the bed.

'I think I can manage.' I counted out a grand in fifties. I could save this for Alice, but it felt too much like dirty money. Paying for my services. I'd always be reminded of this night, of being inseminated with his sperm. I shuddered.

This waiting part was the hardest, especially now we knew that Malcolm and Brenda were only next door. I did not want to hear a thing. I'd turn the TV up if necessary.

'Do you think he's going solo or will he need Brenda's helping hand?' Steve held his stomach as he rolled on his side laughing.

'Ssh, they might hear you,' I hissed, feeling queasy at the thought of it. I pushed away the images it brought up in my head of Malcolm's sperm wearing little V-neck jumpers, struggling to swim towards my egg.

I peered out of the window, cupping my hands around my face to block out the light. The sky here was darker than at home, the stars brighter. I found the brightest and focused my thoughts on it, praying for it to be a sign.

Under a pool of light in the car park, a figure standing alone caught my attention. It couldn't be, surely. 'I think it's that woman again.'

'What?'

'Seriously, it looks just like her, with the curly hair. The one outside work a while ago.'

'It can't be.'

'Come and look.'

He jumped off the bed and pressed his nose to the glass, covering his head with the curtain. 'Where?'

'By the entrance.' I pulled the curtain back to have another look. 'Shit, where's she gone? Why is she following us?'

Steve laughed. 'You must be imagining things. Why would she be anything to do with us?'

'It's just a weird feeling I get that we're being watched.'

'Don't be daft. We're not doing anything illegal.'

I pulled the curtains firmly shut. Maybe he was right.

'Come and watch this film.' He leapt back onto the bed.

'What is it?'

'*The Omen*.'

'Isn't that dead creepy?'

'Yeah, but it's good.'

There was a light tapping on the door, making us both jump. Steve launched himself off the bed and opened the door a crack.

'It's only me,' Brenda whispered.

Steve opened the door wider. Brenda took a sample bottle of Malcolm's sperm out from under her cardigan.

'Not as much this time. I hope it's enough.' It was about a quarter full.

'Only takes one strong swimmer.' Steve took it from her, trying not to look at the contents, holding the lid gingerly with thumb and forefinger.

'I'm sure it'll be fine,' I told her. Brenda gave a thin hopeful smile and we said good night.

'Are you ready for this?' Steve asked when he'd shut the door.

The thought of another man's sperm inside me again brought bile to my throat. It did the other times too and I'd had to get past it, remember what this was all for.

I changed into my nightdress and lay on the bed, my bottom planted in the middle of the towel, legs wide. Steve opened the bottle and using the medicine syringe, he carefully sucked up as much of the sperm as he could. He held it up so as not to let any drip out, then gently plunged it inside me, as far as I said felt comfortable. Slowly, he released the sperm. Once he'd withdrawn it, I rolled back and pushed my legs straight up, steadying myself by putting my hands beneath my hips. I'd read that staying like that for as long as possible could increase the chances of conceiving.

Afterwards, we carried on watching the film, cuddled up together and both fell asleep before the end.

–

After breakfast, we said goodbye to Malcolm and Brenda. As I hugged Brenda, she started to cry.

'She's been like this all night,' Malcolm said and checked his watch.

'I'll do a pregnancy test as soon as I can, I promise.'

'Let us know how you're feeling. Fingers crossed.' Malcolm leaned down and gave me a kiss on the cheek, scraping my face with his beard.

'Eat and rest well, won't you?' Brenda put her arms out again and wrapped me to her warm chest. 'Precious cargo. We'll have to get you a warning T-shirt.'

'Come on now,' Malcolm opened the car door. 'We're in Dubai in a few weeks, Skype us any news, won't you?'

'Of course. Have a lovely time,' I said, waving them off. It wasn't long before we were stuck in traffic. Steve switched the CD player on, midway through 'I'm Not Down' by The Clash.

'I think I might give up work earlier, like Brenda suggested,' I said.

'You don't even know if you're pregnant yet.'

'I know, but I've been thinking it over and I'm definitely sticking to the food and drink rules this time. I'll make sure I rest more too.'

'Do what you think is right for you.'

'We don't know anything about his medical history, do we?'

'Do we need to?'

'There might be something that affects the pregnancy. Maybe why I was sick last time?'

'That's not to do with genes though, is it?'

'Serious morning sickness can run in families.'

'See how you get on and ask Malcolm if you're worried. Do you think it's more Brenda wanting a baby than him?'

'They've been together, what, twenty years? He's used to a good lifestyle without kids. A big old change when you're pushing fifty.' Would he be one of those old-fashioned dads that refused to change a nappy or give the baby a bath? He might find the broken sleep and baby crying too much to cope with. If it was a boy, would he tell him not to cry? I pushed the thoughts to the back of my mind.

We pulled into a busy Welcome Break on the way home for an all-day breakfast. Steve stuffed his pockets with sachets of ketchup and brown sauce. I rolled my eyes at him as usual.

By the time we reached Mum's house, it was late afternoon. She shushed us as soon as she opened the door.

'She's asleep upstairs.'

'Oh, Mum, she won't sleep tonight now.'

'But it is night.'

'Hardly.'

'I used to put you to bed at five p.m. at that age.'

'If she wakes up she won't go back to sleep. Has she eaten?'

'She ate a few carrot sticks with hummus and half an apple after we came back from the park. She was so tired, poor little poppet, she fell asleep at the table.'

Steve brought Alice down, wrapped in her blanket. 'I think she's out for the night.'

Mum handed me Alice's bag.

I opened the front door.

'Not staying for a cuppa?'

I exchanged a look with Steve. 'We'd better get back, thanks.'

'It went all right then?' Mum followed us out to the car. Steve carefully sat Alice in her seat and strapped her in.

'The deed is done. Have to wait and see now,' Steve told her.

'I see.'

'I know you're hoping it won't work, Mum.'

'If it doesn't, you know they'll find someone else, don't you? What I mean is, you shouldn't feel it's your responsibility.'

I climbed into the back seat with Alice before I said something I shouldn't. 'Thanks for looking after her.'

Mum nodded.

I jumped back out and gave her a peck on the cheek. 'I'll be fine, Mum, I promise.' I wished I felt as certain as I sounded.

Chapter Twelve

It was the usual crowd at the club on Friday night. Dan and Carly were already there. The first rounds of pool had started. Steve went to the bar and bought me a lemonade and a pint of lager for himself.

I'd been working behind the bar when I first met him, both straight out of school at sixteen. I hadn't seen the point in staying on to do A levels when I couldn't afford to go to university afterwards. I took on cleaning jobs during the day, while Steve became an apprentice mechanic. He'd come in every night for weeks, eyeing me up. I checked him out too. He was fit. Worked out every morning before work. He wasn't rude like a lot of the lads and best of all he wasn't pushy. We'd often chat while I served the customers. It was a good few weeks before he asked me out and it felt completely natural to say yes. He took me to the Crooked Cat for a posh meal. I wore a red satin dress I'd bought in the sales. He was a real gent. I'd never felt so special. When I introduced him to Mum, I was pleased that she'd liked him straight away.

He put my drink on the table and said hello to my friends. He kissed my neck, then my lips, before he went back to the bar.

'You are lucky, you know that, don't you? Jammy cow,' Milly said, sitting opposite me. I smiled to myself. She always said that. I wished she could find someone special too. We'd been friends since school, but she'd never had a relationship that had lasted more than six months.

'I'm guessing there's no vodka in that?' Carly asked, giving a little wink.

I grinned. 'Got to be careful.'

'So, come on then, spill.' Milly nudged my leg with hers, nursing her half empty pint glass.

I shrugged. 'Nothing to tell yet.'

'How are you feeling though?'

'Fine. At the moment.' I laughed.

'What are these people like exactly?' Milly twisted her red hair until it resembled a rope.

'They run their own business, they're a bit older than my mum and…' I lowered my voice, 'the woman has had eleven miscarriages.'

'Oh my god, that's awful.' Milly looked at the others, who nodded.

'So, what's the husband like?' Shell asked.

'I think he'd do anything for his wife.'

'Ah, that's lovely. I need a man like that,' Milly sighed.

'Me too,' Shell said.

'Hey, won't it be weird to have a baby that looks like you and this bloke? I mean, is Steve all right with that?' Milly pulled a sour face.

'Yeah, he's fine. It's not like we're keeping it, is it?' I laughed.

'If they want a second child, would you do it again?' Milly asked.

'I don't think so.' I shrugged. 'I'll see how this goes.'

Steve came over with a cue in one hand and a pint of lager in the other. I smiled up at him. He finished his drink and shoved his empty glass onto the table.

'I think what you're doing is really kind.' Shell linked her arm through mine. 'Having a baby is not easy.'

'Mmm. Rather you than me.' Milly finished her drink and took her glass to the bar. Steve kissed my hair and went to begin his match.

Milly came back, banging down a tray of drinks. 'Are they proper rich then? What's their business called?' She opened several bags of crisps, put them in the middle of the table and started tucking into them. 'Help yourselves,' she said with her mouth full.

'Premier Properties. You should see some of the houses they sell. They have a beautiful home too. Cream and gold inside, massive rooms. Their kitchen has an annexe with a glass roof.'

'Have you actually been there?' Milly stopped chewing to speak.

'No, silly, they live in Orkney. They come down to see us. They travel all over the world for their business.'

'Blimey, worth staying friends with them. Maybe I should give it a go too.' Milly patted her belly.

I frowned. Maybe the others thought I was doing it for the money too, even though I'd told them about Mum and why I wanted to help Brenda.

'So you've got everything in writing have you?' Milly asked.

'It's in the agreement, yes.'

'I thought you said that wasn't legally binding?'

'It's not but—'

'What if one of you changes your mind?' Carly chipped in.

'I don't think any of us will.' I forced a smile and turned to Shell.

'But it's not going to be easy giving up the baby, is it?' Milly asked.

'I doubt it, but then why would I want to keep a baby that wasn't Steve's?'

Milly nodded and glugged down a mouthful of beer.

'So they won't be able to do as much travelling when the baby's here, will they?' Carly dug her hand in the bag of salt and vinegar crisps.

'I'm guessing they'll scale it back for a while. The husband can probably carry on, but I can't see his wife wanting to travel with a tiny baby.'

'When do you think you'll tell Alice about it?' Milly finished her beer.

'The plan is for her to grow up knowing her half-brother or sister.'

'Oh I see.' Milly stood up.

'I'm going out for a ciggie.' Shell gently nudged me with her elbow.

'I'll come with you, it's stuffy in here.' I gave a little wave to Steve, who was at the far end of the room, about to take a shot.

I pushed open the heavy squeaking door and breathed in the cold evening air. The wind had picked up, but the sky was clear and the stars insanely bright.

'Blimey, Milly's on your case tonight.' Shell lit her roll-up behind her hand.

'And Carly.'

'Neither of them has the first clue about having kids.' She laughed.

We strolled around the side of the pub to a small enclosed garden. Across the road, the off-licence and chippy were busy, with people spilling out of the doors. Shell's cigarette went out. She turned to the wall to try and relight it.

Up the road near the bus stop, a car was parked, a woman in a suit standing next to it. My heart skipped. Could it be her again? Steve would think I was being paranoid. I moved nearer the building, into the shadows, as the woman got in the car and drove away.

As we were going back inside, Steve came out of the hall looking for me.

'You okay?' he asked.

'Yeah, I suddenly feel really tired. I think I'd better go home.' Perhaps this was it, I was pregnant again.

We went and said our goodbyes, then walked home, hand in hand. Mum texted to say that Alice had gone to sleep without a fuss and she'd bring her back in the morning.

As soon as we got in, I undressed and got straight into bed. Steve turned the lights out and put the TV on. *Top Gun* had just started. I cuddled up to him and fell asleep.

As the film was ending, I woke up, my eyes half glued with sleep. Slowly, I became aware of Steve laying close to me. He kissed me, and I kissed him back. We turned towards each other and he gently pushed inside me. He groaned softly as we moved together. Afterwards, I slipped back into a deep sleep.

Chapter Thirteen

The next three weeks floated by. Alice started at nursery twice a week to give Mum a break and I increased my hours at the deli to six a day. I thought I may as well while I was still feeling well. I opened a Junior Savers account for Alice and put my name down for a Teacher Education Info Evening at Bedford College, to find out about the courses starting in September.

By the fourth week, I was up early on Saturday being sick.

'This is it, time to take a test,' Steve said.

I'd guessed I was pregnant a few days before, from my sore breasts and waves of tiredness that came out of nowhere. Steve made us a cup of tea. I texted Brenda to say I'd been feeling nauseous.

Alice played on her mat in front of me, chattering away to herself in a toy mirror. I wanted to get one of those wooden playpens now she was moving around more, but there wasn't enough space when the bed was out. Shell told me to get a travel cot and use that instead so I could fold it away when we weren't using it. I'd have a look online, see if I could get one locally. Trouble was it might have been sicked over, like the pram Mum brought over before Alice was born. One of her worst boot sale finds. A gorgeous sky-blue with various reclining positions, but the material was filthy in places with a faint smell of vomit. I'd tried to hide my upset, but I'd burst into tears. My baby was worth more than that. I'd longed for a brand new one. In the end, Steve bought one on his credit card. At least we'd been able to pay that off now.

I wanted to give Alice a bath before Dan and Carly came over to watch a film. I wished we had an actual bath. She'd grown way too big for the sink. We'd tried showering her, but she cried at the force of the spray and the water running in her eyes. I was terrified of her slipping from my arms.

A reply from Brenda pinged up on my phone.

Can I Facetime you?

Course you can!

Brenda's face appeared. 'How are you?' Her hair was messier than usual and she hardly had any make-up on. She moved closer to the screen, then away again. Malcolm appeared behind her, squinting.

'Paula's been dying to hear from you!' He held a hand up in greeting.

Brenda turned to stone. I swear she stopped breathing. I glanced up at Steve standing next to me and back at Brenda. Malcolm darted looks all over the place.

'Silly old goat. He's just been talking to his sister.' Brenda drew in a sharp breath, then let it out, her hand flat to her chest. 'Getting all muddled up, aren't you?' her eyelids flickered. 'How are you?'

'I… I've only been sick this morning so far. I thought it might be worth taking a test? But maybe I'm just under the weather?'

'We'd like you to take it.' Malcolm smiled and crossed his arms.

'Oh okay. I'll call you back if that's all right. I'll only be a few minutes.'

'That's fine,' Malcolm said.

'Chat soon.' Brenda gave a forced smile. The screen went blank.

'What was that all about?' I swung round to Steve as soon as I'd switched my phone off. 'I don't remember him saying he had a sister.'

'Can you believe he got her name wrong?' Steve wrinkled his nose. 'I mean it wasn't even a slip of the tongue, like say Bryony. Why Paula? That's just weird.'

'Could have been a genuine mistake, but what about Brenda's reaction? Like he'd committed an actual crime.' I shook my head.

'She's old-school though. Manners are important to her. Most of us wouldn't give a shit.'

But I went off to the bathroom, Mum's words ringing in my ears: *How well do you know these people?*

Chapter Fourteen

When we called them back, Brenda's eyes were red and sore, but she wore what I guessed was a fixed smile.

'Good news.' I showed them the new positive test. Tears welled in my eyes. This is what I'd hoped for.

'Oh my goodness, look, Malcolm.' Brenda's hands cupped her mouth.

Malcolm leaned over her shoulder, his face half filling the screen. When he spoke, I wasn't listening, I was staring at his strangely perfect white teeth. Why hadn't I noticed them before? Were they new? I imagined them dazzling out from his skull.

'When do you think it will be, Charlotte?' Steve jogged me with his elbow. 'The first scan,' he said under his breath.

My mind was miles away. 'It's normally at twelve weeks.'

'I pray we get that far this time. Could we come with you?' Brenda asked.

'Should be okay if you don't mind going private. I'll have to let you know the date.'

'Wonderful. I can't wait.' Brenda seemed nervy, her smile dropping every time she looked down at her linking and unlinking fingers.

As soon as they rang off, I leaned into Steve. 'What is going on with them today? Brenda seemed completely stressed out.'

'She probably doesn't want to put Malcolm's hopes up too much. Can't be easy for him with his huge ego.'

Steve always managed to make me smile.

'I'm scared of losing it again, letting them down.' I picked at a button on his polo top. One small tug and it would come off.

'I know,' he kissed my forehead, 'but they have every faith in you, as I do. It's a risk they're willing to take.'

'You're right. It's definitely Brenda who wants it more though, isn't it?'

'Yeah, and I think he's a good bloke doing this for her. He must love her a lot.'

'But they should both want it, shouldn't they?' There was something about Malcolm today that left me with a growing sense of unease.

'He'll probably be more into it the moment the baby's in his arms. Anyway, bit late to have doubts now, hun. You're carrying the fruits of his loins.'

'Don't say it like that, sounds sleazy, like I've slept with him.' I wrinkled my nose and play-punched his arm.

'I know he's not laid a finger on you. Bet he'd like to though.' Steve gave a dirty laugh.

'Stop! That's not even funny.' I jabbed a finger at him. 'You're a sicko sometimes.'

'I've seen the way he looks at you.' Steve laughed and pulled me on top of him, unbuttoning my top.

I pushed his hands away and kissed his lips. 'Later. I need to give Alice a bath, remember?'

He held my wrists and tried to stop me, but I swung my legs round and stood up.

In the bathroom, I filled the sink with warm water and a drizzle of peach bubble bath. I stood at the mirror until it misted over and my face was a shadowy outline. Milly and Carly's questions floated round my head, sending my mind drifting back to the Skype call with Malcolm and Brenda when we were writing up our agreement.

'Come on Malcolm, it's three against one mate,' Steve had said, trying to keep it light-hearted. But Malcolm had sat back on their sofa, legs stretched wide, arms crossed on his chest, shaking his head.

'What are you worried about exactly?' I asked.

'I think he's concerned it will be tying us down.' Brenda placed her hand on his thigh.

'I really want Alice to get to know her half-brother or sister. It doesn't have to be regular visits, just a few times a year, in person, over Skype, whatever suits us all at the time.'

'It wouldn't hurt would it?' Brenda patted his leg. He glowered at her.

'I think the child should be given the chance of getting to know me when he or she is older, if they want to. Isn't that their human right?'

'Come on Malcolm, it's not too much to ask is it?' Steve said, linking his arm through mine.

'Charlotte *is* doing this amazing thing for us,' Brenda said.

Malcolm had nodded his agreement in the end, but I wondered now if it was only because we pushed him into it, if he ever intended to stick to his word.

I wiped my finger up and down the mirror until I could see myself again, like peering through a little window into the future. What would Alice make of it all when she was older, when we told her we'd given away her half-brother or sister? I hoped that if she was able to grow up knowing the child, it would be easier for her to accept. But even if we did keep in touch, the child might resent me for not keeping them. And how would they feel when they discovered I took money in exchange? They might believe it was a heartless transaction –

that I sold them for cash. My gut twisted into a knot because it was true, I *was* taking payments for a baby. Even though it was money for expenses, I'd probably end up having to defend myself.

Chapter Fifteen

The sickness kicked in fully the following week. Relentless nausea that led to throwing up every time I tried to eat. I didn't want to feel sorry for myself knowing that Jack was about to start chemo, but I felt so ill I'd already had three days off work and Steve said Tash was not happy when he went to pick up his lunch.

Tash had never been able to have children, but she'd wanted them dearly. Her husband let it slip to me soon after I had Alice. I thought they should try surrogacy, but I didn't say. They were about the same age as Malcolm. I'd always made sure I didn't overdo the baby talk at work except to Shell, who had two of her own at primary school. She thought Tash was jealous of me having a baby for someone else. I did feel sorry for her.

While I was still off sick, Mum called in unexpectedly one lunchtime. I opened the door still in my pyjamas, my face probably sickly pale.

'When were you going to tell me you were pregnant again?' She bustled in after me, dumping a bag of One Stop shopping on the counter. I slumped on the end of the bed and dragged the sick bucket between my legs. I felt too weak to fight with her.

'It's the last time, I promise,' I said.

She tutted as she unloaded a punnet of grapes, a bottle of orange juice, a pint of milk and a loaf of bread.

'I don't want us to fall out. Please, just let me do this?'

She stopped and stared at me, her lips pulled in tight like she was trying not to cry. Her eyes shut for a long second and I detected the faintest nod.

After a week with no let up, Steve booked me in to see the doctor. I'd lost weight; my jeans were falling off me. Mum didn't say a word when we dropped Alice with her. The worry was right there in her eyes.

'Do you think I should call Brenda?' I asked as we got in the car.

'What's the point?' Steve said.

'I promised to keep them in the loop.'

'She'll only worry. Let's at least see what the doc says first.'

The doctor prescribed anti-sickness medicine and sent me straight over to the hospital for an early pregnancy scan to make sure the baby wasn't affected.

'Now we'll have to call Brenda. You know they're funny about me taking drugs, they don't even want me to have paracetamol. They'll have to accept I need to take these, though, won't they?' I said, wringing my hands.

'Okay, slow down, let's wait and see what the scan tells us first.' Steve pulled into the hospital car park. I didn't know how he always managed to stay so calm. As we parked, I caught sight of a woman in a light-coloured trouser suit hurrying towards the hospital building. I unclipped my seatbelt and leaned forward, straining to see her more clearly, but she'd already gone. Had I imagined the bounce of curly dark hair? It couldn't be the same woman, could it?

'You okay?' Steve asked.

'Yeah, I'm fine, it's nothing.'

In the waiting area, I put a hand to my non-existent bump and wondered what was going on in there. If I didn't drink too much or eat large quantities, I was mostly all right. But the doctor had told me to drink about a litre of water before the scan. God help me if I threw it all back up.

Sure enough, after four large glasses of water swishing about in my stomach, I rushed to the toilet. I was only sick once thankfully. When I was called, Steve helped me to the scan room.

The midwife squirted warm gel on my bare stomach. She pushed the paddle down and swept it steadily across my skin. I reached for Steve's hand. He squeezed mine tight. I couldn't do this without his support. I wanted to cry, praying this baby was okay.

'Well well, look at this.' The midwife's face brightened. She swivelled the screen towards us. 'You're having twins, my darling.'

I drew in a breath, staring in utter wonderment at the two hearts flickering on the dark hazy image. I was unable to speak.

'Two babies.' Steve stared at the screen, mesmerised.

I lapped up the moment until reality pinched my chest. They weren't *our* babies.

'They're still so tiny, which is why we can't see them very well, but they both have strong healthy heartbeats.'

I blinked away tears. Brenda should be here to see this. Steve gawped at me.

'Bit of a shock for you, eh? Double trouble.' The midwife chuckled.

'Was not expecting that for a single second.' Steve touched his forehead.

'Let me measure them for you. Here we are, five weeks, three days. Not too long until the twelve-week check-up so take the medication for the sickness, it will really help stabilise you and allow these two to get all the nourishment they need.

Eat little and often. Most sickness passes by the end of the first trimester.'

I left the room, a mixture of horror and elation swirling inside me.

All the way home, Steve and I sat in stunned silence.

'What will Brenda say?' I said at last.

Steve shrugged. 'I'm guessing she'll be pleased. Not so sure about Malcolm.' We stopped at traffic lights and turned to each other.

'They will want both babies, won't they?'

'Shit. It's not in the agreement.' The lights turned green. He drove on.

'Why didn't we think of it?' I twisted round in my seat, my hand on the dashboard to steady myself.

'I don't know. When are we going to tell them?'

'Today, it has to be today,' I said. 'If it comes to it, we'll keep one, won't we?' I tried to catch Steve's eye.

'Wouldn't we put it up for adoption?'

'What? *My* baby?' My heart thudded against my chest.

'It's not yours though, is it?' His voice was gentle.

A flash of heat surged through me. 'It is if they don't want it.'

We stopped at another red light. I imagined my face flushing the same colour.

'They're sure to want both anyway.' He nodded, probably trying to convince himself as well as me.

'We can't assume they will.' I flopped back in the seat.

'Maybe we could ask for more money.'

I shook my head in disbelief.

'Why not?'

Two kids on the back seat of the car in front of us were jumping all over the place, clearly not strapped in. 'I have to go and say something,' I said, unclicking my seat belt.

'No, you can't.' The lights turned amber.

'But those kids are in danger, right there in front of us.' I opened the door and started to get out.

'You can't fix everyone, Charlotte.'

'What do you mean?' I glared back at his face lined with worry. 'Those children are too young to know it's dangerous. Look at the mother, yacking on her phone.'

'Please leave it, the lights are changing.' He caught hold of my wrist.

'Is that what you think, that I'm some bloody do-gooder?' I shook him off. The car in front moved forward, another beeped us from behind.

'Of course not. I know you can't help caring, but I think there's a point where you have to let things go.'

I swung my legs back in, slammed the door shut and fastened my seat belt. Why hadn't any of us thought about the possibility of twins? I'd seen nothing about it on the forums. 'What if they want me to abort one, like with IVF?' A shiver passed through me.

Steve was silent.

'I'm telling you now, I will not do that for anyone.' I crossed my arms. I'd tried to stay emotionally distant, but it was impossible not to love these two tiny lives growing inside me.

Chapter Sixteen

I texted Brenda and arranged a call with them for when we got home. As soon as I got in, I ran to the toilet to be sick. Steve brought me a glass of water and when I felt better, I took my first sickness tablet.

Steve logged on to Skype. I sat Alice on my lap with her favourite musical book, *Incy Wincy Spider*. Malcolm and Brenda were sitting in what looked like a games room, a snooker table behind them and a bar in the corner. The patio doors were open, showing a lawn I couldn't see the end of.

'Hello, Alice, how are you?' Brenda waved.

'She's got yet another new tooth, haven't you, sweetheart.' I tickled Alice's sides. Her mouth opened when she giggled. 'Can you see it?'

Brenda moved closer to the screen. 'Oh yes, isn't it tiny? Bless her. Is it bothering her much?' She sat back and put her hand on Malcolm's knee.

'Not too bad so far, but she's dribbling like mad.' Steve took her from me and wiped Alice's chin with a muslin cloth.

'We've got some good and bad news,' I said.

Malcolm's face didn't move. Brenda frowned.

'I've been sick again, I mean a lot. I hoped it would pass, but it's been getting worse.'

'When she says sick, she means vomiting all the time, day and night, every half-hour or so,' Steve said.

'I'm so sorry, you poor thing.' Brenda glanced at Malcolm, who wrinkled his forehead.

'The thing is, the doctor had to give me drugs to control it because I can't keep a thing down. Not even water. I've actually lost weight.'

'Oh Charlotte.' Brenda moved to the edge of her seat.

'I know you said no drugs, but I really don't have much choice. I hope you understand.'

'She'll only need to take the pills up to the twelve-week point, with any luck,' Steve added.

'Are they concerned about the baby?' Brenda moved close to the screen again, this time half blocking Malcolm.

'Well that's the good news…' I could hardly contain my smile. 'The doctor sent me for an early scan to make sure the baby is fine, or should I say, babies.'

'What?' Brenda jumped a few inches out of her seat and her hands sprung up.

'How many?' Malcolm burst into a smile.

'You're having twins,' Steve said.

'Oh my lord, I can't believe it,' Brenda cried. She reached forward. 'I so want to give you a virtual hug right now.'

'Me too. Isn't it exciting?' I beamed, delighted at their response. I could almost detect the pent-up tension draining from my body. 'I'm almost six weeks already.'

'This is wonderful. Two babies!' Brenda held her palms to her pink cheeks.

Malcolm nodded, his face creased as though he was trying not to cry.

'I'm so glad you're happy about it. We didn't know if you'd set your mind on having just one. For some reason, we never discussed the possibility of twins.'

'We'd be happy with any number, wouldn't we?' Brenda said.

Malcolm leaned towards the screen. 'We'll pay you an extra ten thousand.'

'Really?' Steve and I looked at each other.

'Absolutely. I'll give you ten at the six-month stage and fifteen when you hand them over. Thirty-five total.'

'That… that's just brilliant, isn't it?' Steve grinned at me stupidly.

'It's really not necessary, but thank you.' My stomach tightened.

Steve stared at me wide-eyed as though I'd lost my mind. He pulled at my hand, but I tugged it away.

'I insist.' Malcolm leaned back in his chair, pressing his palms together.

I let out a deep sigh, but no one seemed to notice.

'I know it's early days and if anything goes wrong it will hurt all the more,' Brenda turned to Malcolm and cupped his face in her hands, 'but I want to enjoy each moment along our journey, even if it ends… differently. I want to celebrate these tiny lives every step of the way.'

Malcolm's face softened. He took her hand in his and kissed it. I realised how worried and tense he must have been all along and I'd made out he didn't care about this as much as Brenda. How mean of me to think that.

'We'll do everything in our power to protect them, we promise, don't we?' I linked my arm through Steve's. He was unusually quiet. He cleared his throat.

'We're made up for you, we really are,' he said.

–

By Monday, I was well enough to go back to work. Tash didn't say much at first, but I explained to her why I'd tried again for this couple, that being their surrogate was important to me because of Mum.

'Well, I hope they appreciate it,' Tash said, wiping down the countertop, collecting breadcrumbs in her cupped hand.

'They do, honestly. I'm sorry for the time off. I'll try and make it up.'

'All right, but you can't overdo it, can you? It's not just yourself you need to look after.'

Shell told me after our shift that Tash had been going on about replacing me if I had any more days off.

'She can't do that, can she?' I said.

Shell stubbed her cigarette out on the wall behind the bus stop. 'I told her, that's unfair dismissal, that is. Charlotte could make a claim against you.'

I giggled. 'What did she say to that?'

'Nothing.'

'She was actually all right to me today.' I hoped I'd put her mind at rest.

The nausea came back every now and again, but not enough to keep me off work. The weeks merged into each other. I hadn't told anyone else I was expecting twins, not even Mum. I'd been avoiding telling her, knowing what her reaction would be. It seemed like such a big thing to say and for Mum in particular to take in. Double the pressure for me to produce two healthy babies and twice as disappointing for her.

I went up to Jean's flat to collect Alice after work.

'Come in, come in,' Jean said, holding Alice on her hip, 'we've just finished playing on the tambourine.'

'She loves music, don't you, darling?' Alice put her hands out to me. I lifted her into my arms. 'She's obsessed with her little keyboard. It mainly plays the songs for her, but she loves it.'

'Do you want a cuppa? I've just made a pot.'

'Oh yeah, go on then. I wanted to ask your advice about something.'

She brought two mugs of tea into her living area and passed one to me. We sat on the sofa bed covered in a throw. Even though she minded children every day, her flat was far tidier than ours.

'I found out I'm expecting twins.'

'Oh my god, Charlotte. How do you feel about that?' She put her mug down with a clonk, sloshing a bit of tea over the side.

'Little bit shocked still, but not as shocked as Mum will be when I tell her.'

'Ah… of course.'

'Do I tell her? She's going to be so upset with me.' I sipped my tea. It tasted strong.

'From what you've told me, it's a really big deal for her, isn't it?'

'Completely and I get all that, of course I do, but maybe I should leave it a few months?'

'Until she guesses? And she more than likely will. I think that would be cruel. You need to be honest with her now.'

'I suppose so.'

'This is your decision and you have to stand by it, whatever the outcome. This is you, her grown-up daughter, deciding for herself to have babies for a childless couple. She will respect you for it in the end.'

'Do you think so?'

'I do. But that's just my own take on it. I'm not the one expecting twins for someone else. You need to do what you think is right for you.'

Deep down I knew she was right, but it didn't stop me worrying about upsetting Mum all over again.

Chapter Seventeen

The twelve-week scan was booked in for Thursday at 1 p.m. I'd have preferred Brenda to come on her own, give us a chance to have a girly chat, but I didn't say. We met at Debenhams café in Bedford town centre so that Brenda could have a look at prams first. She rushed forward and gave me a hug, squealing with delight when she saw my bump was starting to show. I'd done my best to eat healthily and take my vitamin pills.

'Almost time to meet your kids.' Steve shook Malcolm's hand. We took the lift up to the baby section. Brenda made a beeline for the Silver Cross pram and pushchair combination display.

'This is the one I saw online. There's a double option over here, see? Isn't that clever?'

'It's really smart, and versatile.' I tried to sound enthusiastic. It cost over sixteen hundred pounds. 'Don't you think you should wait a bit longer though?' It was still so early in the pregnancy, even though it was further than last time, it felt like she'd be jinxing it.

'I suppose so. I just wanted to show you, see what you thought.'

'It's the perfect choice. Does everything you want it to.' I hoped I came across as excited. Steve was loitering around the toy section while Malcolm seemed to be on his phone.

'Let's have a quick look at outfits. I'm allowed to buy a few little things, aren't I?'

I didn't answer. I followed her, trying not to notice the other pregnant women holding baskets of beautiful clothes for their unborn babies.

'We'll need these, won't we, for the hospital?' She picked up a pack of newborn baby nappies and another of muslin squares.

'I have lots of those at home you can have.' I still used some to wipe Alice's face and hands or mop up any mess she made.

'There's no harm buying new ones though, is there?' She added a second pack to the basket. 'Oh my, will you look at these sleepsuits. Aren't they cute?'

'Yeah, really sweet.'

She took down two designer outfits, with baby rabbits in lemon and white and mint and white. I would have loved to have had something so beautiful for Alice to wear, instead of the bundle of used clothes I'd bought at a boot sale.

'That's probably enough for now, isn't it?' I didn't want to tell her what to spend her money on, but I was nervous of her buying so early.

Malcolm cleared his throat. I hadn't noticed he was standing right behind us. 'We need to get a move on.' He tapped his watch.

-

At the hospital, I was called in quickly. Malcolm had paid for a private scan so they could both come in. We'd agreed not to explain who Malcolm and Brenda were. It was simpler that way. This was our business. In any case, Malcolm said they didn't want to have to answer a load of questions.

I watched the midwife's face weighing them up. Probably wondering if they were my parents or Steve's, but too professional to ask.

The image on the screen couldn't have been clearer. Two tiny babies, each moving in their own little space. This time I could see their delicate fingers and toes. My love for them was instant, a big whoosh right through my body. For a few precious moments, I forgot they weren't mine.

'Oh, Malcolm, just look at them.' Brenda clung to his arm.

'A healthy pair if ever I saw them,' the midwife said.

Steve stretched back in his chair, hands linked above his head.

'Are you going to find out the sex?' The midwife wiped the gel off my stomach.

Brenda smiled. 'Yes, I think we probably will.' I wondered why Brenda hadn't checked with me before we came in, although I had to remember, it wasn't my decision.

The midwife switched the lights back on and left the room to fetch a printout of the scan. Steve held his phone up and took a photo of Malcolm and Brenda, but when Malcolm saw what he was doing, he jumped out of his seat and made a grab for the phone. Steve stood up too quickly for him and staggered back a step, trying to catch his balance, the chair tipping over as he held the phone far out of reach.

'Delete that,' Malcolm's voice was more like a growl.

'What for?' Steve stayed standing.

I stole a sideways glance at Brenda. She'd frozen to her seat, eyes fixed on Malcolm. Why didn't she say something?

'I told you we want to keep our privacy.' He spoke through clenched teeth.

'I'm not going to show it to anyone, it's only for us.'

'Delete it.' Malcolm spoke in a more threatening tone this time.

Steve scratched his head, half frowning half smiling, clearly as taken aback as I was.

'All right mate, calm down.' Steve clicked a couple of buttons.

'Show me.' Malcolm held out his hand.

Steve flashed the screen at him. 'There, all gone.'

'Swipe back so I can see.'

Steve did as he asked. Malcolm gave a nod and sat back down, his hand resting on Brenda's leg. They exchanged a look that I tried to understand. Why had he flown off the handle like that?

'We're sorry, aren't we, Steve, we thought it would be a nice memento for you, that's all. No harm done.' Steve could have airdropped it to them before deleting it. I looked to Brenda to at least acknowledge that we didn't mean them any harm, but she stayed silent.

The midwife brought the scan picture back into the thick silence and handed it to me. I put it in my bag, my hands visibly shaking. We said our thank yous and shuffled out, heads down.

In the car park, Malcolm patted my shoulder. 'I'm sorry. I didn't mean to upset you.' He shook my hand, then Steve's.

'Goodbye,' Brenda said at last, her face drawn with an injured expression. She waited until Malcolm was ahead of her, almost at the car. 'I'm sorry he got so angry. He doesn't want anyone knowing our private business, judging us for not being able to have our own children or for using a surrogate.' She sighed. I imagined the kind of friends they had, ones with impossible standards, who only used hand-picked nannies to bring up their own, beautiful children.

'It's okay, it's not your fault.' I hugged her, but as Brenda drew back from me, she was shaking. 'Are you going to be all right?'

'I'll be fine, it's just my nerves. The pressure gets to him sometimes and it affects me. We've wanted a child for so long.'

I gave a nod. 'Does he often get angry like that?'

'No, no, not at all.' She shook her head.

We hugged again and said goodbye.

Back in the car, Steve finally spoke. 'What is his fucking problem?' He smacked the wheel.

'I don't know, I'm in shock. How overboard can you get?'

'I was doing them a favour.'

'Although they did say no photos. We need to respect their wishes. Why be aggressive though?'

'Well ha! I still have it.' He stabbed his finger at his phone and showed me.

'What?' I sat up straight.

'I emailed it to myself before I deleted it.'

'What for?'

Steve shrugged. 'Why not? Can't tell me what to do.'

'He seems to think he's in charge of us.'

'Didn't have to try and grab it off me.' He started the car.

'Brenda said he's not normally like that, but she was shaking. He can't be like that with kids around.'

'Better not be.'

'He needs to control himself. It's not like we're going to run to the papers and sell our story, is it?' I dug into my bag for my phone. Steve hadn't meant any harm. 'Oh no, look at this.' I plucked the scan picture out of my bag. 'I meant to give it to them.'

'Why didn't they ask you for it?' Steve frowned.

'I don't know, I suppose they forgot because of the photo business.'

'But if that was us, we'd have been dying to see it, wouldn't we?'

'Yeah.' I nodded.

'I don't remember them even looking at it.'

'Well, to be fair, we were in the middle of arguing. They must have forgotten. I did, didn't I?' But he was right, we would never have left without it.

He shook his head and drove us over to Mum's in silence. When we arrived, Mum was playing with Alice on the living-room floor. Plastic cups and farmyard animals were scattered across the cream carpet.

'Hello, sweetheart.' I scooped Alice up and held her tight.

'Everything well with the baby?' Mum asked, turning *The Archers* off.

'All good.' Although I was still yet to tell her it was twins.

'What is it?' Mum asked. 'Is there something else?'

'If I tell you, please try not to be mad at me.'

Mum crossed her arms. I handed Alice to Steve. He took her to the window to point out a robin on the fence.

'I'm having twins,' I said.

'Oh no.' Mum opened her hands out in front of her, as if to catch the world falling apart.

'They're pleased and we're pleased.' I knelt down and collected up Alice's toys. I counted up the animals but one of the baby piglets was missing.

'My grandchildren and you're giving them away?'

'We're getting more money for having two,' Steve said.

Mum and I stared at him. If I'd had a gun in my hand, I think I would have shot him in the foot.

'So, selling them for more money makes it better, does it?' Mum asked. 'If it's about your finances, I've told you before I've got a bit put by, I'm more than happy to help you.'

'And like I've said before, that's very kind of you, but I don't want to rely on you for money.'

Mum looked away.

'*Alice* is your grandchild,' I took the half-chewed baby piglet from Alice's hand, 'these babies are not mine.' I spread my fingers over my barely-there bump.

'Don't you feel anything for them?'

I shook my head, but a fizz of excitement and love had shot through me at seeing the new lives. Two babies tumbling together. Two peas in my little pod.

'I remember every single one of my babies. I knew every kick, every pattern of their movements. I spoke to them, sang to them… even though I was never blessed with meeting them.' Mum's voice was filled with a haunting sadness.

'Oh, Mum. That's why I'm trying to do something good, to bring joy to this couple.' I kissed Alice's chubby toes.

'These babies, Charlotte, they're our flesh and blood.'

She wasn't listening. My jaw set rigid. I turned away from her accusing face. Words backed up in my mouth. If I let them spill out, I'd never be able to take them back.

Steve quietly played peep-bo with Alice. I realised I still had my coat on. It was time to go.

'We're off,' I said, pulling at Steve's arm.

'Oh, already? Bye bye, poppet,' Mum kissed Alice as we bundled out of the door. Alice waved and made a b-b-b-b sound.

'I knew I shouldn't have told her,' I whispered as soon as we crossed over the road.

'She'd have found out.' Steve strapped Alice into her car seat.

'Why can't she understand that I can make my own judgements and my own decisions? That I'm grown up now, and this is a good, kind thing to do.'

'She'll get used to it eventually, hun.' Steve pulled me to his chest. The warmth of his musky aftershave calmed me. I shut my eyes and tried to imagine what it was like for the babies hearing all the muffled shouting, sensing my stress.

'I think I'll get Jean to babysit more for us. Might be easier while the babies are growing.'

'Isn't that the last thing your mum would want?'

'I have to put me and the babies first. I can't have them picking up on all this upset.'

'I'm not sure that's a good idea.'

'I don't know. I'm too tired now.' I leaned back in my seat, cupping my arm around my tiny bump, still shocked at the aggressive side we'd seen in Malcolm. Was it something we needed to worry about? The only thing I was certain of was that the twins were my priority, and for now they belonged to me.

Chapter Eighteen

I kept in touch with Brenda by text, updating her on my progress with selfies. It wasn't until a month after we'd last seen them that we Skyped again.

Brenda gave one of her finger waves. 'How are you? I hope you're well.' She seemed her usual glam self. They were sitting on a corner sofa on their patio – a huge lawn behind them, enclosed by trees and bushes, more like a park. I could just make out an arch near the bottom, which Brenda had told me led to her rose garden.

'Thank you, I'm fine.'

Malcolm smiled, relaxed in his chair. I searched his face for traces of anger from the day of the scan. I needed to know I could trust him, that it had been a one-off.

'How are you both?' Steve asked.

'Been so busy. We flew back from Saudi on Monday,' Brenda said.

'I'm lucky if I go to Brighton beach.' I darted a look at Steve. He shook his head slowly, as though I was making it all up. But the truth was we hadn't been able to afford a holiday for ages.

'You two okay?' Brenda frowned at us.

'We're fine.' I linked my arm through Steve's.

'Let's see your bump then.' Brenda clapped her hands.

I stood in front of the screen sideways and smoothed my hand down my T-shirt, holding it close to me at the bottom to emphasise the full roundness of my tummy.

'Gosh, getting so big already.' Brenda's eyes flashed.

'Only a month until the twenty-week scan.'

'Yes. We wanted to talk to you about that.' Brenda turned to Malcolm for a second, then back to the screen. 'We'd like to be there please, to find out the sex of the twins.'

I wanted to say no after Malcolm's outburst last time, but I didn't want to let Brenda down. 'As long as everyone stays calm this time.'

'Thank you, we appreciate it, don't we?' She nudged him gently with her elbow.

Malcolm seemed distracted, glancing behind him as though she was talking to someone else. Probably had some big business deal on his mind.

'Will you still be going on these business trips when they're born?' I asked.

'Probably not straight away. We might need to hire a nanny,' Brenda said, glancing at Malcolm, who nodded.

'I'm thinking of giving up work a bit earlier than I planned to. I'm managing my shift at the moment, but at the rate these babies are growing I wonder if I'll need to stop sooner.'

Malcolm rubbed his chin. He seemed more relaxed, but I couldn't pinpoint why. Maybe it was because I was past the first trimester. Brenda was right, he was more sensitive than he let on. I felt satisfied that it had been his way of showing his love for the twins.

-

I fainted at work the following Monday. The café was packed at lunchtime and, maybe because of the confined space and the air filled with the musty smell of damp bodies from the unexpected rain shower, I couldn't breathe.

Shell told me later that when I fell, everyone let out a collective gasp. Several people jumped up from their seats to help me. Fortunately, I slumped onto my side and was only out for a few seconds. Tash called Steve while Shell made me a cup of sweet tea. I soon felt better.

Steve finished work early and drove me home. He made me go to bed while he warmed a tin of tomato soup. Mum got wind of the incident and came knocking within the hour. Steve wasn't thinking and let her in.

'I know you don't want me here, and I'm not stopping, but I had to come and see how you are. Glenys called me. A friend of hers was in the café when you fainted.' She barged past Steve and plonked herself on a chair by the bed. 'How are you feeling?' She touched my forehead with her warm hand.

'A bit spaced out.' I didn't have the energy to argue or ask her to leave.

'Haven't you been eating properly?' She glared at Steve. 'Are you looking after her?'

I remembered the time she looked after me when I was off sick from school with flu. She'd snuggled up with me on the sofa under my duvet and we'd watched *Toy Story* and eaten a bag of popcorn.

'I'm eating all the time, Mum. These babies need so much food. I'm constantly hungry.' I had to smile at Steve, standing to one side of the sink, trying to hide the pile of pizza boxes, my latest not-so-secret craving.

'Who's been looking after Alice for you?' Her voice became as high and taut as a violin string.

'Jean, from upstairs. She's babysat for us before and I used to look after hers, remember? It's easier at the moment with her so close by.'

Mum's face fell. It took a second or two for her to speak. 'I hope these people are paying for all that. You could have had me for nothing.'

'We thought you'd like a bit more time to yourself now you're going to the gym more often, didn't we, Steve?' I needed help here, but he was staying shtum.

'Did I ask for any?' Mum fussed about with my duvet, pulling it up to my chin. Any moment she'd knock the bowl of tomato soup with her elbow and murder would be committed on my clean white sheets. When Mum became uptight, her head moved in a jerky way, like a chicken. I realised that it's not until you grow up that you notice your parents' flaws. And then they bug you like hell.

'Well no, but… look, I'm sorry.' I could tell her we didn't want the hassle at the moment – that sometimes it was easier not having her around because she had a knack of invading our space, taking over wherever she went. How much longer could I prevent her from meeting Malcolm and Brenda? No doubt there'd be something about them she'd find alarming or that gave her 'cause for concern'. Why couldn't she find the good in people?

Ever since Dad had walked out eight years ago, then met and moved in with Sandra four years ago, Mum had become bitter and suspicious of everyone new. If Sandra had been a twenty-something bit of skirt, I think in some ways Mum could have dealt with it better. But Dad's unexpected choice of a fifty-year-old widow, size fourteen with greying hair and glasses, Mum could not fathom. It was so much more insulting for a woman like Mum, only in her mid-forties, trim figure, appointments pre-booked for the coming months at the beauty salon.

'What does he see in Sandra?' Mum often still asked. 'Is it because I'm a hairdresser and she's clever – a doctor of something or other – is that it?'

I would half nod, not wanting to take sides. But I liked Sandra and her intelligent beauty. She encouraged me to think about going to college, the good I could do in the world with a better education. I couldn't tell Mum that. She would see it as my endorsement of her rival; a betrayal.

'I think they just clicked,' I'd told her, 'they're friends, they laugh together. She's not fussed if he wears blue with brown or leaves his clothes on the floor now and again. He cooks and keeps the garden tidy, takes the bins out.'

'He never did any of that for me,' she'd said.

I don't think she'd realised how miserable she'd been to be around towards the end of their marriage. Her deep unhappiness had to leach out somewhere, and it was Dad who'd suffered the brunt of it.

'I'll leave you both to it.' Mum got up to go.

'I'm sorry.'

She swung round and pointed her finger at Steve. 'Make sure you take good care of my daughter, please.'

'You have my word, Gloria.' He walked with her to the main door. I sighed. I shouldn't leave things like that, but I was struggling to find the energy to make peace with Mum.

I'd been thinking lately about going to visit Dad, see his new house, but I didn't fancy the heat in Portugal when I was so uncomfortable already. I'd promised to Skype him. As soon as I saw Mum drive off, I decided to call him. He was sitting up on a sun-lounger by the pool, cowboy-style hat shading his face.

'Hi Charlie, how are you, sweetheart?'

I smiled, hearing his special nickname for me.

'I'm fine, Dad, how are you? Looks lovely there.' I propped my phone up against a mug.

'Hot today. When are you coming over? It's been ages since we've seen you and Alice.'

'I'd love to, but I'd be so uncomfortable in that heat.'

'What's wrong, darling?'

I twisted the edge of my cardigan. 'I fainted at work.'

'Oh, darling, are you all right?' He sat up and moved into the shade.

'I should be okay now.' I felt the tears gathering.

'Hey come on, sweetheart. Is it your mum?' He took his hat off. His face came closer to the screen, clear blue eyes deep set in weathered mahogany skin. I remembered a time when there wasn't a line on his face. I'd run my tiny fingers up and down his stubble then onto smooth skin.

'You know how it is.' My hands linked into a fist in my lap.

'I wish she'd support you, put her own feelings aside.'

I gave a single hopeless laugh.

'You're doing a brave and noble thing and it's completely your choice. It's your body.'

'Try telling Mum that.' After Steve, it was Dad who I'd confided in about wanting to be a surrogate, how helpless I'd felt growing up, watching Mum go through one loss after another. I'd told him about Kerry having a baby for her brother and how good it made me feel thinking I could do that for someone too. He'd admitted he was worried in case anything went wrong, but said risks came with anything worth doing.

'She's worried about you. You're still so young, our little girl. And after everything, it's…'

I nodded. 'But I'm healthy. I've had a baby. I've researched it to death. I tick all the boxes.'

'There you are then. As long as you're happy about it, it doesn't matter what we think.'

Silence.

'Except it does to me, Dad.' Tears spilled onto my cheeks.

'Oh, sweetheart. I don't know what else to say, except that you're your own person now. Your mum knows you're trying to help someone who suffered like she did. She's just taking a bit longer to get used to that.'

I nodded and brushed away the tears with my fingertips. I wasn't sure Mum would ever change her mind.

-

I fainted again over the weekend. I was in our flat and Steve was there to help me. The doctors' was shut so he rushed me to A & E. They took a series of tests and found I had a kidney infection. I was sent home with a course of antibiotics.

Sometimes I wished the pregnancy was over. Time dragged. I lived minute by minute. When both babies moved at the same time, it was as though I lost control of my body. At work, Tash wouldn't give me any slack. I texted Brenda about going on maternity leave. She called me back on FaceTime, later that day.

'You poor thing,' Brenda said as soon as I told her all about the trip to the hospital and the tests.

'I'm so sorry, but I'm on yet another load of medication. I promise you I didn't have any of this trouble when I was pregnant with Alice.'

'It's not your fault. It must be miserable for you. You look well though.' Brenda was sitting in the sunshine further down her garden than before, on a tiered decking area with sofas and oversized silver herons either side of a hot tub.

'I don't feel it. I have to drink loads of water so I'm on the loo half the day. My boss keeps going on at me, even though I can't help it.'

'Look, if you do decide to stop work early, this week, next week, whenever, then just do it, we'll support you in every way we can.'

'I'll talk to Steve and Tash and decide on a finish date.'

'Great. Now, how are my little babies?'

'Moving well. I think they're responding to your voice, your unusual accent.'

'Yeah, I've been here too long.' She laughed.

'You never said whereabouts in America you're from.'

'Sorry, I thought I had. I was born in New York, came over here about fifteen years ago.'

'Oh, so you met Malcolm there?'

'We met here but decided to live in Manhattan for a few years.'

I held my phone so she could see my bump. It was the first time I'd properly talked to her without Malcolm being around. What if she decided to go back to the US? How would I be able to keep in touch with the twins?

When I looked at the screen, expecting to see Brenda beaming at my growing bump, she was crying.

'They'll be all right,' I tried to reassure her. It must be hard being so far away and not having any control. She had to rely on me completely, which was why I was determined to do the best I could. I'd been going to the grocers on the corner of the high street every morning on the way to work, buying myself a small selection of fruit and veg to graze on. I'd cut out our weekly Chinese takeaway because of the MSG and high salt content. I'd even made the switch to decaf coffee. Not one single drop of alcohol this time either. I didn't want to take any chances with these precious babies.

Brenda kept checking over her shoulder.

'Are you sure you're okay?' I asked.

Brenda nodded, pressing her lips together tightly. Malcolm started up the mower at the end of the garden.

'You'd tell me if it was something serious, wouldn't you?' Brenda said. I could ask her the same question.

'Honestly, it's just an infection. The babies aren't affected. This course of tablets should clear it up. Anyway, it'll be time to find out what sex they are soon. Is it one of each you want?'

'That's what I'd like, but…' Brenda hesitated, looking over at Malcolm again. He had his back to her. 'The thing is… he'd prefer boys.'

'He never said that before. You know I can't guarantee what sex they're going to be. Surely what matters is that they're healthy? I think they will be. Look at the size of me.' I blew my cheeks full of air to make her laugh.

A faint smile crossed her lips.

'Seriously, he'll be happy whatever they are, won't he?'

But her gaze dipped to one side, eyelashes flickering as though she was a robot shutting down.

'Brenda?' But I was looking over her shoulder, at Malcolm striding towards her.

'I'm not supposed to say I… I'd better go.' She stared at me for a long second, close to the screen, so I could almost feel her short breaths on my skin.

'Talk to me.' I tried to read her face, her eyes. Malcolm was right behind her, his face out of shot.

She reached out, fingertips skimming the screen. Then it went blank.

Chapter Nineteen

I tried calling Brenda back several times, but she didn't pick up. Now I knew Malcolm could lose his temper, I understood why Brenda seemed so anxious sometimes, as though she was trying not to upset him. Why had neither of them mentioned he wanted a boy when I was pregnant before? What if it had been a girl? What if I was carrying two girls now?

Steve brought home pizza and chips for dinner. Not the healthiest choice, but I had mine with a couple of pickled onions to cut through the fat.

As it was a warm evening, we took a grizzly Alice to the Forest Centre in her buggy to help her fall asleep. Another new tooth had been bothering her all day. Now the sickness and fainting had passed, I was getting to know the twins better. Their movements and kicks were often the highlight of my day, although sometimes the full tumbles stopped me in my tracks. Alice liked to watch the imprints of their feet as they pushed out my skin. In some ways I wished they were brothers or sisters for her. I'd asked the doctor if having the twins might affect my chances of giving birth to one of our own in the future, and she said it shouldn't do, but that nothing was guaranteed. The last thing I wanted was for Alice to grow up as a lone child like me.

I'd never forgotten the excitement of looking forward to having a brother or sister to play with. On the last weekend of the summer holidays, I'd ridden my bike to the park for the first time with Mum and Dad. They carried the picnic basket, a handle each, while Dad whistled all the way to the edge of the lake, a rolled-up blanket under his arm. We ate lunch, then played football, while Mum sat under a tree, balancing a book on her bump. But she wasn't reading, she was staring into the distance at the shimmering water.

They'd kept the first two stillbirths from me. I was only five so I wasn't aware that anything could go wrong, that this baby brother or sister I longed for with all my heart and made Mummy look comically fat, could be born sleeping.

It was the last time I remembered us being happy all together. Funny how you don't realise at the time; that life is never going to be the same again.

Steve and I sat on a seat carved out from a felled tree, painted with mermaids. I told Steve about my call with Brenda and what she had said about Malcolm wanting boys.

'I don't remember that ever coming up before.' Steve sat back with his legs stretched out.

'I'm worried that if I have girls, he won't want them.' I picked a buttercup from a patch of wild grass. Alice's eyes sparkled as I twirled it between my fingers. 'And, on top of it, they don't seem to be getting on at all. Brenda looked really upset, like she was almost scared of telling me.'

'It's stressful for all of us, so it's bound to put a strain on their relationship.'

'They must have argued about it. He'll probably be even more mad at her now.'

'He should have said at the beginning.'

'We wouldn't have gone ahead though, would we?' I held the buttercup under Steve's chin. Alice giggled at its yellow glow.

'I suppose not.' Steve took the flower and held it under Alice's chin.

'Well, now they'll have to wait until the twins are born to find out what sex they are,' I said.

'Why's that?'

Alice reached forward and took the buttercup from him.

'Because I've decided not to tell them the date of the twenty-week scan.'

Chapter Twenty

For the next four days I switched off my phone. I hadn't sulked like this since the day Dad left. We went down the club one night with Dan, Carly and the gang, but mostly we stayed in. I resisted the urge to turn my mobile back on. On the fifth day, I was on my laptop when an email arrived from Brenda saying she didn't blame me for being upset, but please, please could I call her.

Without waiting to speak to Steve, I switched my phone on. More than twenty missed calls from Brenda flagged up and several texts, begging me to answer or call straight back.

I knew I should wait until after the scan, but I couldn't bear the thought of Brenda being so upset. I was on my lunch break so I texted Brenda to FaceTime me. She called straight away.

'Charlotte, thank god! I thought we'd lost you.'

'What do you mean?'

'I thought you'd changed your mind after what I told you, I thought you might have had an abortion.' Her hollow face filled the screen. There were smudges under her eyes, her skin pale and blotchy. I hadn't meant to upset her, it was Malcolm I was mad at. I should have turned my phone on sooner.

'God, I could never do that! These babies are far too precious.' I could feel their movements every day. I liked to talk to them while I was walking or washing up. I suppose I took it for granted that we'd already built up a bond, whereas

Brenda would have to start from scratch, from the day they were born.

She squashed a tissue into a tight ball, hands trembling.

'Is everything okay?' I asked.

She propped up her tablet on the table in front of her and pulled at her cuffs like she usually did. The clothes she wore were always smart but slightly too big for her. She was crying now, head bowed, turning the tissue in her fingers until it grew smaller and smaller, more tightly compact. 'I honestly thought it was all over.' Her voice faded as if she were disappearing in front of my eyes.

'I admit I was upset and I'm sorry for blocking your calls, but I needed space to think.' I held a hand over my bump. 'We all have a responsibility to these babies. I'd hate to think they were unwanted because of their gender. It would be wrong and it would totally break my heart.'

'I completely agree. Whatever sex they are we should take them.'

'*Should*? Should isn't enough, Brenda. And what about Malcolm? Does he even know you're calling me?'

'No, but I will tell him. He knows I'm not happy about it.'

'I don't understand. Why would he only want boys?' The words I'd been wanting to say, spilled out. 'And what if they're both girls?'

Brenda's eyes swelled with tears.

'I'm sorry to be blunt, but I need to know because, to be honest, I think it's awful, especially as he never mentioned it before.'

Brenda rested her face in her hands. The top of her head filled the screen. Her roots were coming through. Not a natural blonde after all. The new growth was most definitely ginger.

'Is there something else you want to tell me?' I asked more gently.

Brenda didn't seem able to look at me. She shook her head, her lips quivering.

'We should all meet up. Discuss this face-to-face.'

'Yes, we must. I'll tell Malcolm.'

'And you think he'll be all right with that?'

'He'll have to be.' Brenda glanced up, a flash of determination in her eyes.

'He can't dictate to us like this.' I wished I could reach out and put my arms around her. Perhaps he really was only doing this for Brenda. But if his heart wasn't in it, how well would he treat the children?

'You're right. We need to get back on track.' She sniffed and dabbed her eyes with the balled-up tissue.

'I was thinking it would be best if I go for the scan on my own...' I brought my phone closer to my face, '...and not find out what sex they are.'

Brenda didn't speak for a moment. 'I suppose it's for the best.'

'And once the babies are here, none of this will matter. I bet we'll all be laughing about how silly it was.'

Brenda stared at me. 'I shouldn't be telling you this, but he's had it in his head about having a son for a long time. It's because he had a younger brother who died when he was a teenager. I hoped he'd got past that.'

My stomach tightened. 'I'm really sorry to hear that, but I'm wondering what you want, Brenda?'

She blinked a few times. 'I... I don't mind... one of each?'

'Then you tell Malcolm, he'll have to accept whatever sex the twins are.' Part of me wondered what else he was holding back.

Chapter Twenty-One

I drove to the hospital on my own for the twenty-week scan. Steve couldn't get away from work and there was no way I was going to ask Mum. She'd be in tears seeing what she only thought of as her grandchildren.

I was the first to be called into the small dim room. I made a point of never mentioning that I was a surrogate mother to any of the midwives or doctors I saw, so I didn't have to answer any questions. It was no one else's business.

'Let's have a look at these babies for you.' The midwife squirted gel onto my skin. The stretch marks looked like red jagged tears, as though something had clawed at me.

She stared at the computer screen for what felt like ages, without saying a word.

I bit my finger. *Please be all right, both of you.*

'Here we are, they're both moving around nicely.' A screen on the wall came to life and there they were, two perfect babies, swimming in their individual sacs. 'This one on the right is a bit smaller, but that's perfectly normal. Do you want to know what sex they are?' The midwife blinked at me over her glasses, her smile encouraging me to say yes.

'Please,' I found myself saying. What was I doing?

The midwife smiled all the more and my face lit up too. The stress of the last few days fell away. Right now, it was about me and the twins. I wanted to know everything I could about them and keep them safe. And it would be my little secret, even from Steve.

'This smaller one on the right is a boy and the bigger one on the left is a girl.'

I covered my smile with the back of my hand, but I couldn't stop the tears coming.

'Aw, is one of each what you wanted?' The midwife passed me a tissue and a sheet of paper towel to wipe the gel off.

'Yes, yes it was.' I had to stop myself blurting everything out about how happy this would make Brenda, but I managed to hold it in. 'Thank you,' was all I could say when she handed me a scan of the twins with my notes. I couldn't take my eyes off the picture. It was going to be harder than I thought giving them away, especially to Malcolm. Would he keep the girl as well as the boy? What kind of childhood would the twins have with a father prone to angry outbursts and controlling behaviour? But perhaps he was overreacting because the babies were so precious to him and it had taken him forever to become a dad?

As soon as I got outside, I texted Brenda to say all was well and that we needed to meet up with them as soon as possible. I'd do whatever I could to keep the twins together.

Chapter Twenty-Two

The following Saturday, we took Alice up to Jean's after lunch. Steve drove us to a Welcome Break restaurant on the outskirts of Peterborough. Brenda looked like she'd lost weight and Malcolm's face was a slab of chiselled granite. We didn't do our usual hugs and kisses and shaking hands but sat on opposite sides of a table scattered with crumbs and ordered our own hot drinks.

'How's Alice?' Brenda asked, her head dipped.

'She took her first steps the other day.' I wanted to reach out and take her hand, ask her what was going on. Instead I sat back.

Malcolm pulled out a folder of papers. 'You went to the twenty-week scan without us?'

I let out an audible sigh.

'I think you'll find that's in breach of our agreement.' He handed round a copy to each of us.

Steve ignored his. 'You know why.' He made a big show of ripping off the top of two sachets of sugar. Once he'd emptied them into his coffee, he rattled the spoon around the mug, the muscle in his cheek hammering the whole time.

'Did you find out the sex of our children?' Malcolm folded his arms and fixed his eyes on me. Brenda stared at the floor, her fingers picking at the leather strap of her bag.

I shook my head.

'Why didn't you tell us you only want boys?' Steve asked as soon as Malcolm opened his mouth to speak.

'Who doesn't have a dream of what their family will look like?' Malcolm pulled a wide Joker grin. 'That doesn't mean to say I wouldn't want a daughter. That's why Brenda was a bit confused.' He patted her leg and shot her a sideways glance. Her pained expression was becoming permanently etched into her skin. I wished I could understand what these looks between them meant.

'What if I have *two* girls?' I shoved the table with the heel of my hand, jogging the drinks. A black puddle of coffee spread around the base of his mug. 'Won't you take them? What do you think of all this, Brenda?' I needed her to back me up here, but she only shrugged and reached up to touch her hair. The cuff of her jacket shifted an inch, showing the purple green stain of a bruise on her wrist. We stared at each other for a second, but she darted her eyes away. Her arm snapped down, hands under the table.

'Of course we'll take them.' Malcolm batted the air.

'What is your problem then?' Steve stood up, leaning towards Malcolm, knuckles pressed into the table. Someone behind us tutted.

'There is no problem, I told you, Brenda got muddled up.' Again Malcolm slid a glance towards her. She was being way too quiet. These babies were hers. Why wasn't she fighting for them?

'Best you get that in writing then, ASAP.' Steve stabbed his finger at the sheets of paper. Malcolm glared at him.

'I don't want the twins split up.' I looked again to Brenda for support, but her head was down, finger dabbing at grains of sugar.

'They won't be.' Malcolm's mouth twitched. Brenda squinted at him as though she was expecting an explosion. I hardly dared to breathe in the billowing silence. I couldn't work out when things had changed. At the start we all seemed to get on. We came up with an agreement that was fair all round but now everything seemed to be in question. We had to get past this – and soon. There was a strong chance the twins would be early. I was already the size of a house at twenty-one weeks.

'Glad we're all back on the same page.' Steve gathered up all the papers and piled them in the centre of the table.

The waitress topped up our mugs of coffee. The smell of frying food caught in my throat.

Malcolm slipped the papers back in his folder. 'I'll get my lawyer to write it in the agreement then give you a call, go through all the paperwork with you. Would that help to settle your minds?'

Steve and I looked at each other in surprise.

'Yes, it would, thank you,' I said. 'By the way, I forgot to give you the picture of the twins from the twelve-week scan.' I handed Brenda an envelope.

'Oh yes, I was going to ask you for it.' She peered inside.

'There's one from the twenty-week scan too. The twins are doing really well.' I touched the top of Brenda's hand and she forced a smile. She took the scans and slid them into her bag without looking.

–

It took half the drive home for Steve to calm down.

'What is that bloke's actual problem?' He leaned forward, almost headbutting the wheel.

'It's like he's not bothered what the rest of us think.' I knitted my fingers together. 'Did you see the bruises on Brenda's wrist?'

'No.' He frowned.

'She looked scared.'

'Maybe they had a row and he grabbed her a bit too hard. At least he knows now that he can't dictate to us like that.'

'I hope so.' But why would Brenda hide the bruises if it was an accident? Did Malcolm hurt her on purpose? I tried to picture the moment I'd hand the babies over to them, but right now I wasn't sure I'd be able to do it. Would he try and take them from me because they were half his? He might stop me from seeing them altogether. I took a deep breath and tried to calm down, cupping my bump, stroking it, but my mind shifted back to the neglected baby Mum told me about. I pictured it crying, dirty and hungry and its poor little buckled toes.

Chapter Twenty-Three

Mum pulled up outside our flat at 8.30 a.m. on Sunday. I waved to her from the kitchenette window, the sun already warming the worktop.

'You sure you feel up to it?' Steve propped himself up on his pillow. I sat Alice next to him with a pile of her favourite books.

'I feel fine. Anyway, I promised.' I grabbed my bumbag full of change. 'Mummy will see you two later.' I kissed the top of Alice's head. 'Bye, bye.' I waved and she waved back saying, *ba-ba, ba-ba.*

'Don't forget the bag of stuff by the door,' Steve called.

–

We always tried to be one of the first onto the field. Nan used to love doing boot sales with Mum, but when she died, I said I'd help out once a month. It was a good way of having a clear-out and making a bit of extra cash. I loved the thrill of walking round the stalls, scanning for a bargain, particularly clothes or toys for Alice. So many were practically new and only a few pence each.

I helped Mum open the trestle table and fix the clothes rail together. She'd organised all the clothes ready on hangers, each individually priced. Since she'd started going to the gym a year ago, she'd dropped two dress sizes so most of her old clothes didn't fit.

The field started to fill up with cars around us. We carefully unwrapped old kitchen plates and knick-knacks that Mum had found in her loft.

'I've never seen any of these things before.' I placed a glass clown ornament next to a set of black coffee cups with gold rims.

'It's all from when your dad and I got engaged. Our families gave us loads of bits and pieces for our first flat together. I'd forgotten it was there. No point keeping any of it.'

'What's this?' I asked, although I'd already guessed. I unwrapped a small silver-plated box with 'Charlotte' engraved on the lid and my birth date.

'How did that get in there? Open it.'

Inside was a curl of blonde hair. 'Is that really mine? It's just like Alice's.'

'It is, isn't it? I gave you your first haircut.' Mum smiled, taking it from me to look closer. 'Dad sat you on his knee in the kitchen and Nan photographed it. Honestly, your little face when you saw your curls on the floor.' She handed it back to me.

'Can I keep it?'

But Mum was staring into space.

'Mum?'

She blinked. 'Oh yes… of course.'

I zipped it up in my bag and tried not to think about the other five silver boxes I'd once found in a drawer while snooping in her bedroom. Each with a name and date of birth: *Rachel, Victoria, David, Oliver* and *Anne.* All had had the finest tufts of fair hair. All born sleeping.

Neither of us spoke for several minutes.

I cleared my throat. 'Any in here I've not read?' I tore open two boxes of paperbacks and propped them up on a pair of old plastic garden chairs.

'Only the Dan Browns. You should try one.'

'I might do,' I said, but we both knew they weren't my taste.

Once we were all set up, Mum unfolded two camping chairs while I poured us both a cup of tea from her flask.

'How much for the vase?' asked a man with a sleeping baby strapped to his chest.

'Five pounds,' Mum said.

He thought for a moment, then whispered to the woman behind him, also carrying a baby in a sling. 'Will you take three?'

'Yeah, go on then.' I put my hand out and he dropped the coins in. Mum frowned at me and sat down.

'Are they twins? How old are they?' I wrapped the vase in bubble wrap and put it in a plastic bag.

'Eight weeks tomorrow.' He grinned.

'They're so beautiful.' I had to suppress the urge to reach out and kiss their miniature toes.

'They're being really good for us, so far.' The woman beamed.

'Looks like you haven't got long to go yourself.' The man took the bag from me.

'Another nineteen weeks. I'm having twins too.'

'Really? That's wonderful,' the woman said. 'Honestly, I was so uncomfortable in those final weeks, but it was worth it to have these two at the end of it all.' She leaned against her partner, gazing up at him, the babies side by side. My face dropped; this was never going to be me and Steve. I had to give my babies away. How on earth was I going to do that?

'Good luck!' they both said and moved on.

'What was all that for?' Mum asked in a loud whisper. I'd forgotten she was behind me.

'Nice family, weren't they?'

'We're not going to make any profit if you give stuff away,' Mum said, not that that was what she really meant.

I finished my tea and went for a wander before it got too busy.

A few stalls along from ours, a woman was selling baby clothes, equipment and toys, but I couldn't find anything suitable for Alice except a T-shirt similar to one she already had.

'I've got some nearly new baby clothes if you want to look through before I put them out?' The woman nodded at my bump.

Without waiting for an answer, she laid out a pile of newborn babygros in front of me. I picked up two in a creamy colour with *Dreamy* and *Perfect* printed in small writing on the front. How was I supposed to resist them? They were too adorable.

'A pound each or two for £1.50.' She turned away to get some more.

I checked the label. John Lewis. No wonder they felt so soft. I'd seen their sets of three but had never been able to justify the price.

'Only worn once, you can see for yourself there are no stains,' the woman said. 'Honest to god, my daughter had that many early-baby and newborn clothes, we could have opened a shop. Why don't people buy bigger sizes they can grow into?'

I nodded, still holding one in each hand. It wouldn't hurt to buy these now I was past the halfway mark. 'How much is the T-shirt there?'

'Fifty pence.'

I shouldn't really buy anything at all. And Brenda would probably have outfits ready for the twins. 'I'll have all three please,' I heard myself say, dipping into my purse for some coins.

'Do you want a bag?'

As I looked up, I caught a flash of dark curly hair out of the corner of my eye. I spun round, scanning the crowd, but she was nowhere to be seen. 'Sorry. Just a small bag, please.' I handed her the correct change.

'Good luck.'

Mum was in full haggle mode when I got back, so it gave me a chance to squirrel the clothes away in the car.

'See anything good?' Mum asked.

'Nothing special.' Had it been the same woman as before or was I becoming paranoid?

-

When I arrived home later, Steve was building a multicoloured brick tower with Alice. She got straight up and toddled towards me. I caught her in my arms for a hug.

'Clever girl! Mummy's bought something for you.' I took out the T-shirt. 'Do you like the sparkly unicorn?'

Alice nodded.

'What else have you got there?' Steve asked.

'Just a couple of babygros.' I held them up.

'Seriously, do you need to buy them clothes?'

I shrugged. 'I couldn't help it.' They were my babies, growing in my body, so why should I feel guilty?

He shook his head and went back to the game. By this point in my pregnancy with Alice, he'd been touching my bump several times a day, kissing my bare skin, talking to her. We'd laughed at him trying to listen for the smallest sound of her moving. He'd even gone through a list of names, bought little

Chapter Twenty-Four

When I was at the clinic for a check-up a few weeks later, the local radio station was there, running a week-long mother and baby special. The presenter made a beeline for me. I turned away, pretending I hadn't seen her.

'Hi, I'm Lucy Carter from the afternoon show. You look mighty uncomfortable. Are you due any minute?' She stuck the microphone under my chin. Her smile was so wide it was almost a laugh. I waved my hand to show I wasn't interested, but she moved the microphone even closer to me, flicking her long blonde curls behind her shoulder as if to say she wasn't giving up that easily. I shook my head, I didn't want to talk about it, but one of the other mums piped up, 'She's having twins.'

'Are you really expecting twins? How exciting. When are they due, err…?' She sat on the bench next to me and tugged down the skirt of her bright coral suit. 'Charlotte.' She read my name on my folder of notes.

I sighed. 'I've got ages yet, fifteen weeks.' I thought she'd lose interest and move on to someone else.

'And is this a natural conception or IVF?' She cocked her head at me so it was difficult to look away. All the mums around me were quiet, waiting for me to speak.

Then, without meaning to, I blurted, 'Actually, I'm having them for someone else.'

Lucy's eyes popped wide. 'You mean you're a surrogate?' She said it in such a loud comic voice that the whole roomful of expectant mums turned to gawp at me. Murmurs swept round the room.

Shit. I was tempted to lie, say I was only joking. I shouldn't be doing this. I wanted to shrink into the chair. But instead I leaned into the microphone and the words tumbled out: 'Yes, I am.' *Look at my amazing body growing two babies.* I sat back like a mother hen preening her feathers, imagining all the people agreeing that being a surrogate was an incredible, selfless thing to do. Lucy nodded, her face still stretched in surprise.

'And what made you want to be a surrogate?' Lucy held the red microphone closer, her voice softer now, rising at the end in a question I couldn't avoid. Malcolm's angry face flashed up in my mind. A stab of fear hit my chest. As long as I didn't say their names, it would be okay, wouldn't it? They'd never hear this up in Orkney, surely?

'Um, this is only local radio, isn't it?'

Lucy pointed to the pop-up banner behind her, *Bedford FM – Turn up the feel-good!* She gave me a nod to continue.

'Well, after I was born, my mum had several stillbirths. I was old enough to remember the last ones. When I was about fourteen, I remember thinking that one day I'd like to help a woman like Mum, someone who was struggling to carry a baby to full term. I had my own daughter last year and when I held her that first time, I knew that this was the moment that my mum had longed for, to hold a live, healthy baby in her arms again. For me it confirmed that this is what I wanted to do.'

Lucy's face melted. The other mums said a collective, 'Aww.'

'That's so sad and beautiful at the same time. What a wonderful thing to do. Look, I've got goosebumps all up my arms.' She pushed up her jacket sleeve.

I wished my mum had had the same reaction.

'And how old is your daughter?'

'She's eleven months.'

'Is she aware that her mummy is pregnant? I mean, it's hard not to notice this magnificent bump.'

'I think so. She likes to touch it as it gets bigger especially when the twins are kicking out or turning over.'

Lucy gave a cautious laugh. 'So, tell me, how did you meet the lucky new parents?'

'My partner and I met the intended parents online. I trawled round a few surrogacy websites and mentioned on various forums that I wanted to be a surrogate.' All the other mums were listening and smiling at me. I was proud of myself for doing this.

'And how did you decide who to choose? I'm guessing there are lots of people out there who sadly can't conceive and decide to go down the route of finding a surrogate to help them?'

'Yes, there are. It was hard choosing, but I liked this couple. Their story broke my heart. It reminded me so much of what my mum had been through. They'd been trying for years to have a baby and their last chance was to try surrogacy.'

'And so you met up with them, got to know them?'

'That's right. We chatted online, then my partner and I met up with them. We all clicked straight away.'

'And how long did it take you to get pregnant?'

'After two failed attempts with them I got pregnant the third time but miscarried early on. We had one final try and here we are.' I smiled at my bump and gave it a gentle rub, imagining the twins listening in. I'd tell them all about this day when they were old enough to understand.

'Can I ask, because I know our listeners will be wondering too – are the twins biologically yours?' Lucy pulled a face, probably unsure how far she could go with this line of questioning.

'Yes, I self-inseminated with the help of my partner.'

'Oh I see!' She gave a nervous laugh and held up her hand in a stop sign. 'Let's leave that part right there. Family show.'

I scanned round at the mixture of reactions from the other mums. Some were pulling faces as though they'd smelt something bad.

'So, I'm guessing your mum is proud of your grand gesture for this lucky couple?'

I didn't answer. Should I lie? Lucy raised her eyebrows.

'Um, she's not all that keen actually.'

'Ah, that's a shame, isn't it? So, there we have it, falling pregnant is not easy for everyone, sadly. Well, thanks for talking to me, Charlotte. I'm afraid we're out of time. Hopefully we can catch up with you nearer the big day?'

'Yeah, okay, thanks.' At that moment, it was as though I'd been jolted from a dream. I'd agreed total privacy with Malcolm and Brenda, but here I was telling thousands of people my story.

'Thank you to all the mums-to-be we've spoken to today at the North Bedford Antenatal Clinic. And now it's time for the four o'clock news.'

Lucy switched off the microphone and handed me her business card.

'Would love to keep track of your story. We're already getting loads of great comments about you on social media.' She pointed to a few on the screen in front of her.

Her voice sounded more normal now she was off air.

'That's good, but please, don't say my full name or the names of the intended parents because they want to keep their identity private.'

'I understand, we can do that. Good to meet you, Charlotte.' She took my mobile number and we shook hands. Wow, people I didn't know were saying they respected me for being a surrogate. I just wished Mum was one of them.

-

Later at home, when I told Steve about it, he went ballistic.

'That's one thing we did agree on with Malcolm, no publicity.'

'I only used my first name. I didn't say their names or yours.'

'What show was it on?' He opened his laptop.

'The Doctor's Surgery, a medical show every Wednesday afternoon.'

Steve jabbed at his keyboard.

'Brenda and Malcolm are hardly likely to hear it in Orkney, are they?'

'Anyone could copy it and send it round the internet. What if it goes viral?'

'It's unlikely.' But I was shaking as I lifted Alice into her high chair.

'Here it is, let's have a listen, shall we?' He turned up the volume and folded his arms. When it had finished, he swivelled his chair until he was facing me. He cocked an eyebrow as if he was a teacher about to tell me off. 'What do you have to say now, Charlotte from Bedford?'

'I told you, it's fine, there are no pictures of me and they didn't say any of our surnames.'

'It only takes one person to post this on Twitter.' He squeezed his thumb and forefinger together as though that was how small I should feel. 'It wouldn't take much for people to work out who you are.'

'I'm sorry, I thought it wouldn't do any harm. The woman sort of pounced on me, probably because my bump is the size of a potato sack.'

'You should have said no. Malcolm will go mental if he finds out.'

'Exactly – if.' I stood in the kitchenette staring into the fridge.

'Lucy is it?' He held out the crisp business card. 'Lucy Carter, Radio Presenter.'

'You went in my handbag?'

'What's this for? A follow-up interview?'

'You don't care about what I think, do you?'

'Don't be ridiculous.'

'You're only interested in the money or that you might not get any more.' I slammed the fridge shut. How could he be so heartless? I'd enjoyed sharing my story in front of all the other mums, they'd really seemed to admire what I was doing.

'Now you really are being silly.' He came towards me, but I backed away.

'Stop talking to me like I'm a stupid child.'

'I'm not.'

The phone's sudden insistent ring interrupted us. Steve picked it up.

'No, she isn't bloody here. Don't call again.'

'Who was that?' My voice cracked.

'*The Evening* bloody *Advertiser*. See what you've done?'

Perhaps I had got too carried away. I pressed my palm to my forehead. I hoped to god Malcolm didn't find out.

Chapter Twenty-Five

We went over to Mum's for lunch on Sunday. I took the opportunity to take a long soak in her bath while she was cooking roast beef. Alice had a splash around first, with a basket of plastic fish and a mermaid doll Mum kept there for her.

Steve looked round the door without knocking, a big grin on his face, still trying to make up for having a go at me about the radio show.

'Is she finished?'

'Yeah, you can take her. How long's dinner?'

'Your mum said half an hour, so get a move on.'

'Charming.' I passed Alice up to him.

'Her words, not mine.' He grabbed a towel and took her from me, wrapping it around her.

'I'll be down in a bit,' I told him and let myself slip under the water as he carried Alice away.

My hair snaked out from my head across the surface and my hands automatically found my bump, an island sticking up in the water, almost the size I was when I gave birth to Alice. I let my mind drift away to a beach in Portugal, floating in the sea on my back, the sun sparkling across the surface of the water.

The tune of the dripping tap brought me back to Mum's blush pink suite. The baby girl on the left side was moving a lot, tumbling and kicking, making me smile at the wonder of the strange but magical sensation. This tiny person trying to get comfortable, maybe sucking her thumb, giving her brother a playful kick.

I smoothed my hand over the right side, but there was no movement. I waited a few moments, but it was completely still. 'Come on, wake up sleepyhead.' I tripped over my words, spoken aloud into the echoey room. I circled my palm around and around, pressing a little firmer each time to rouse him. My heart beat faster, into my throat. He must be fast asleep.

I sat up, shivering. The water was cooler than I'd realised. I hoisted myself onto my knees and held onto the sides of the bath. A shadowy image of myself reflected back at me from the murky water. The sweet jasmine smell had faded. All that was left of the bubbles had drifted to the other end. My belly seemed bigger than ever, hanging down ripe in front of me, the skin silently stretching into more angry, jagged tears.

Still the boy didn't move. I stood up, water cascading from my skin. I reached for the plug and pulled it out, watching until the last of the soap suds collected and gurgled around the plughole as it sucked them down. My head swelled in its own bubble. Everything was happening so slowly, the dripping tap seemed too loud. Now neither baby was moving. I made a grab for the towel on the radiator, but no matter how hard I stretched, I couldn't reach it.

A gentle knock at the door gave me a start. Steve opened it a few inches and peered through the gap. I shivered, my teeth chattering.

Worry etched itself into his face in a second. He wrapped the towel around me, holding me, as I let myself collapse in his arms.

As the tears began to subside, Steve dried me. He tried to rub warmth into my skin, but the cold was deeper than that and I couldn't get warm.

He led me to Mum's bedroom where I'd laid my clothes out. He helped me into my dressing gown.

'What's happened?' He knelt in front of me and pushed his fingers between mine, clasping my hand tight.

'One of the babies… is not moving,' I whispered.

Steve's eyes darted back and forth, searching my face in case he'd missed something. I opened my dressing gown. He raised a hand, trembling as it hovered above my bump. We glanced at each other as he touched my skin. I placed my hand over his and moved it round. His pressure was light. For a crazy moment, I willed him to push and prod, not to worry about hurting me, but to do anything he could to wake the babies up, remind them they were inseparable, together forever. But Steve was gentle, feeling every inch. I could hardly breathe. I longed for the boy to give him an almighty kick, but there was no movement, not even a flutter.

I dressed in silence. Mum called out to us up the stairs. Steve told her we'd be down in a few minutes. He telephoned the midwife and left a message.

I couldn't eat lunch. Mum sat opposite me, her face blank after I told her one wasn't moving. All her tears spent long ago for her own lost babies. I sat in front of the TV while she cleared the plates of the half-eaten meal. She said she'd keep my roast covered up for later. Alice curled up on me while she watched *Peppa Pig*, Steve next to us, holding my hand. I could tell he'd run out of the right words, worried he'd say all the wrong ones.

I wouldn't let myself think beyond that moment. I moved Alice onto Steve's lap and every so often I gently pressed my bump, then smoothed my palm over and over it. A flutter ran through me as the girl shifted position, but still nothing on the other side.

Mum came and sat in the armchair furthest away, her eyes small and red.

'Do you want tea?' I asked, springing up. I had to remember I couldn't do that any more. The weight of the twins made my back ache.

'Please.' Mum wouldn't look at me. I could not cope with her pain too.

In the kitchen, I boiled the kettle and filled the teapot. As I turned to take a spoon from the drawer, a movement in my bump took me by surprise. I clung onto the counter with both hands and took a deep breath. The girl moved in what felt like a half-turn. A few seconds later I was certain I could feel the tiniest of flutters on the other side. I waited, hardly daring to breathe. Steve came in and rushed over to me.

'What's happening?' His arms slipped under mine, propping me up.

Had I imagined it? I let my head rest on the counter. Then it came, one enormous kick, the boy's tiny foot pushing out my skin, making me half gasp, half cry. I pulled up my top so Steve could see.

'Ha! There it is,' Steve said, 'I think that one's going to be a footballer.' He hugged me and we cried together.

Mum stood at the doorway. When I looked again, she'd gone.

Steve sat me in a chair while he finished making the drinks. I didn't think it was a good idea to tell Brenda about this. And I couldn't tell anyone how desperately upsetting it was for me when the babies stopped moving, that they felt like my own. They were a part of me and only existed because of my decision. Now they were sharing the same cocoon as my own little Alice. Steve and I would have to separate ourselves from them emotionally when the time came, but for now, they were embedded in me and deserved all the love I could give them.

I joined Mum in the living room. She was sitting in the window seat, pale-faced. The pink light of the afternoon gave the whole room a surreal glow. I didn't know what to say to her. I doubted she'd ever be able to see my side of it.

'We're going home in a minute. Thanks for dinner.'

Mum gave a deep sigh. 'This is heartbreaking for me.'

'I'm sorry.' There was nothing I could say.

'Every step of it tears me apart.'

'I shouldn't have told you.'

'What and have me believe this pregnancy was yours and Steve's? Find out the truth after you'd given them away, sold them?'

'We're not selling them, Mum.'

'You are as far as I can see. Who are this couple?'

'They're good people.' I stood up. I could feel the weight of her questions bearing down on me.

'Nappy's changed,' Steve said, carrying Alice in. When neither of us replied, he looked from me to Mum. I bolted for the door.

'When do I get to meet them?' Mum's voice was shrill as she followed me out to the car. I was surprised it had taken her this long to ask. What would Brenda and Malcolm make of her?

When I opened the car door, she held it while I strapped Alice in. I could see the grip she had on it, determined not to let go until she got the answer she wanted. But I walked round and sat in the driver's seat.

'You're driving then?' Steve closed Alice's door and got in.

'Try and talk some sense into her.' I heard Mum say to him. It took all my strength not to react.

I put my foot down and drove off, leaving her standing on the pavement. I thumped the steering wheel. A flash of heat swept through me. I shouldn't have left her like that.

Steve was silent on the way home.

'Agree with her, do you?' I asked. He should be making more effort to stick up for me.

'Course not. It's all getting a bit messy though, what with the radio station as well.'

'I don't see the problem. Malcolm and Brenda will never know.'

'Unless that newspaper prints something.'

'How can they when they haven't spoken to me?'

'Quite easily. How many other mums were in the clinic that day? All they need to do is tell them what you said.'

'Why are we going over this again?'

'And now your mum's upset too.'

'I can't help that. It's not like I can change my mind now, is it?'

'You've got to see it from where she's standing though.'

'Whose bloody side are you on?'

'Yours of course.'

We pulled into our parking bay just as Alice fell asleep.

'I'll sit with her a while. You go in,' I said.

'You sure? You should be resting.'

'I'll rest here.' I shut my eyes. As soon as Steve had gone, the tears came again. I'd been stupid thinking Mum would change her mind and see me as some kind of heroine. Perhaps she was right to be worried. Could she tell I'd had doubts? What if I did come to regret giving the twins away?

Chapter Twenty-Six

At three o'clock, the first guest arrived through the side gate to Mum's garden. Hayley, one of the mums from nursery, handed me a present and card.

'Happy first birthday, Alice.'

Her little girl, only a few months older than Alice, gave her a hug.

'Aw, that's nice, say thank you,' I said to Alice. But she turned her face towards my leg.

'Looks gorgeous out here,' Hayley said.

'The warm weather helps, doesn't it? Steve's been decorating it all morning.' He'd tied bunting and balloons to the fence, refilled the sandpit and laid out a selection of toys and rugs in a picnic area under a small marquee. Alice's new mini slide and tent from Mum was set up in the middle of the lawn. Alice put her arms up to me. 'Come on, sweetheart, don't make Mummy pick you up today. You're getting such a big girl now.'

Steve was busy greeting a couple of the other mums and dads. He caught my eye and came over.

'I think the birthday girl wants her daddy.'

'Do you want to sit down?' he asked and picked Alice up.

'I'll be all right. I'll go and see if Mum needs a hand.'

Mum was busy in the kitchen preparing all the finger food. She'd spent half the morning icing the teddy bear cake she'd baked.

'Let me do something to help, Mum.'

'How about taking the serviettes and plates out to the trestle table?' She looked round at me and smiled. She was in her element doing this. She'd always been brilliant at organising parties, taking time and care to give me the best she could. All my friends at school had been desperate to be invited.

'It's good of you to do all this. I'm sorry about Sunday.'

She shut her eyes and shook her head, which meant I wasn't to worry about it.

Outside, Alice was playing in the sandpit, surrounded by three of her nursery group friends and their parents.

Mum and Steve brought the food out.

'Come on, poppet, time to eat,' Mum said to Alice, putting her hands out to lift her out of the sand. 'Look, here's a bowl of soapy water to wash your hands. Do you think your friends want to join in?'

Alice nodded. It was hard to believe that this time last year, Alice was only a few minutes old. I'd never forget Mum's face when she first saw her; the picture of love at first sight. Someone should have captured it on video. She'd cupped Alice's face and kissed her forehead, then did the same to me. 'She looks just like you did,' she'd said, tears in her eyes. And when she held her, as though she was the most delicate, perfect thing she'd ever seen, I selfishly pictured Mum cradling me like that as a newborn. Then I'd realised it was the last time she'd held a live baby.

One of the twins kicked my side. I touched my bump. Silent tears fell down my cheeks. I hoped no one noticed with my sunglasses on. Where would these two be on their first birthday? Would we be invited? I hoped so. But I hadn't thought about what Mum would be missing out on, had I?

-

Brenda and I chatted every few days on FaceTime or by text. I kept them updated with weekly selfies so they could watch my bump grow. I'd started counting down the days at work. In the end I'd stayed on as long as I could. I would miss chatting to the customers, the banter with Shell and, in some ways, I'd even miss Tash. She treated me like everyone else, pretty much, which was fine, except when I got out of breath or there was anything heavy to lift. Shell kept an eye on me and didn't mind helping me out. In return, I balanced the till at the end of the days when Tash went home early. She'd started working part-time too. I had the feeling she couldn't stand being around me with my hormones oozing out of every pore and the babies looking more and more like two bags of shopping strapped around my middle. It must be hard for her. She kept her comments to herself, but her eyes had lost their shine.

'Charlotte's only got four more days until she goes on maternity leave,' Shell said aloud, to no one in particular.

I glanced up from mixing chopped eggs with mayonnaise. Tash kept her head down, scrubbing out the bottom of the display cabinet, only pausing for a second. I covered the mixture and put it in the fridge. Out the back, I stood by the window. In the afternoon sunshine, droplets of rain on the glass lit up like a string of seed pearls. These had been the longest weeks of my life. Sometimes I wished things were like before the pregnancy: simple, straightforward, happy. Why did my decision to do something good have to upset so many people?

I opened the door to the yard and breathed in the fresh smell of washed earth. The babies were stirring from their afternoon nap. I smoothed my hand over my bump. This was our special time together, the three of us. I hadn't meant to bond with them, but it was impossible not to. Part of me was already grieving the day they would no longer be mine.

Steve picked me up from work at 5.30 p.m.

'You're quiet,' he said. Nothing passed him by. He'd been able to read me from day one.

'In some ways I'm going to miss being pregnant.'

'After all the trouble you've had?'

'Yeah.'

'You mean you'll miss the babies.'

See, I couldn't even twist it. He knew exactly what I meant. When Mum said men were dumb and unable to pick up on women's feelings, she hadn't met Steve. I had this idea that he could look at me like an X-ray and any feeling I tried to smuggle away, he'd search it out.

'I know I'm not meant to.'

'Why wouldn't you love them? I'd be more worried if you didn't. They're growing out of your love.'

I'd miscarried because I didn't let myself love the baby. How stupid of me to think I could grow a new life without connecting to it, without letting my love wash through my body to every cell and fibre of theirs. 'I want to see them grow up and for Alice to get to know them.'

'And you will. Wait and see who's in charge once they're born.' He winked. I hoped and prayed Brenda would speak up once the twins were hers.

-

On my last day at work, Shell decorated the café with pink and blue balloons and streamers. I smiled to myself, knowing how appropriate that really was. As soon as I came in the door, I was crowned with a sparkly tiara and a sash saying, 'Mum-to-be'.

'Thank you, Shell.' I gave her a hug.

Tash stayed behind the counter grinning. What was she after? It wasn't like her to allow all this fuss, especially for me.

'Made you a cup of tea.' Tash pointed to a pink Mum-to-be mug by the till. 'You take it easy today.'

I thanked her and hung my coat up in the back room.

'What's put her in such a good mood?' I whispered to Shell.

'Dunno, she's been excitable ever since she got in.'

'Can't wait to see the back of me, I suppose.'

'She's a dried-up old cow, don't let her ruin your last day.'

'Don't say that, Shell. You'll come and see me, won't you?'

'Course. Here, I got you a little something.' She held out a package in silver paper. 'Kept it all neutral, you know.'

'Thanks, Shell. Can I open it now?'

'Yeah, go on then.'

I ripped off the paper. Inside was a memory picture frame, a box-like space covered in glass to display things, decorated at the top with a stork holding a baby in a basket.

'That's so beautiful, Shell, thank you.' I hugged her again.

'Thought you might want to keep a few bits in there to remind you of the babies.'

I started to cry. 'I didn't know how hard this would be. Every day feels a little bit worse. I'm their mother, protector, but I can't be either of those things.'

'Oh, babe, I didn't know you felt so bad.' Shell wrapped her arms around me. I could hear her swallow hard. 'You know,' she said, hesitating, 'you can change your mind.'

I stepped back and looked in her eyes. If it were that simple I might be tempted.

'I can't do that, Shell.' I stretched both hands across my bump. 'These two deserve a good life, with everything easy. Steve and I can't give them anywhere near that.'

'Alice is doing well, she doesn't need material things.'

'We don't have the space. Anyway, it's all agreed. It would kill Brenda if I kept them. They're her babies, not mine.' But still I ached at the thought of giving them away when my mind, body and heart were screaming at me to keep them close and protect them.

'Running this place by myself, am I?' Tash called, but it wasn't in her usual grouchy voice, more of a light sing-song tone, which meant there were people in the shop.

'We're coming,' Shell called.

As we stepped through the door, we were blinded by flashes of bright lights. Two photographers were standing in front of the counter, aiming their cameras at me. I shielded my face with my arm.

'What are they doing here?' I shouted.

Tash was sitting at one of the tables behind them. A smile swept across her lips.

'Come on Charlotte, give us a smile,' one of the men called.

I turned back, slamming the door. Shell came after me, shouting at the men to get lost.

'What the hell's going on?' I asked.

'No idea. She's a sneaky one, didn't have a clue she had that planned.'

I stormed back into the shop. 'What has she told you?' I shouted at the photographers, pointing to Tash. 'This is nobody's business. You do not have my permission to print those photos, do you hear me?'

'We're just the shooters.' The older man held his hands up as if I were pointing a gun at him. They packed up their stuff and left out of the main door.

'What have you done, Tash?' Shell asked.

'You'd better tell me, right now.' I crossed my arms.

'A bit of publicity never did anyone any harm.'

'Don't talk rubbish. This is all about you, isn't it? Getting your shop in the papers on the back of my pregnancy.'

'It's a lovely story. What you're doing is a generous thing. People are curious, interested to know why anyone would do it.'

'You can't bear that I'm having babies for someone else, can you?' I practically spat the words out of my mouth.

Shell held me back.

'You need to calm down, Charlotte.' Tash moved backwards. 'I don't know why you're so upset.'

'What have you told them?'

'Only about the wonderful thing you're doing.'

'But you don't think that, do you. You're trying to get me in trouble.' I waggled my finger at her.

'What sort of trouble?'

'With the intended parents. I told you I was worried about the radio interview because they don't want publicity, and you do this!' I shouted. 'Now they're going to think I've been stringing them along, trying to cash in on my story.'

'Do you want me to call Steve?' Shell took hold of my hands. Customers had started to come in for the mid-morning rush.

'You need to tell me which papers you've spoken to.' I picked up a small knife and stabbed all the balloons, making everyone squeal and cover their ears.

'I'll drive you home.' Shell offered.

Tash stared at us, mouth open. The twins were squirming about like nobody's business.

'I can't pay you for today if you leave early,' Tash said.

'Do I look like I care? You need to get on the phone to those newspapers, tell them that everything you said was wrong.'

'Who are these new parents anyway? I bet they're celebs, aren't they? That's why they're so fussy about remaining anonymous.' Tash gave a crooked smile.

'They're successful business people who don't want everyone knowing about their private lives. I promised I wouldn't tell anyone who they are.'

'That's all right then, we won't say, will we, Shell?'

Shell rolled her eyes and picked up the bag of presents. 'Come on, let's get you home.'

The dark outline of a person moved away from the window.

'How long has someone been standing there?' I pointed.

'Dunno,' Shell said.

I opened the door, checked up and down the street, but whoever it was had gone.

Chapter Twenty-Seven

That evening, after dinner, we snuggled up on the sofa and watched *Bridget Jones's Baby*. It was the first time we'd properly spent time alone in days. Steve had been to visit Jack and said he was doing well, staying positive. The doctors were confident the chemo would zap any remaining cancer cells.

When I came back from the bathroom, Steve had put the bed out and scattered the duvet with silk rose petals.

'You're so romantic.' I kissed him and tried to turn towards him, but the bump was in the way. 'It'll soon be over.' As soon as I said it, tears filled my eyes.

'What's wrong?' Steve asked.

'I can't stop thinking about how much I'm going to miss them.' I lay my hands on the tight drum of skin. Only I knew that they were a perfect pair – a boy and a girl. I'd like a son of my own one day.

'You'll have to start getting used to life without them, hun. It's going to be strange.'

'I think I might feel actual grief.'

'It'll be a kind of loss though, won't it? You doing all this hard work then coming home without them.'

I looked down at my bump, a hand on either side. 'I'll wish them well in their new lives, but I hope to god we can be at least a small part of their future. It'll break my heart if we can't.'

'Brenda will make sure you are, you know it, right?' He kissed my forehead. I wasn't so confident any more. Malcolm probably saw us as kids in a way, not long out of nappies ourselves, Nan would say.

'Should be getting that second cheque tomorrow.' Steve took a Coke out of the fridge. 'I thought we could go away on a little weekend holiday, just the two of us.'

'Really? Do you think we can afford it?'

'Course, why not? All the bills and rent are up to date. Jack's got his money and the business is doing okay without him, so far.'

'But I want to save most of it for Alice this time.'

'We can and still have a good time.'

'Let's do it then. Where shall we go?'

'How about Brighton? This weekend?'

'Oh could we? That'll be so romantic.'

'You deserve it.' He pushed my hair back from my face.

'I feel better already. I love you so much.'

–

It was a beautiful hot Indian summer day when we packed up a picnic and took off for Brighton. The second cheque had arrived and I'd paid it in a couple of days before we left so we'd have money in the bank. Mum was pleased to have Alice for us so we could have a much-needed weekend by ourselves.

By lunchtime, we pulled up outside the old-fashioned bed and breakfast Steve had booked. After we'd checked in, we went straight down to the packed beach to eat our sandwiches and drink bottles of cola. We strolled along the pier in a refreshing sea breeze and spent the afternoon mooching around The Lanes, going in and out of quaint and funky shops and a massive flea market, full of both unusual and everyday objects from past decades. Steve wanted to buy a wall-mounted phone complete with the original circular dial. I loved an art deco style diamond ring, but it cost four hundred pounds.

As we were coming out, I spotted a fortune teller sitting in a pop-up tent alongside a juggler and a fire-eater. A man covered in tattoos and piercings stood outside, taking money for a reading.

'Oh, can I?' I pulled on Steve's arm and made him stop. 'I've not been to one since I met you.'

'Don't believe in all that tripe, do you?'

'Some of it can be true,' I said. 'The one I saw told me I'd meet you.' I snuggled into his chest.

'What, me specifically? Had a photo of me, did she?'

'No, but she said a man with a name beginning with S was going to come into my life and turn it around.'

'Yeah, did that all right.' He blew on his fingernails and pretended to polish them on his T-shirt.

'She also said that you'd be my protector. See? Not so daft.'

'Go on then, how much is it?'

'Five pounds.' I took a note out of my purse.

'I'll pay. Put your money away. My little treat.' He handed the tattooed man the money. 'Make sure it's good.'

The man showed me into the tent and velcroed the door shut behind me. The psychic was dressed in the usual garb: headscarf full of stars and moons with shiny mirrored sequins, and a crystal ball in front of her on a purple velvet table cloth.

'What's your name, my lovely?' Her wrinkled hands snaked across the table towards me. She cupped her cold fingers around mine.

'Charlotte.'

'Ah, yes, Charlotte, I've been waiting for you.' She shut her eyes and lay one hand on the crystal ball, her sparkly purple nails tapped the glass. 'You're an only child, aren't you, dear?'

'Yes.' I frowned.

'But you did have brothers and sisters.'

'Yes.' A shiver ran through me.

'And you're going to have a baby...' She stopped abruptly.

'What's wrong?' I asked.

'I can't say.' Her eyes flicked open. She pulled her hand away from mine and shook her head as if to clear away a bad vision.

'Please tell me, even if it's something awful, I'd rather know.'

'Not everything will go smoothly for you, Charlotte, that's all I can say.'

I sat back, trying to work out what she could mean.

'But you're going to have a healthy baby girl.' She grinned at me, flashing her broken yellowed teeth. She grabbed my hand again and closed her eyes, her other hand on the crystal ball. 'I can feel the vibrations in your heartbeat. Good and strong. I can see a little girl.'

'That'll be my daughter, Alice.'

'No, it's you, you're seven years old and you're crying because your mother is sad, but you can't do anything to help her.'

I pulled my hand away. The psychic opened her eyes.

'I can see that you're trying to build a new relationship with your mother. Don't let the past dictate your future, my dear.'

I stood up to leave. How could she know any of this stuff?

She put her hand firmly on my arm. 'Take care won't you, dear?'

'Thanks.' I frowned at her, wondering what she was holding back, why she hadn't mentioned my baby boy.

I stepped out into the sunlight and stood there blinking. Did that really happen? I shivered, frozen to the core even though it was baking hot.

'How'd it go?' Steve came over with a bag of freshly cooked cinnamon doughnuts. We found a bench and sat down to eat them.

'Some of it was too accurate to be true. It must have been a wild guess. She said I'm having a girl, which is strange considering I'm expecting twins. It's left me with a weird feeling. There was something bad she didn't want to tell me.'

The smile slid off his face. 'I don't think they're allowed to.' He bit off a piece of doughnut. 'You know it's a load of rubbish, don't you?'

'She seemed genuine to me.' I touched my bump. I couldn't bear it if something bad happened to one of my babies.

Steve took my hand. We found a café with chairs and tables outside and sat near a street artist, sketching a cliff edge in chalk on the pavement. I ordered two coffees and a slice of chocolate cake from the waiter. We sat back, watching people go by.

'Don't let what she said bother you. It's nearly over now.'

I took his hand and laid it on my bump, but he pulled away.

'Why won't you touch it?'

Steve folded his arms over his chest. The waiter brought our order.

'You don't love them like I do.'

'It's difficult for me. They're not mine, are they?'

I nodded and stared at the sugary sponge.

'I know it's hard for you though. Are you feeling any better about giving them up?'

'I don't know. Do you think they're going to be good parents?'

'Yeah. Malcolm will mellow out once he's a dad.'

'These two will have everything they could ever want, although I hope they don't spoil them.' I circled my palm over my bump. 'I know every twist and turn and kick from each of them.'

'Do you think they'll be identical? Same sex or one of each?'

A woman on the next table was breastfeeding her baby under a lightweight scarf.

'I already know,' I said.

'Do you?' He did a double take.

'I wanted to find out for me. I suppose it was sticking two fingers up at Malcolm over him only wanting boys.'

'So, come on then, what are they?' His eyes brightened.

'A boy and a girl.' A child with short hair strolled past swirling a shiny streamer on a stick.

'Nice. What Brenda wants.'

'Exactly.'

'What about Malcolm though, do you think he'll stick to his word?'

'When I spoke to Brenda a couple of days ago, she said he's really looking forward to being a dad. He said he'll accept whatever they are, so we have to believe him.'

'Too bloody right. He can be weird sometimes.'

A kettle drum band started playing nearby.

'What's so bad about having a girl anyway? Bit old-fashioned, isn't it?'

'Brenda thinks it's something to do with him losing his brother when they were growing up.'

'Mmm, maybe it's that then. He's softer than he likes to make out.'

I couldn't shift out of my head what the fortune teller had said. How could she have thought I was only having a girl when everything else she said about me was so spot on?

I sat up straight. At the end of the road near a jewellers, stood a woman in a suit with curly hair and dark glasses.

‘Look,’ I said, not quite believing my eyes.

‘What?’ Steve twisted round in his seat. Scores of people were meandering up and down in different directions.

‘That woman over there in front of the furniture shop. I think it’s the same one I keep seeing round our way.’ Was I imagining it because of my baby brain, or was I becoming paranoid?

‘Hey, calm down, don’t be daft. It can’t be the same. What would she be doing here?’

But I was already out of my seat. ‘Are you sure you haven’t upset someone or owe them money?’

‘No, of course not,’ Steve called after me.

I hurried down the road, dodging people who were in my way, not taking my eyes off her. As I grew nearer, I let the other shoppers and tourists shield me, so I could get a closer look, see her face more clearly; heavy tan make-up, thick dark eyebrows, nude filler lips. She started to do a runner down the street, glancing back over her shoulder. Steve ran after her, catching up as the crowds slowed her down. Enough time for him to take a photo of her. Definitely the same woman as before.

Chapter Twenty-Eight

'Are you certain it's the same woman?' Steve showed me the photo he'd taken.

'A hundred per cent.'

'Hey, you're shaking.' He slipped his phone in his back pocket and took my hands. 'Let's get you back to the B&B.' Steve hailed a taxi.

In our room, I lay on the bed, propped up on pillows. My mind sifting through all the possibilities. Who would waste their time and money following us around?

'It can't be a coincidence. Not this many times. Are you positive you've not upset someone, because I'm starting to feel pretty scared.'

He shook his head, pacing up and down the room.

'Would anyone you know have a reason to set someone onto you?'

'No, honestly. I'm wracking my brains here.'

'It wouldn't be to do with Malcolm checking up on me, making sure I'm not smoking or drinking?'

'No way.'

I swung my legs off the bed, but they felt wobbly.

'Look, maybe we should tell the police.'

'What can they do?'

He slumped down on the end of the bed. 'I don't know, but at least it would be on record.'

-

The next morning we had a late breakfast, because I felt nauseous and my head was pounding. I put it down to stress and not drinking enough water. I took some tablets and we set off to the Brighton Pavilion.

It was like stepping back in time with the beautiful silk wall paintings and wide staircases. I imagined myself in long flowing dresses, gliding down the stairs. I couldn't wait to be thin again. The babies were growing fast now, my stomach was so wide and the skin itched where it had stretched. Would I ping back into shape this time or was my figure ruined? I knew I shouldn't worry about it, but I wanted myself back at the end of all this.

By lunchtime, my headache was worse, and my ankles were swollen from all the walking in hot weather. We sat in the Pavilion garden sipping a bottle of water, but I wished it was ice-cold so I could drench my feet in it; they were near to bursting out of my canvas shoes. The pain of my headache pierced the side of my eye, blurring my vision. But it was too soon to take any more tablets.

'I'm not sure I can make it to the beach, this has turned into a migraine.'

'It's not far, do you good to walk it off.'

'I don't think it will. Look at my puffy feet and ankles.'

'Walk barefoot for a while?'

'I won't be able to get my shoes back on.'

'You need to soak them in the sea, cold salty water will help.' Steve took my hands and pulled me up.

'You're not listening. My head's killing me. I feel really awful, like I might throw up.' I couldn't even say a whole sentence without running out of breath. I leaned the side of my face on his chest and he put his arm around me. How was it possible that my little body could grow two whole human beings? My bump was so tight I doubted they had much space left to grow. Perhaps it was getting too much for my body. I wanted this pregnancy to be over, even though I wasn't anywhere near ready to give the babies up.

So many times, I'd pictured the moment I'd hand them over to Brenda and Malcolm. I'd had a recurring dream of waving them off and the babies screaming without me there to protect them. The umbilical cords would be cut, but I would always be connected to them. They were part of me. No one could ever take that away. It was strange to think of me having children with Malcolm though. Our DNA combined forever. A bitter taste came into my mouth. My features mixed with his. The thought of it made me grimace. How would Steve react when he saw the reality of it?

–

I still felt sick the next morning, so we decided to leave Brighton earlier than planned, but when we came to pay the bill, our cards for the joint account were declined.

'Shit,' I said under my breath. Steve turned his back on the receptionist and kicked our suitcase. Why hadn't the second payment cleared yet? I dug deep into my handbag and pulled out our chequebook. At times like this, it was a lifeline. Malcolm must be playing games with us; he certainly didn't have money problems.

Fortunately, the hotel accepted a cheque with my banker's card number written on the back as well as our address and full names.

'What if it doesn't clear?' I whispered, wringing my hands.

'I'll bloody throttle him, that's what.' Steve gripped the steering wheel so hard, I thought it would snap.

Chapter Twenty-Nine

When we reached Mum's, I was so tired I lay down in the spare room and fell asleep.

When I woke up, I felt odd, not quite there. My ankles were still swollen and lights flickered in my eyes.

The next morning, Steve drove me to my hospital appointment after we'd dropped Alice at nursery. I told the midwife straight away how strange I'd been feeling. She sent me off to do a urine sample. When I came back, she unscrewed the bottle and dipped a small strip of paper in it.

'Right, let's check your blood pressure.'

I sat by her desk and she slipped the cuff onto the top of my arm and pulled it tight.

'You're what, thirty-five weeks now?'

'And four days.'

She smiled and pressed the button which inflated the cuff, squeezing my arm until it hurt. I detected a slight squint in her eye as she read the result. The machine deflated.

'Let me just check that again. I still prefer the good old manual machine.'

But when it inflated again and she saw the result, her face pulled up tight. Without another word, she undid the cuff, slipped it off my arm and dragged the manual machine over. She didn't look at me this time as she squeezed the black rubber bulb until I thought my arm would burst. For what seemed like ages, she stared at the result. I glanced sideways at Steve as she left the room. A moment later, a male nurse followed her in with a wheelchair.

'Your blood pressure is sky-high, Charlotte. Your top line is 196 and there are traces of protein in your urine. We need to keep you in under close observation for the next few hours.'

'Are you worried she's going to have a heart attack?' Steve stood up.

I put my hand on my chest and blinked at her. She leaned on the desk towards me.

'I'm worried you'll have a stroke. You have pre-eclampsia, which means we may need to deliver the babies early.'

'Oh god.' I grabbed Steve's hand and took a deep breath to calm myself.

'That's dangerous, right?' Steve asked.

'It can be. For the mother and the baby.' She helped me into the wheelchair and whisked me off to a room on the maternity ward. Steve followed alongside me. I'd heard of pre-eclampsia, but I didn't really understand what it was. I knew how serious it could be though – a woman at work had had it a couple of years ago and lost her baby.

The small room had a bed and a fan on a low cupboard. Two nurses and a doctor came in after us.

'Let's get you strapped up to the monitor, see how these babies are doing,' the doctor said, indicating for the nurses to help me onto the bed and turn me onto my side. Steve clasped my hand as a pain crept along my right side under my breast.

'You'd better go and call Mum and Brenda,' I told him, trying not to let the panic seep into my voice.

-

Mum blustered in an hour later, still in her salon work clothes. 'I got here as quickly as I could. How are you?'

'I'm fine, no change.' I sipped a bottle of water and rested it on the huge mound of my belly.

'Why I didn't notice the signs yesterday, I'll never know.' She pulled a chair up to the bed and hooked her handbag over the back of it.

'They're still struggling to get her blood pressure down,' Steve said, pushing a loose tendril of hair away from my face and back under the clip.

'I'd never forgive myself if...' Mum took in a breath.

'They said they'll whip me in for a C-section if necessary. The nurse will be back in a minute, if you want to ask her anything.'

Mum waved her hand at her face as if fanning herself, but she started to cry.

'I'm going to be okay.' I reached for her hand, hoping I sounded confident.

'What would we tell Alice?'

'Let's try and stay positive shall we?' Steve clenched his jaw.

'But we need to discuss this. Literally anything could happen.'

'I've tried calling Brenda,' Steve said.

'I'm not talking about them, I mean Charlotte. If something... goes wrong.' Mum's face flushed red. She gulped a mouthful of air. 'Do we tell Alice that her mum has gone away forever... because... because she wanted to have babies for someone else?'

My stomach tumbled out of control.

'Stop right there,' Steve shouted, holding both hands up, 'Charlotte is stressed enough without this.'

'But how would you look after Alice and keep your business going?'

'Gloria, we are not having this conversation!' Steve looked on the verge of tears.

I couldn't find any words to say.

'Where are those people anyway? Do they have any idea what they're putting you through?'

My head felt like it was floating away from my body. Were they really talking about me not being here? I didn't want to die. I couldn't bear the thought of Alice growing up without me. I'd miss out on too much. I wanted to be there for her birthdays, when she grazed her knees, started school, got married. She needed me.

'Everything all right, Charlotte?' The ward sister looked straight at me as she strode in, registering my hot cheeks and tears beginning to spill down my face.

Mum stood up. 'I'm concerned about my daughter.'

'So are we, I can assure you. Now, you don't want to be the cause of Charlotte's blood pressure rising any higher, do you?' She opened the door and guided Mum towards it. 'If you wouldn't mind waiting outside for a moment, please.'

The sister came back in and checked my blood pressure, then the babies' heartbeats on the monitor.

'They're steady for now.' She smiled and laid a hand on my arm. 'Shall I send Mum back in?'

I nodded. 'Thank you.'

'I'll give you a few minutes together first, then I want you to have a rest once your mum's gone.' She rearranged my pillows and left.

Steve smoothed my hair back and tipped his forehead against mine. I gazed into the darkness of his eyes. We blinked at each other, probably having the same thoughts.

'I'm sorry for not taking it more seriously, when you said you felt unwell.' He pulled back slightly, head bowed.

'You weren't to know. I thought puffy feet and ankles was fairly normal, especially as it was a hot day and the babies are so heavy.'

He cupped my hands in his warm and sturdy ones, so used to fixing things, finding solutions.

'Maybe we should make plans. Just in case,' I whispered.

He gave a solemn nod, his eyes darting to mine and away again.

'You know I'd want Alice to stay with you, of course. But I wouldn't want you doing everything, you must let Mum help you.' My voice tangled on the words and I had to repeat them, more slowly.

He nodded silently and wove his fingers through mine.

'Whatever you think is best. You know if it came to it, I'd take good care of her?' His lips trembled. 'I'd never let her forget you… her brave and beautiful mum.' He buried his face in my hair and sobbed. But I didn't feel brave at all, just scared.

Chapter Thirty

I spent half the night caressing my bump, whispering to the twins how much I loved them and that soon we would meet each other at last. I tried to settle down and sleep, but the chatter in my mind wouldn't slow down. Everything that had happened in the last few days, every conversation, re-ran in my mind. Should we have gone to hospital in Brighton, or as soon as we got to Mum's? What if I had a stroke and couldn't care for the twins or Alice?

I'd made Steve go home for a rest. I promised to call him if there was any change. He texted to say the cheque had cleared, which was the least of our worries.

My blood pressure still wouldn't go down. If it didn't shift soon they were talking about inducing me.

At three in the morning, a nurse and doctor came to check my blood pressure and the babies' heartbeats. The doctor had been quite chatty, but now she was quiet. At first I guessed it was because it was the middle of the night, but I caught sight of her face which had visibly fallen. A few seconds later, three or four nurses rushed into the room.

'One twin's heart rate is dipping and not recovering, Charlotte,' the doctor said in a low, steady voice, 'we're going to deliver your twins now, by C-section. It's not safe to wait.'

The words swam in my head. Was I dreaming? Had I heard her right?

A nurse smiled at me as she lowered an oxygen mask onto my face. I grabbed her wrist and tried to push her away. I must have fallen asleep. This had to be a nightmare.

'Come on, Charlotte, this is to make sure the twins are getting enough oxygen.'

The cold seal of the mask startled me. I pulled it off and whimpered,

'Please call Steve.'

I was wheeled into the operating theatre, where I was lifted onto the table. The anaesthetist asked me to lean forward and curve my back over as best I could. A nurse held my hand. A small poke in the middle of my spine meant the needle was going in.

I soon started to feel tingly and warm in my legs. The nurses helped me to lie down, then applied heart monitor pads to my chest. A catheter was fitted and a small pillow slipped under my right hip so I wasn't completely flat.

When Steve arrived by my side wearing a gown and mask, hot tears ran down my cheeks. He kissed my forehead.

'Carly and Dan have got Alice. I called your mum and I finally got through to Brenda. She said they'll be here as soon as they can. They can't get a boat or a plane from Orkney until the morning.'

But I wasn't thinking about any of them. It was me and the twins now and their safe delivery. More nurses and doctors arrived. A spike of pain shot through the side of my head. I groaned and pushed my palm to my temple.

'We'll soon be ready, Charlotte, you're in safe hands,' the nurse said in a soothing tone. 'I'm going to wash your abdomen now with an antiseptic solution.'

'Just got to do this last important bit now,' Steve said, stroking my hair.

When the nurse finished, she put drapes up across my chest so we couldn't see what was happening. My breathing became rapid. I wasn't ready for this. Was I going to die?

'Can you feel this, Charlotte?' the surgeon asked.

'No, what's that?'

'I'm pulling the skin on your stomach. Are you sure you can't feel anything?'

'Nothing at all.' I'd never stepped out of a plane before, but I imagined a similar level of trust was needed in the parachute as well as the pilot.

'Good. I'm going to start the incision. You may feel a little pressure on your abdomen.'

I gripped Steve's hand as tightly as I could. We fixed on each other's eyes.

'Here comes the first one.'

We heard two little yelps like a kitten. My mouth fell open. Steve looked up. I followed his gaze.

'Your baby boy, Charlotte.' The surgeon held the tiny mite above the drapes for a moment, to a collective cheer, before whisking him away to be assessed.

'Did you see him?' I cried.

Steve nodded and kissed my face.

Moments later, my crying baby girl was lifted up to another cheer from everyone in the room.

'She's got a good set of lungs,' Steve laughed, his face wet with tears.

'Your son weighs five pounds one ounce, Charlotte.' A nurse handed him to me, wrapped in a blanket.

'Hello, little man.' I took him in my arms and my heart blossomed. 'You're here at last, safe and well.' I kissed his cheeks and button nose. He felt so light. I couldn't stop smiling as I gazed at his grey-blue eyes. He blinked up at me as though he recognised me.

'And your daughter weighs five pounds six ounces,' the nurse said, bringing her over. 'Is Daddy going to hold his baby girl?'

Steve glanced at me before putting his arms out. 'Look at her,' he said, 'isn't she perfect?'

'They're both beautiful, aren't they?'

We held them side by side and my smile wilted into tears.

As soon as I was wheeled into recovery, I had the chance to hold the two of them together. The boy was just big enough not to have to go into special care. The girl cried until her face was deep red. Steve couldn't take his eyes off her. How on earth was I going to let them go?

'Are you starting off breastfeeding?' a nurse asked.

I shook my head. 'But I'd like to express some milk and bottle-feed them please.'

She went off to find a breast pump. When she came back, she helped me to bottle-feed them as well as dress them and put on their nappies. I didn't want to miss a single moment of their first few hours, but I was so tired, I couldn't keep my eyes open. Steve went home for a nap too. I woke up three hours later and had a shower and washed my hair. The cut under my stomach seemed a fitting wound for what I'd been through. As if I needed a scar to remind me.

The Bounty photographer came round offering to take photos of the twins. I thought what a lovely surprise present it would be for Brenda and Malcolm. She showed me the snaps on the screen of her camera. It took me ages to pick one of the twins side by side, one wrapped in a blue blanket, the other in a pink blanket with matching stripy hats. So perfect. Tears blurred my eyes. I ordered an extra copy for myself.

There was no one I could talk to about the warm rush of love I felt for them. Perhaps Steve found this as hard as I did. I had an overwhelming urge to hold them in my arms and keep them safe forever. But there was no choice, no going back. I had to begin distancing myself from them emotionally.

After lunch, the nurse came to tell me that both babies had a touch of jaundice and needed to go under heat lamps. They could stay by my bed, all the equipment would be brought to me. I couldn't bear to let either of them out of my sight.

In the afternoon, Steve came back in with Mum and Alice.

'She insisted,' he mouthed, knowing he couldn't overrule her. He sat Alice next to me and I hugged her tight. She showed me an indistinguishable picture she'd scribbled of me and the twins. 'Mamma, baba,' she said, pointing at it.

Mum handed me a gift bag.

'Aren't they adorable?' Mum cooed. 'Won't you reconsider?'

Here we go. 'You know that's not possible, Mum,' I whispered.

'Aren't you going to open that?' Mum perched at the end of the bed.

'You didn't need to buy anything, they won't be with me for long.'

'That's what this is for.' She pointed at her present.

Steve took Alice while I ripped open the paper and took out a hand-printing kit.

'Oh, that's a good idea. Thanks, Mum.' I kissed her cheek. It was such a thoughtful gift, giving me something of them to treasure. It reminded me that Mum never got this chance with her own babies.

Malcolm and Brenda appeared at the gap in the curtains, giving me a start. How long had they been standing there? Had they been listening?

My eyes darted to Mum. I'd been trying to avoid them being here at the same time.

'Come in, come in, congratulations.' Steve moved Alice over his shoulder and shook Malcolm's hand, then half hugged Brenda with his free arm.

Mum stepped backwards to the corner of the small space, her face tight and staring. I took in a breath and held it there, examining each of their faces, hoping Mum wouldn't say anything awkward.

'Oh my lord, will you look at these two?' Brenda touched the side of the cot, then came over and hugged me. Malcolm gave me one of his odd little smiles.

'They've only just gone to sleep, I'm afraid, and they have to stay under the lamps for as long as possible.' I wrinkled my nose, anticipating Brenda's disappointment.

'That's okay, we're staying nearby so we can see them every day until they're ready to come home.'

I flinched at her comment and hoped no one had noticed. *Home.* Tears started to well up, but I pressed my nose as though I was about to sneeze and managed to keep them at bay. When was I going to start getting used to the fact that I couldn't keep them?

'This is my mum, Gloria,' I beckoned Mum to come closer, but she didn't move, giving only a hint of a smile that pinged back into a straight line. 'Meet the new parents, Malcolm and Brenda.'

'Lovely to meet you.' Brenda held out her hand. Mum offered her a limp-wristed effort. 'I know this must be so hard for you,' Brenda said.

Mum nodded but didn't utter a word. I was silently grateful. She collected up her bag and coat and slipped away through the gap in the curtains. I let her go. I didn't call her back, although part of me wanted to. But there was no point. It was too much for her. This was the opposite of what I'd wanted. I'd hoped so much that doing this would bring us closer, but it had only seemed to push us further apart.

Malcolm loomed in the corner, chatting with Steve, his eyes meeting mine every so often. His chest puffed out, proudly talking about his twins. I'd done this service for him, growing his children. He was the sort of man who was used to getting his own way, paying for what he wanted. A man almost fifty years old having babies with a twenty-four-year-old. In some twisted way, did it feel like a conquest to him? One over on the younger, more handsome Steve?

At that moment Malcolm turned and stared at me, as if he knew what I was thinking. The hairs on my arms bristled. Steve stood by, completely unaware. I tried to look away, but my eyes kept finding Malcolm's, even though I did my best to focus on what Brenda was saying to me. Then a smile slid up one side of Malcolm's face.

Chapter Thirty-One

I treasured the time I spent feeding the twins and hated having to put them back under the lamps. Their having jaundice meant I was keeping them with me for longer than expected. Deep down I was pleased to have these extra days with them. I secretly named the boy Robert. He was already beginning to fill out. The girl I named Rose, and she was still the noisiest and hungriest of the two. Both tiny versions of Alice. The shape of their eyes were from me, their noses a bit like Malcolm's. I'd named them after two of my favourite nurses. Every day I tried to memorise their faces, their tiny distinguishing marks: the tiny freckle on Rose's ear, the pink birthmark on Robert's shoulder. I took photos of them in their nappies, together and on their own, wide awake, little fists and feet pumping into the air, then fast asleep wrapped in blankets. I probably wasn't supposed to, but who would know? They were only for me. For now, they were mine. I needed to make sure I stayed in their lives to reassure them that I loved them.

I fed one at a time and changed their nappies, chatting quietly to each of them, telling them all about Alice and her favourite toys. Before I put the lamps back on, I held them close to me, one in each arm, and breathed in their warm baby smell. I felt no different to the first hours after Alice was born, when I'd gazed into her eyes and kissed her golden tuft of hair. A rush of love washing through my body. How would I fight the urge to keep them safe under my wing? Would I be able to let them go? I lay them under the lamps side by side and kissed their miniature hands. All the time, I was screaming inside at the little time we had left together.

Malcolm and Brenda arrived again at lunchtime, carrying two helium balloons in the shape of storks, one carrying a baby boy and the other a baby girl.

'They're nice.' I didn't want to say thank you because the babies were theirs, so the balloons were more for themselves than for me.

Brenda placed the weights of the floor-length ribbons either side of the cot. She kissed me on both cheeks. Her perfume was different, sweeter. I coughed and pulled back.

A frown passed over her brow so quickly I wondered if I'd imagined it. She stood by the cot, head tilted. 'They're doing so well. Do you know when we'll be able to take them home?'

'I'm not sure, not till the end of the week at least, I think. They want them to be fully recovered from jaundice and the boy to put on a bit more weight.' I hoped the doctors didn't discharge them earlier.

'And what's happening about the parental transfer document?' Malcolm asked. He'd barely glanced at the babies, perhaps because they were asleep.

'Steve's filling our part of it in, that's why he's not here yet.'

Brenda took off her raincoat and folded it neatly at the end of my bed.

'I'm due to feed whichever of them wakes up first, if you want to help?'

'I'd love to.' Brenda settled on the edge of the bed to watch them.

'Great, I'll go and sort out their formula.' I left them watching the sleeping babies while I went in the ward kitchen and took two ready-mixed bottles of milk from the cupboard.

I could see Malcolm and Brenda through the partition window. Leaving the babies with someone else made my stomach flip over and over. I was all fingers and thumbs screwing the teats to the bottles, while looking up every few seconds, checking that everything was okay. I didn't know why I was so worried. It wasn't as though they would harm them or run off with them. I had to get used to this. A few more days and I'd be handing them over forever. The reality of it winded me. I leaned over the counter choked up, fist to the ache in my chest. The storm building inside me finally broke; tears dropped on my hands. I slipped to my knees, giving in to it, in long heaving sobs.

When I dragged myself up, I looked through the partition window, but there was no sign of Malcolm and Brenda. My heart leapt to my throat. Where were they? Had they stolen my babies?

I dragged my sleeve across my eyes and rushed back, my dressing gown billowing behind me in what seemed like slow motion.

The babies were still tucked up asleep. Malcolm and Brenda were standing at the window, holding hands. What was I thinking? Of course the twins were all right. How could I have thought such a terrible thing? All they were trying to do was memorise these precious moments, take in that they were finally parents. What was wrong with me? I couldn't blame tiredness. I had to let the babies go, trust that Malcolm and Brenda were going to be the best parents.

As they turned, the light obscured their faces so they appeared blank. The silence between us was brittle. Someone stepped towards me. The woman who'd come to take my babies and keep them forever. I swayed back and forth and put my hand out to the bed to steady myself. What was happening to me? My heart beat fast enough to burst.

'Are you okay?' The woman's lips moved slowly, her face distorted. Her red lipstick had bled into the thin lines around her mouth. As she came closer, all I could see was her skin caked in foundation. Instead of hiding her pores, it showed them up with every criss-cross wrinkle.

'Who are you?' I asked, my vision blurring. What was I saying? Their frowning eyes fell on each other in a way I couldn't read. She came up closer to me and held my wrist. I tried to pull away. She spoke so quietly, I couldn't hear.

'What's going on?' Steve shouted, striding into the room. Brenda let go of me and I collapsed in his arms. 'What's happened?'

'I don't know,' Brenda said, backing up, 'one minute she was fine, getting milk for the babies and the next—'

'I think you'd better come back tomorrow,' Steve said.

I clung to him, sobbing.

'I hope you're all right, Charlotte. I didn't mean to...' Brenda touched my elbow, but I moved my arm away.

They dipped their heads at each other, picked up their coats and left.

'What's going on?' Steve tried to detach me from him. I shook my head. He sat me down on the bed. 'Tell me slowly what happened.'

I explained about going for the milk and how I panicked at leaving the twins for the first time and when I looked up I couldn't see them. 'I thought they'd gone, taken the babies. But it's not their fault, they didn't do anything. I just got so upset.'

'It's okay.' He held me and kissed my temple.

'They were standing out of sight at the window. Their faces blanked out by the bright light. I panicked. For a second I didn't know who they were.'

'You're tired and anxious about giving up the twins. It's understandable. Have you spoken to any of the nurses?'

'I don't want to tell them. I've been mostly fine until now.'

'I could ask one of them to come and speak to you?'

'No! I don't want to talk about it.'

'OK, but you need to rest. I'll do the next feed.' His leather jacket creaked as he took it off.

I lay on the bed staring at the ceiling, a bottle of baby milk still gripped in my hand.

Chapter Thirty-Two

In the afternoon, Malcolm and Brenda stopped by again. Steve was there and helped Brenda hold Rose and give her a feed. I sat on the bed and took long slow breaths to control my anxiety. We'd had a cat once that'd had kittens and, as each one was sold, the mother gave long mournful meows, walking in circles, tail quivering in the air. Now I knew how she'd felt, and the twins hadn't even left yet.

'You look like an old hand at this, Brenda,' Steve said, looking round at me, 'don't you think?'

She smiled at us watching her.

'Yeah, a natural.' As much as it pained me to see her holding my baby, I was grateful for that. How much worse it would be if she found it awkward, or was worried about dropping the baby, like some women did. Malcolm looked mesmerised by his wife feeding their very own daughter. He seemed so much calmer, like something had changed between them for the better. At last they were content. They had the family they'd dreamed of and my heart swelled, knowing that I'd helped them.

'See, it's all going to be fine,' Steve whispered, his back to them as he leaned over the bed. He pushed my hair behind my ear and kissed my cheek. I took my hand away from my mouth. God knows how I ever thought this would be straightforward. But they *were* good people and Brenda was going to be a wonderful mum.

After they'd gone, Steve sat with me, holding my hands.

'Wasn't that bad, was it?'

'Not really, I suppose. I just need to get my head around it.'

'I thought you were okay with it now.'

'I am, in theory, but it's still going to be hard letting go.' As soon as I was feeling like myself again, I'd try and move on with my life, see about starting college.

'Yeah, I know. It's weird for me too.'

'Did you go and see Jack?'

'Yeah, he's doing well. Looking forward to finishing the chemo.' He stuck his hand in his jacket pocket. 'I forgot to give you this, it's from Jean. She sends her love. Says she'll wait and see you when you come home. And your dad emailed to say he'll call.' He passed me an envelope. I ripped it open and read a quote framed by flowers on the front of a card: *Do things for people not because of who they are or what they do in return, but because of who you are. Harold S. Kushner.* Inside she'd written: *Dear Charlotte, I think what you've done is extraordinary, I know I couldn't do it! Take good care of yourself. I'm here if you need anything. Love Jean xx*

'That's kind of her,' Steve said.

'Yeah, isn't it lovely.' I tried not to let myself cry. 'Has Mum said anything to you?'

'Nah, I drop Alice off, pick her up, she talks about what they've done that day, asks how you are and that's it.'

'We knew she wouldn't like Malcolm and Brenda. She'd have been the same whoever they were because she's so dead against the whole thing.' I closed my eyes. I needed to fix things with Mum. I couldn't let this come between us. But I didn't know what to do.

Chapter Thirty-Three

Malcolm and Brenda were already parked outside our flat the day we brought the twins home. The hospital would only release them into our care, as they weren't aware of the surrogacy. My pulse accelerated as soon as I saw their car. Part of me wanted to grab the steering wheel and drive away.

We unstrapped a baby each and lifted them out of the car. Malcolm and Brenda came straight over, but I wouldn't let go of Robert. Steve clocked the look on my face and narrowed his eyes at me.

'Come in,' he said to them cheerily, carrying Rose in her all-in-one coat.

'How are they?' Brenda asked, gently pulling Rose's hood to the side to see her darling face.

Both twins still had grey-blue eyes, their lashes long like mine. I'd taken my time dressing them both that morning, in the *Perfect* and *Dreamy* babygros and dear little stripy cotton hats from the hospital. They'd kicked their legs and made little mewling sounds the whole way through.

'They're doing so well,' I said, trying to swallow down the lump in my throat.

'And you?' Brenda touched my elbow. 'How are you feeling?'

'I'm... better, thanks.' I turned away from her. I needed to snap out of this.

Inside, Steve and I took the twins out of their coats. Steve handed Rose to Brenda and switched the kettle on.

'Thought we could have this instead?' Malcolm held up a bottle of bubbly.

'Great. Not sure we've got the right sort of glasses though,' Steve laughed, searching the cupboard, knowing full well we only had tumblers.

'Doesn't matter, anything will do.' Brenda's face was flushed. I imagined mine was a pale shade of grey.

'Here we go.' Steve switched the kettle off and brought over four small glasses. 'Paperwork's all signed for you, just need your signatures and it'll be ready for the court.'

'We can sort all that out.' Malcolm popped the cork and poured out the champagne. Rose started to cry. Brenda rocked her backwards and forwards, whispering to her and she soon calmed down.

'You really do have the knack,' Steve said, downing half his glass. 'Have you looked after children before?'

'A long, long time ago. I suppose you never lose it.' Her eyes glistened. 'I can hardly believe they're coming home with us.'

I held onto Robert, smelling his sweet skin, watching his eyelids flicker with dreams. I wished I could hold onto this moment. I'd never be ready to let them go.

'Cheers everyone, especially to you, Charlotte, we'll always be in your debt.' Malcolm raised his glass and we all hugged and congratulated each other. 'It's incredible that this day has finally come. For us, it's a miracle.' He took Brenda's hand and kissed it. He wiped a tear from his eye with the back of his hand. I was glad to see how much he cared. Such a shame he wasn't always good at showing it.

I gazed down at Robert. He opened his eyes and blinked up at me. My breathing quickened. I held him tighter, kissing his face and hands. My mouth opened to tell them to take all the money back, I needed to keep my babies, but no sound came out.

'So, you've got your car seats sorted then?' Steve asked.

'Yes, all ready to go.' Malcolm topped up our glasses. 'We'll bring the final payment once the paperwork is signed off.' He took the envelope from Steve.

'Fine by us, isn't it, Charlotte?' Steve put his arm around my waist.

'Can I hold him?' Malcolm asked. I was taken aback, wondering if I'd heard him correctly, but he had his arms out ready. He'd never asked before, maybe because he was nervous of holding a newborn? As I passed Robert to him, a gnawing click sounded in my head, as though part of me had detached itself. Malcolm took him in his arms and Robert curled his fingers around Malcolm's thumb. I turned away, pulling two made-up bottles of formula from my bag. Steve warmed them in the microwave and handed one each to Malcolm and Brenda.

'The start of things to come,' Steve said, holding up his phone, 'let me take your first proper family photo.'

'No,' Malcolm's sharp tone cut through me, making me jump. He quickly tempered it by saying: 'It's okay, but thanks.'

Steve pulled a face at me. He stuffed his phone back in his pocket.

'So, have you decided on names?' I rubbed my palms together, watching the babies being fed and having nothing to do felt strange. They asked me to show them the best way to hold the bottle, but I wanted to take over. The twins were used to me doing it. They'd be wondering where I was, why I wasn't holding them, comforting them.

'We've not decided yet.' Brenda gave a guarded smile.

'Oh.' I frowned. I thought they would have planned names long ago.

Seeing them all together, the four of them, this new family I'd helped create brought fresh tears to my eyes. This very moment was what I'd imagined, what it had all been about for me, seeing the joy on the faces of two new parents. But I hadn't expected to feel so cut up, as though they were taking them from me against my will. Yet, all the difficulties I'd been through throughout the pregnancy, all our disagreements, didn't seem to matter any more.

'Hey, you okay?' Steve whispered, putting his arm around me.

'They look so happy together, don't they?' I whispered back.

Malcolm and Brenda looked up and held their smiles as though posing for a camera.

'I know we keep saying it, but we really can never thank you enough. We'll be grateful to you for the rest of our lives,' Brenda said, 'and we'll bring them back to see you as often as we can.'

'Of course.' Malcolm gave a broad smile. Any worries about him vanished. It was plain how elated he was. He must have been so worried before, with the health scares and tantrums. I'd been too judgemental about him.

Once the twins had finished feeding and had clean nappies on for the journey, we followed Malcolm and Brenda out to the car. I hugged and kissed each of the twins goodbye, trying to memorise both of their faces, the soft sweet skin, the little snuffling sounds they made. I stepped back, but my legs trembled. I clung to Steve's arm. Then I lunged forward and touched Robert with my outstretched hand. His tiny fingers gripped mine. Brenda gently moved him away and strapped him in his seat. Malcolm strapped Rose in on the other side.

Brenda gave me a big hug, then Steve, her eyes welling up.

'This is it,' Brenda said, her hands either side of her face, 'the moment I've dreamed of for so long.'

Malcolm gave me a kiss on one cheek and shook hands with Steve.

'We'll take good care of them,' he said, looking directly into my eyes.

I nodded, holding my fist to my mouth, biting my skin. The two little faces in the back seat, Robert blowing a bubble with his lips, Rose sucking the edge of her coat.

'Will it be okay to call you?' I asked Brenda as I gave her a final hug.

'Of course. We'll be down again before you know it. I can only imagine how hard this is for you, Charlotte. I really can't thank you enough.'

As they drove away, the world seemed to shift sideways. My knees buckled and a mournful sound escaped from my throat. Steve's arms reached out to save me.

Chapter Thirty-Four

Back indoors, silence filled the flat, sweeping into unseen corners. I stood still, listening for signs of life. The smell of baby lotion clung to the air. The wrinkle of Rose's outline left on the changing mat. I wished I could capture all of it, keep it with me forever.

'That's it then.' Steve seemed as lost as I was. He stood next to me, hands on hips, elbows out like clipped wings.

I flung my arms around his neck. 'I'm so worried they'll forget to feed them or not hold them properly.'

'Brenda knows what she's doing. They'll be fine.' He spoke into my hair, muffling his words as though he only half believed it himself.

'Did I tell them that both babies like a cuddle before they go down for a nap?'

'I'm sure you did, hun.'

'They will ask me if they're not sure about something, won't they? I can't bear the thought of the babies suffering.' My breasts ached, still engorged with milk. Another set of pads soaked through. I sank down on the sofa, staring into space. I should feel better about this. It's what I'd wanted.

'Let's go and pick Alice up,' Steve said.

'Can you go? I can't face Mum.' I'd have to see her soon, but not now, not today.

Steve gave a single nod. Without speaking, he picked up his keys and left.

I fell forward on the sofa and let myself sob until I was exhausted. I must have dozed off because when I woke up, Steve was kneeling in front of me, smoothing back my hair.

'Where's Alice?' I sat bolt upright, scanning the room.

'She's fine, fast asleep.'

I stayed awake most of the night; emptied out, paralysed by a deep sense of loss, despite Brenda texting to reassure me they'd arrived home and the twins had settled in. How would I ever get over this?

Chapter Thirty-Five

The weeks until we saw them again dragged. I'd wanted to start college, but I was too late for this year and I couldn't get enthusiastic about anything. I snapped at everyone. I went back to work and for a while found myself getting along better with Tash, but it didn't last. I couldn't forgive her for calling the local press, even though they hadn't run the story. It didn't take much for her to sack me – for overcharging a regular customer and then telling them they were wrong.

I dreamed of taking the twins back, but I knew it wasn't possible. For a start we didn't have the space. And how would we afford to feed and clothe three children after the money had run out?

We agreed to meet Malcolm and Brenda at the Holiday Inn for lunch, to see how the babies were and collect the final fifteen-grand cheque. The parental order had been signed off by the court, which was much sooner than we expected. I still wasn't prepared in my head. The twins were not legally ours any more.

We arrived first and waited for them in the restaurant. It seemed quiet for a Friday. I picked up a menu. I fancied a fresh salad with grilled salmon, but I didn't feel that hungry.

Steve ordered me a vodka and orange and a beer for himself. I thought back to Brenda tapping on our room door with Malcolm's sample. I shuddered. I didn't want to be a surrogate a second time. The cold sperm of a practical stranger being squirted into my body was not something I wanted to go through ever again.

I spotted Malcolm first, pushing the double buggy with the twins fast asleep. My heart stopped. They'd changed so much already in three weeks. Their darling little faces were fuller, cheeks a bit more rounded, their hair had grown in longer wisps. I wondered if they'd recognise me. Maybe my smell? I knelt down to them and, as if they knew it was me, their bright eyes fluttered open. I thought I'd burst with happiness and sadness at the same time.

'How is everything?' I asked, offering my little finger for Robert to grab onto.

'Hard work of course, but they're good babies,' Brenda said, coming up behind him. 'So good to see you.' She seemed more like the bubbly Brenda we'd first met. I hoped Malcolm was being good to her, but when he put his arm round Brenda's waist, she flinched. I looked away, pretending I hadn't noticed.

'We're at the table in the corner if you want to sit down?' Steve said.

'That's perfect, thanks.' Brenda headed straight towards it.

Malcolm caught my eye, throwing a warning stare, which morphed into a smile. He must have seen me notice Brenda flinching at his touch.

'Shall we order some drinks first?' Steve said when the waiter came over.

I couldn't fault how well the twins were being looked after, decked out in new coats and mittens. They must have grown out of the ones they'd left in.

'What have you named them?' I asked.

'Julia and Joseph.'

'Oh, nice.' I tried not to sound disappointed. To me they'd always be Rose and Robert.

Brenda fussed about, moving chairs to fit the buggy closer to the table. She sat on one side, Malcolm on the other with the twins in between. Having two demanding babies was probably affecting their relationship. No wonder they were a bit tetchy. They were so used to lavishing their time on each other, doing what they liked when they liked, it must be a shock. It was early days, they probably needed more time to adjust, especially at their age.

The waiter brought the drinks over. For a few moments we sat in a bloated silence. The last time we were all here was the start of these two tiny lives. It hardly seemed possible. For weeks now, I'd been in a kind of limbo, waiting to officially be told they weren't mine any more. I'd slipped into a deep sadness, not having the motivation to do much of anything. I hadn't wanted to talk about it or listen to Mum. I'd wanted to read up about the teacher training course, but at the moment my heart wasn't in it.

Steve winked at me, wondering where the cheque was, no doubt. Perhaps we could start afresh after today. The trouble was, I'd never really be able to put any of this behind me. I'd been through so much anxiety and pain bringing these two precious babies into the world, giving them up would haunt me forever. I'd always miss them.

What was the point in telling Brenda that I'd hardly got out of bed for the past few days since I lost my job at the deli? The woman from the radio station, Lucy, had called and left several messages. I'd lain under the duvet listening. *Would I like to give her a call? She'd love to know how it all went. Were the babies well? What had the new parents called them?* In the end I'd switched it off. So many questions – *what did it really feel like giving your babies away to virtual strangers? Any regrets?* I could write a whole book about that one.

Malcolm cleared his throat. They were all staring at me. I wished they could see the dark shape of my thoughts, what I was really going through. I faked a smile.

'You look so pale.' Brenda touched my arm. There was something different about her that I couldn't pinpoint. Her American accent had virtually gone for one thing.

'How have they been?' I asked, wanting and not wanting to know.

'They're good most of the time, settling down to a routine.'

What did she do when they cried? Was she letting them feed on demand? But it wasn't my place to ask. She was their mother now.

'Will you keep your promise to stay in touch?' I wished I didn't sound so desperate, but I couldn't imagine my future without them in it.

'You'll always be part of their lives, Charlotte. You're their birth mother. No one can take that away from you, whatever happens.'

What did she mean? Where had this inner confidence of Brenda's come from?

The twins yawned and wriggled their arms and legs, their tiny fingers finding and grabbing each other. I scooted closer and touched the sides of their faces. I longed to hold them. If Brenda didn't offer in a minute, I'd have to ask.

'Can I take a photo?' I stood up ready, whatever the answer.

Brenda darted a look at Malcolm as she said, 'Yes, of course, why not.'

I took several snaps. Malcolm turned away, but I caught them both either side. I'd crop them out anyway, get it framed and keep it by my bed, forever.

'Are we ordering food?' Steve picked up the menu.

'I'm not really hungry,' I said.

'Why aren't you eating?' Brenda sounded alarmed.

I shrugged.

'It's been really hard for Charlotte,' Steve said.

Brenda held out her hand to me and our fingertips touched.

'I miss them so much.' I watched Joseph rubbing his eye and Julia yawning. They were nice names. 'But I don't want you to worry, I'm sure it's natural. I'll get over it,' I lied.

'I'm so sorry, I don't know what to say.' Brenda's face was full of worry lines. 'Is there anything I can do?'

'Not really, except… love them with all your heart and please, please let me see them, send me photos, updates on their progress.'

Brenda gave a nod, not looking me in the eye.

None of us ordered food. Malcolm took the papers out of his pocket and handed a copy of the parental order to Steve. I imagined wrestling it from him, ripping it up in a moment of madness. But I could never do that to Brenda after coming this far, giving her what she'd always dreamed of. I had to follow my head, not my heart.

Brenda unstrapped little Joseph and handed him to me with a bottle of milk. I sighed and held him close, high on my chest, under my chin so I could inhale his smell mixed with a bath scent I wasn't familiar with, but it still intoxicated me. I couldn't stop smiling. His golden hair had thickened and he lifted his hands to the bottle, almost holding it. The tiny scrap I'd given birth to.

Brenda fed Julia. She was the smaller of the two now. Was she getting as much attention from Malcolm? Was she being fed as much milk as Joseph? I ached to ask.

'He's caught up now, so they're on the same quantities,' Brenda said, guessing what I was thinking.

'Strange that she's the tiny one now, isn't it?' I hoped I didn't sound like I was accusing her; I wasn't expecting an answer, it was just an observation.

'The health visitor is happy with her.' Brenda's tone was defensive. I supposed she didn't need me telling her what to do. She was holding the baby almost at arm's length, as though she didn't really want to be doing it. Maybe I was being hypersensitive, but when Julia started to cry, Brenda became flustered, moving her to standing then sitting, over one shoulder then the other. Perhaps they hadn't bonded yet, or it was me making her feel nervous? I handed Joseph to Steve.

'Can I?' I said gently, offering to take Julia. Brenda seemed relieved and lifted her into my arms. Julia stopped crying straight away. My heart lifted. Did she recognise my smell? I shut my eyes as I rocked her.

'You have something else for us then?' Steve said, not able to resist asking any longer.

Malcolm didn't say a word at first, pretending he hadn't heard. Then he opened his wallet and took out an envelope and handed it to me.

'Open it,' Steve said to me, 'make sure it's kosher.' His laugh was uneven, forced. Brenda threw him a stony look.

I carefully ripped the flap open and took out the final cheque for fifteen thousand pounds.

'Who's this L. Brown?' Steve asked.

'My professional name,' Malcolm said.

'Are you a writer or something? I thought you were in property.'

But Malcolm had turned away, glancing from Brenda to Julia.

'I'll take her.' Brenda came towards me with her arms out. I didn't really have a choice as she leaned down and prised Julia away from me.

'So, you're coping okay then?' I said.

'Can't you see we are?' Brenda snapped back.

'I'm sorry, I didn't mean…' A distant voice in my head heard them saying: *No, sorry, we're not, can you take the twins back please?*

'Sorry, I didn't mean to snap. It's all going smoothly. Thank you. Like I said, we're very grateful.'

Her expression told me otherwise. I'd expected her to look exhausted, but she appeared surprisingly fresh. Was she hiding it well? Perhaps they'd hired a nanny after all. I wished she'd open up to me.

'Right, I think that's everything we came to do.' Malcolm slapped his knees and stood up.

'Off so soon?' Steve finished his beer and banged the empty glass on the table. 'Have one more?'

'We need to get going, it's a long journey.' Brenda answered in this strange way she had today, as though all her answers were practised.

I stood in the car park, watching helplessly while they belted the twins in, arguing about the correct position of the straps. I made a move to help them, but Steve reached for my wrist and held me still.

'Let them find their way.'

We waved goodbye as they drove out of the car park. I wanted to run after them as though part of me was being torn away. My whole body wavered. Steve wrapped his arms around me in an instant.

Would I ever get over this? Mum's voice echoed in my head, *What have you done?*

What have I done?

I buried my head in Steve's chest. He held me while I wept.

'What was wrong with them?' I managed to say at last. 'They were acting strangely, weren't they?' Or was it me, not wanting to let go?

'I suppose they are the parents now and don't want to be told what to do. To be honest, I get the feeling they don't really want to stay in touch.'

'No! Don't say that. Brenda promised.' I grabbed his sleeve, pulling at him, slapping his arm, as though it was his fault.

'It doesn't mean they'll stick to it, they're not bound to it by law. You've seen the forums, sometimes the new parents want to cut off from their surrogate completely and go it alone.'

'I don't believe that. Brenda made a promise to me. You heard her.' I swung my arms like a belligerent teenager.

'Maybe they will, but to me it felt like they were paying us off, that this was final.'

'Not. To. Me,' I shouted and started crying again.

'Okay, okay.' He raised his hands. 'Maybe I'm wrong.'

He led me to the car, grabbed a blanket from the back and laid it across me in the passenger seat, tucking me in. But nothing would stem my tears. I couldn't imagine never seeing the twins again.

Chapter Thirty-Six

I didn't drag myself out of bed until Tuesday. My eyes felt puffy and sore from crying. Steve had gone to work early and I'd promised him I'd take Alice out. It wasn't fair to neglect my own child because I was grieving for the twins.

I paid the cheque into my current account and walked past the deli on my way home. It was empty, long after lunch, so I called in as it was Tash's day off and Shell would be holding the fort.

'How are you?' Shell came rushing towards me, stripping the tight plastic gloves from her hands.

I threw my arms around her. On the wall behind her was a photo of me when I was ridiculously huge, full of two babies, a blissful smile on my face, in my eyes.

'How's this little missy? High five.'

Alice giggled as I raised her hand and Shell clapped it with hers.

'What is it, babe? You don't look well.'

'I miss the babies *so* much, I know I'm not supposed to, but I don't know if I can carry on,' I sobbed, the loss still so fresh, like a blow to the stomach, folding me in two.

'Come here.' Shell pulled me into her chest. 'It's only been a few weeks since you had them, you're bound to feel emotional still. It's a huge thing you've been through. And you've been so brave. I can understand how hard it must have been giving them away.'

There weren't many people I could be so open with. Shell understood loss. Her first baby had been stillborn. I dug in my pocket for a tissue. Often through the day, I'd find myself staring into space, an image of the twins as they were when they were born, vivid in my mind. My stomach had already shrunk into an empty purse, the scar like a zip. My breast milk had dried up so at least I didn't wake up with a soaked top any more. Soon there would be no outward sign that I'd had twins at all.

'You're grieving, babe.'

'I wake up in the night wondering if they're okay, if they're fed and warm, if they're crying for me. What if they're in a room on their own, down a long corridor with the door shut and Brenda can't hear them? What if one of them is sick in the night and chokes and no one comes?'

'Oh babe.' Shell squeezed me tight. 'You just have to trust. You have to believe they're being well looked after and cared for by parents who love them.'

'I know. I try to.' I hung my head, shameful thoughts evaporating. 'I can't completely though, it will take time.'

'Try and focus on something else. Find a new job, until you start your college course.'

'I will. Let me know if you hear of anything. Work's picked up at the garage. We need a new car, but I want us to wait for the last payment to come through first otherwise we'll be left skint.'

Shell made us coffees while I gave Alice pieces of banana.

'How's things with your mum?'

'Not great. We're barely talking.'

'She'll get over it. It wasn't her decision to make.' Shell brought our espressos over.

'Try telling her that.'

'You make your own decisions now. The sooner she realises, the better.'

'I hope she does.' I drank my shot of coffee. Alice was dozing off. 'I'd better get back. Thanks for listening.' I hugged Shell and left.

I walked by the park on the way home and sat for a while on Nan's thinking bench. She'd often brought me here when I was little, when Mum was pregnant or had lost a baby. She said that if you sat close enough to the weeping willow and really concentrated, you could hear it whisper. She believed that the gentle movement of its hair-like branches dipping and swaying in the stream had helped her forget her worries.

Today, the murky water was half frozen. Nan would have had something to say about that. You'd have backed me up, I know you would have. In little over four weeks, it would be Christmas. This time last year we'd been about to do the third insemination attempt, and I wondered if I was going to get pregnant at last, if my life was about to change. I'd been so naïve. What's done is done, Nan would say. I'd been determined to help Brenda and I'd achieved it.

As soon as the final cheque cleared, I'd buy a real Christmas tree and some new tinsel. I'd make a list of toys for Alice's stocking and one main present. We wouldn't go mad; a few extras here and there would be enough to make it feel special. Then once we'd put some away for my courses and in Alice's savings, we could think about renting somewhere a bit bigger, with a separate bedroom and maybe a little garden. I needed to focus on my own family now. I'd done my good deed.

I wormed my finger under Alice's warm, sticky hand. The past year had turned into a nightmare. But as long as I made sure this money amounted to something good in our lives, it would have been worth it.

'Time to move on, don't you think?' I stroked Alice's sleeping face. I hoped the twins were happy in their new family. But my mind kept dragging me back to the last time we met them at the Holiday Inn, how awkward they were with us, Brenda's defensive behaviour. Was Steve right about them not really wanting to stay in touch? I had to trust they were doing a good job of bringing up the babies, but I couldn't escape the unease churning in my stomach, how it had suddenly felt like we didn't know them at all.

Chapter Thirty-Seven

The next day I visited Mum. I needed to tell her the twins had gone to their new parents. I wanted to smooth things over with her somehow, get past this.

'Wasn't expecting to see you in a hurry. I'm about to go to the garden centre,' Mum said when I opened the door. Was it an excuse? She didn't have her coat on. I swallowed down the thought and followed her into the kitchen.

'I wondered what you were doing for Christmas, if you'd like to come over to us?' I put down a box of fresh cream cakes from the bakery.

'Mary next door has asked me to go there.' She leaned against the kitchen bench, arms folded. We were two different people now, poles apart.

'Oh.' She didn't even like her. Not really. Always moaning about her. But then she probably moaned about me too.

'But I'm not keen on her grandchildren jumping all over the place, I won't get a moment's peace.'

'So you'll come?' Why did Mum always have this round-about way of accepting an invitation as though she was doing us a favour?

'Why don't you come here instead? Only because of the space.' She unfolded her arm and opened the cake box.

'All right, but we're buying the turkey.'

Mum's face dropped. 'From your baby money?'

'Once it clears.'

'I don't think so.' She turned away and patted a pile of folded washing.

Here we go again.

'Where are the twins? Given them away already, have you?' Her voice went up a key.

'It was time, yes.' I braced myself. I wasn't going to cry in front of her. I couldn't admit how hard it had been, that she had been right about lots of things.

'Once that money's gone, what have you got to show for it except stretch marks?'

I sighed.

'You'll see it my way when you're older. Whatever you think now, the fact is you sold your babies and you'll come to regret it.' She waved her finger at me. I shut my eyes, doing my best to stay calm, zone out.

'Do you have to say that?' I said under my breath.

'Yes, I do, no one else will. I don't think you have a clue how this is affecting me.' She stalked off towards the living room.

'Why can't you try and accept it now it's done?' I asked, following her.

She faced me in the doorway. 'I've told you, they're my grandchildren. Look how ill you were. You could have died.' She drew in a sharp breath and stood by the sofa, facing the patio doors.

A pain pulsed in my eye.

She made a big show of carrying a box of decorations from the sofa to the table. Dad had brought home a whole selection of brand-new baubles one year. Each one beautifully handcrafted in different metals, wood and glass. Mum pulled out bushy lengths of tinsel and a pair of silver glittery reindeers. I'd been right about the garden centre being an excuse.

'Don't just stand there, help me with this.' She lifted out a package of pink tissue paper. Inside was Alice's glass bauble with her name, date of birth and the words, 'New Baby', captured inside in silver letters. It was so delicate and precious, I wondered if I should keep it in the box. Mum passed me each decoration and I hung them on the tree with Alice's bauble in pride of place at the top, under the star. Finally, I draped a red piece of tinsel over the frame of a family photo – an eight-year-old me on the swing in our old garden, the solitary child between two warring parents.

'Do you really believe those people want you around?' she asked suddenly, finding something to stare at in the box.

God help me, she hadn't finished yet.

'Yeah, they do actually. They said they'll send us photos and come and visit.' I pushed away Steve's words about it being final. I couldn't accept that.

'Have you looked in the mirror lately?'

I glanced down at my ripped jeans and studded black T-shirt.

'They're hardly going to want you associating with their kids. Probably don't even want to admit to their wealthy friends that they used a surrogate.'

'You don't know them like we do. They're not the kind of people who care about that sort of thing. If anything, it made them feel good that they were able to help us out.'

'Mutually beneficial? Mmm, we'll see.'

I couldn't listen to her a moment longer. 'Right, that's your last bit of tinsel up. Looks lovely doesn't it? I need to shoot off now. See you on Christmas Day, Mum.'

In the car, Mum's words swilled around my mind. We probably wouldn't fit in with Malcolm and Brenda's posh friends, I'd give her that, but I gave birth to their children.

Chapter Thirty-Eight

On Friday morning, I wheeled Alice back round the park towards the corner shop. Before I went in, I counted out enough change for a pack of big brand nappies; it felt good splashing out. Steve had booked a table in China Town for Saturday evening. I needed to buy our train tickets online. It had been too long since we'd had a proper night out. He'd wanted to book a swanky hotel too, but there was no point chucking money around, we had to make it last. I made my way back home.

Even before I put the key in the door, I could hear the phone ringing. I dashed in but reached it too late. I didn't recognise the number at first, but it was a local code, so I called straight back. I told the woman I was returning their call. She said she was calling from my bank and before I could ask what it was about, she ran through a load of security checks with me. Perhaps they wanted to talk to me about saving account rates for the money I'd paid in.

'Let me see what it was about for you.' She fell silent as she tapped away on a keyboard.

I held my breath, scanning my head for what it could be. We'd paid off all our debts with the first cheque. It couldn't be anything bad.

'Ah yes, here we are. You paid in a cheque on Tuesday, for fifteen thousand pounds?'

'That's right.'

'I'm afraid that cheque has been returned to drawer.'

My stomach lurched. I leaned into the wicker chair. 'Are you telling me it's bounced?'

'I'm afraid so, Mrs Morgan.'

I almost dropped the phone. This was insane. 'What shall I do? Will you contact the person and get them to send another cheque? I don't understand.' I pushed the heel of my hand to my forehead.

'You'll have to contact them yourself, I'm afraid. They'll need to send the funds to you by an alternative method.'

Alice started to cry. This had to be a terrible mistake. I mean, Malcolm and Brenda weren't short of cash. I ended the call and immediately texted Brenda. She'd sort it out. I took a couple of deep breaths to try and steady my pounding heart. Malcolm must have forgotten to put funds in that account. There would be some simple explanation. I rolled the buggy back and forth, trying to calm Alice, who was wailing, *mamma, mamma*, louder and louder. She was due a drink and a snack but my whole body was a live wire, I could barely see straight. Steve had ordered a new vacuum cleaner online only last night, thinking the money would be cleared by today.

I lifted Alice into her high chair and chopped up an apple for her while I sang, 'One, two, three, four, five, once I caught a fish alive...' She joined in, clapping. I switched the TV on for her and checked my phone.

No reply from Brenda.

I tried calling, then texting again. Nothing. I opened my laptop and called them on Skype. No one picked up. I logged onto the surrogate forum and left them a message to call me. All afternoon I kept trying. This couldn't be happening. I phoned Steve and asked him to come straight home.

The tiniest slither of me wasn't surprised. Maybe Malcolm had done it on purpose, to make us sweat, have to beg for the money. I gave Alice a digestive biscuit and a beaker of milk while I paced up and down the flat. A sense of unease settled in my stomach, as though I'd done something awful, like leaving the twins somewhere and forgetting them. If Malcolm could mess this up or do it just to rile us, what else was he capable of? My motherly instinct told me the twins could only really be safe with me.

When Steve walked in, I ran at him, virtually headbutting his chest. I could hardly speak.

'Try taking some slow breaths,' he said, rubbing my back. 'I'm sure it's not as bad as you think. They're probably out of the country again or forgot to move some money around.'

'Gone away on business with two small babies?'

'They'll have hired a nanny. Anyway, I'm sure they'll transfer it to us as soon as they realise what's happened.'

I nodded and tried to take in a slow stream of air, but my chest wouldn't stop heaving up and down.

'Right, let me have a go. What's Malcolm's number?'

I pointed to it on my phone. Steve pressed dial. I watched his face, waiting for it to light up, but it didn't. His eyes narrowed. He ended the call and dialled again. After the fifth time, he threw the phone on the sofa.

'Their bank will tell them it's bounced, so we're bound to hear from them before too long,' he said, taking a can of beer out of the fridge.

I wrung my hands together. None of it seemed right. I tried to think of reasons why they weren't picking up. I dialled Brenda's number again, but this time her answer machine wasn't even kicking in. 'It's like that time before, when I tried to get hold of them after the miscarriage.'

'Yeah and they'd gone away, it was all fine.'

'But what about when the second cheque took ages to clear?'

'Look, we don't know anything for sure.' He picked Alice up. 'How are you today, little lady?' They danced around the flat to the *Peppa Pig* theme tune. I wanted to scream.

'Why aren't you taking this seriously?' I shouted.

'I am, but we can't do anything else right now. They're not answering their phones for whatever reason and the banks are shut now. It's bloody odd, I grant you. But we'll get it sorted.'

'What if you're right about Malcolm not wanting me to see the twins? And why would Brenda go along with it? Although she was really short with me on that last day.'

'Have you tried Skyping them?'

'I've tried everything. I've messaged them on the surrogate forum and even sent them an email pleading with them to call me.'

'Let's leave it tonight, hun. There's nothing else we can do now.' He patted the sofa for me to sit next to him, but I wouldn't be able to sit still. So much for going to China Town. We'd have to cancel.

I warmed up left over corned beef hash and added a fried egg on top of each.

I lay awake that night hoping it was a mistake, and that Brenda would call me back in the morning.

Chapter Thirty-Nine

For the next two days, I tried calling Brenda. At first it would ring and ring, never clicking onto the answerphone. In the end, the line went dead. Malcolm's was the same. I checked my emails every five minutes. I re-sent my message, blind copying it back to myself. It arrived in a second. At least I knew it had been delivered.

While Alice was at nursery, I logged on to the surrogacy forum. My message hadn't been opened. I sent another, trying to swallow down my growing panic. Telling myself Steve was probably right, they'd flown off somewhere exotic and couldn't get a signal. They'd hired a live-in nanny. Why hadn't I asked more questions? Found out what their plans were? Too bloody polite for my own good. Mum had always told me not to be nosey.

I paced up and down the flat. What else could I do? I held my arm around my stomach when it rumbled. I didn't feel like eating but I needed to have something. I took a yogurt out of the fridge. Our copy of the court order was sticking out of the letter rack like a tongue. As they weren't answering my emails, I could write them a letter. I put the yogurt down, pulled out the papers and copied their address onto a plain envelope and ours on the back. I sat on the sofa with a piece of paper balanced on a book and wrote to Brenda. I worded it as calmly as I could, saying I guessed they must be out of the country, but that the cheque had bounced and I couldn't help worrying about the twins as I'd not heard from her for a while. All I wanted to know was if the twins were doing well and if they wouldn't mind sending another cheque or transfer the funds to my account. I ended by saying how pleased I was that they were a little family at last.

I called in at the post office on my way to pick Alice up and sent it first class, hoping it would reach them the following morning.

Over the next few days, we tried to carry on as normal, but I checked my phone and email every few minutes. I wanted to believe they were on holiday and would get in touch as soon as they got back. Almost a week later and there was still no reply from them. It didn't make sense.

Steve came home, but I hadn't cooked any dinner. I wasn't hungry. I fed Alice scrambled egg, mashed carrot and baked beans warmed from the fridge. I found it impossible to stay still for a second. Steve and I shared the last beer.

'They must have got my letter by now, why haven't they replied?' I said.

'Did you check the address?' He opened his laptop and clicked on the Royal Mail website.

'Of course I did.' I read it out while he typed. It came up in a list of properties with the same postcode.

I leaned over his shoulder. He opened a map of the UK and zoomed in to where a little red flag was planted. It showed a large property near a hotel and restaurant. He clicked on Streetmap.

'That's it, the Victorian-looking one with all the trees.' I took a deep breath. 'I think we should drive up there.'

'Really?' Steve said.

'How else are we going to find them?'

'It's a hell of a long way to Orkney and I bet they'll be back from their travels any day.'

'Seriously? I do not have a good feeling about this. We need to make sure the twins are okay.'

'We should wait a bit longer, it's only been a few days. If they're away on business and we roll up demanding to know why they're not answering our calls, they'll think we're obsessed or crazy, that we don't trust them. They might have second thoughts about us being in the twins' lives.'

'I don't want to wait,' I shouted.

'Let's see if they answer your message on the forum. If they don't, then we'll ask around, see if anyone else has heard from them recently or has any other contact details we could try.'

'That might be ages.' I stomped off to the bathroom and banged the door shut. This had set off every kind of alarm bell within me.

Chapter Forty

I moped about at home the next day, checking and rechecking my phone and the forum every few minutes. I'd kept the twins' little blankets because Brenda had bought her own. The photo the Bounty lady had taken of them when they were barely a day old arrived in the post. I cried when I took it out of the envelope. I'd ordered two copies, one for us and one for them. So much for my surprise gift.

Still no new messages. I pressed my hand to my chest, but my heart wouldn't stop racing. I could barely sit still, going over and over every possibility as to why they didn't – or perhaps couldn't – answer my calls. What if they'd been in a car or plane crash? I pushed my fingers into my jelly belly and let the tears fall. My hormones were still all over the place, but the longing was deeper, more physical. My insides buckled at the real possibility of never seeing my babies again. I missed the feel of them in my arms, their smell of new dewy freshness. Steve had a photo on his phone of me holding them, one in each arm. I'd never forget how wide my smile stretched at the sight of them, or the lightness of the two tightly wrapped bundles, their sleepy eyes and cherry lips.

'You're freezing,' Steve said, giving me a warm hug when he came home.

'I don't feel well. I think I'm getting a cold.' My head hurt and my throat had become grainy and sore. He tucked me up in bed with a hot-water bottle.

'I'm going to check the forum, see if I can find the original thread from when we first hooked up with them. Chances are it's still there.'

'It's pretty old.' I hid under the bedcovers.

'I'll see if they've replied to our message.'

'They hadn't when I checked.' Where the hell were they? Did they know how much grief they were causing us? I'd so wanted to buy a real Christmas tree this year, but I daren't spend any money. Alice was much more aware now she was older. I couldn't bear to let her down.

'Shit.' Steve banged the desk with his fist.

'What is it?' I peeped out, not wanting to hear more bad news.

'That thread's been deleted.'

'Why?'

'I don't know, but both their profiles have been deleted too.'

'I didn't think to check. I assumed they were still there. What about my messages to them?'

'All gone from your inbox. Not a single trace.' Steve smacked the keyboard.

'Why would they do that? Why is this happening?' I sobbed, pressing my throbbing forehead. 'They can't do this to us.'

'That fucking agreement is a joke. I bet Malcolm never intended to stick to it.'

'What if he planned to dump us all along? How could we have been so trusting?'

'So stupid you mean.'

'We have to try something else. What about their office number? I think it's on their website, PremierProperties.com.'

Steve typed it in. I was half expecting it not to be there, but it came up straight away. I typed the phone number from the bottom of the homepage into my mobile. One click, and it went straight back to the dial tone.

'Let me try on mine.' Steve tapped it in. A second later he held it away from his ear. Nothing, not even a connection. He tried emailing but got a 'not delivered' notice straight back. 'Now what?'

'Google their names? Something's bound to come up.' My head was killing me. I climbed out of bed and put my dressing gown on. 'Any luck?'

'How long have you got? There are over thirty million results.'

'You're joking? Any obvious ones linked to property?' I pulled up a chair and we spent the next hour clicking on as many results as we could, but nothing linked to the Malcolm Stewart we knew.

'I know.' Steve jumped out of his seat, a finger in the air as though he'd worked out the meaning of life, 'Google images!'

'What?'

He clicked on the images button for results to Malcolm's name. Photos of the same sportsman came up on page after page with the odd other person thrown in. None were of the Malcolm we knew. We frowned at one another, completely puzzled. Without another word, Steve searched under Brenda's name. The same. Not one picture of either of them. What did this mean? Everyone was on Facebook, Twitter or Instagram these days, weren't they?

'They're private people. They might have had any pictures or information about them taken down before they started the surrogacy.'

Steve stretched his arms above his head. 'Then why be so secretive?'

'Maybe their clients are famous and they can't risk publicity about the twins?' Even to me it sounded lame.

'I'm sick of this.' He stood up and took a can of beer out of the fridge. 'Want one?'

'Water please and some paracetamol.'

He handed me a glass and a box of tablets. I swallowed two down, wishing they could cure more than a headache.

'All I wanted was to help someone like Mum. And now this. Poor Brenda.'

'Hang on, poor Brenda? She could have warned us. She had the power to stop him doing all this, if anyone did.'

I wasn't so sure. 'What about the bruises on her wrist? I should have asked more about how she got them.' I sat back down on the bed and buried my face in the duvet. I wanted to scream. 'Have you still got their photo, the one you kept from the hospital?' I sat bolt upright.

'What about it?'

'Post it on the forum.'

'What for?'

'See if anyone recognises them, knows where they are. I'm sure Brenda said they contacted at least two other couples before they decided on us. Surely someone must have their details.'

'It's not a great photo, it's quite dark. What about the one you took of the twins, with them either side?'

'Good point, we can post that one too. Hopefully someone will know how we can contact them.' I scrolled through the photos on my phone.

'Not much good if they've been given the same details as us though.'

'We need to try something.'

Steve uploaded both photos straight away, asking for anyone with information about Malcolm and Brenda to send us a private message.

'I could contact the reporter from the local radio station, see if she can help.'

'What can she do?'

'She wanted to know how the birth and everything went, so I'll tell her we have to find the new parents. We need to try everything we possibly can. If she can broadcast my story, it might reach someone who knows them. At the very least it may stop another woman making the same mistakes we've made. I don't think people realise how outdated the law is. It needs to change, to protect surrogates and the babies.' As soon as I said it, I'd made up my mind. This could be our best chance. We had to see the twins again, make sure they were okay. I jumped out of bed and took Lucy's business card out of my purse. I checked the time. I might just catch her if I called right now.

-

We met in a small café in town the following morning. It was empty except for a couple of builders sitting by the window, heads down, scoffing their full breakfasts.

Lucy sat back from the pine table, legs crossed, skirt carefully arranged to reach the lower part of her thighs. The lime green suit was bright enough to give me an instant headache.

I told her all about my health problems leading up to the birth and everything that had happened since, including Malcolm and Brenda's disappearance.

'Charlotte, this is truly awful.' She cupped her coffee in both hands. 'Would you be willing to come on air and talk about it?'

'I was hoping you'd ask. I feel so powerless. Someone listening might have information which will help me find the twins. The new parents agreed to keep in touch. I'm desperate to know how they're getting on. Babies grow so quickly.'

'Do you have any standing legally?'

'We made an agreement between us, but it's not legally binding. The only part that seems to be covered by the law is the parental order – transferring my rights to them.'

'I see, so you don't have parental rights any more?'

'No.'

'Are you saying that in the eyes of the law they've not done anything illegal?'

'Yes, but…' I twisted my hands together. She was going to tell me there wasn't any point going on air with this. *Come on, think of something.*

She glanced at her watch.

'So… I'm starting a Twitter campaign… #ChangeUKLawOnSurrogacy, and I'd like to launch it on your show.' I hoped she couldn't tell I was making this up as I was going along.

'Oh, I see. That does sound good. We could do a phone-in, ask people what they think about the current law on surrogacy and whether it should be reviewed.'

'All I wanted was to keep in touch with the twins. It's been such a wrench.' I sipped my coffee, keeping my eyes fixed on her.

'It must feel something like bereavement.' She tilted her head to the side.

I nodded, trying to hold the tears in. 'I suppose the new parents might have worried that I'd interfere, try and take over, perhaps in the future, but I'd never do that.'

'There's probably more to it that isn't about you at all.' She gave a quick smile and patted the back of my hand. 'I'll see if the station is willing to pay you a fee for this interview, but I can't promise anything.'

'Oh, thank you...'

She was already distracted by her buzzing mobile. She stood up.

'Hang on, hang on, Gordon,' she yelled into the phone. 'Sorry, going to have to leave it there, Charlotte. Got to dash back to the office, something's come up. I'll get back to you as soon as I can.' She picked her bag up and left me sitting there with her half-drunk coffee.

–

Back at home, Steve barely looked up when I came in. He was still sitting at his laptop, while Alice was scribbling on her chalkboard. I kissed the top of her head.

'What are you drawing?'

She pointed at her picture and chewed the end of the chalk.

'Is it a duck? Well that's lovely, and is that the pond?' I pointed to a squiggle of blue. She smiled and nodded.

I rested my arms around Steve's shoulders and kissed the side of his face.

'How'd it go?' he asked.

'Good. She's going to let me know when she has a slot available to go on air. I've told her I'm starting a campaign to tighten up the UK surrogacy laws. You never know, Brenda might hear it and have a change of heart.' I gave a pathetic laugh.

Steve swung round in his chair so he was facing me, his skin slate grey, as though someone had died.

My heart gave an unsteady leap. 'How've you got on? Has someone replied?'

'I think there might be a lot more to this than we realised.' The words fell out of his mouth. He stared ahead, not quite at me, but beyond, to somewhere I wasn't sure I wanted to go.

'What do you mean?' I scanned the surrogacy forum page.

'There's more to Malcolm not wanting us to have contact with the twins.' His voice wavered, fighting to keep tears at bay. I'd only seen him like this once before, when the police caught him speeding.

'How do you know?' I frowned, my whole body frozen to the spot. He drew in a deep breath.

'There's a woman on the forum…' he said, pointing at the screen, taking a shorter breath to carry on, '… she… she recognises Malcolm.'

'That's good, isn't it? What we wanted.' I wedged my hands on my hips.

'No. It isn't.' He clicked on the message the woman had sent us.

I leaned forward and read it aloud: "This is the same man who was the intended father of the baby I had last year. His name is Ian Turner. His wife was called Sheila. I gave birth to a boy. They chose not to stay in touch with me, didn't give a specific reason. Their choice. Nice enough couple. They offered more money than anyone else, so I wasn't bothered.'

I stood up straight. 'I don't understand. That's not possible.' I swept my hand out in front of me. 'She's mistaken him for someone else.'

Steve shook his head, holding me with hollowed-out eyes, sending chills right through my body.

Chapter Forty-One

'She's dead certain it's him,' Steve said, his face even paler now. I hoped it wasn't true because I couldn't even process what it meant for us.

'It's not the clearest photo though, is it?'

'The one at the hotel is. I was expecting a reply from someone who'd thought about having a baby for them, not someone who'd actually *had* one.'

'Ask her if this man contacted her first, or was it the other way around? That might tell us something.'

Steve typed in the question and sent it. Within minutes, the reply came back.

'She says he contacted her. It was the first time she'd posted about wanting to be a surrogate. "Ian" was the first person to reply.'

'Similar to us.' My vision skittered around the room.

Steve gave a forlorn nod.

'Ask her to describe him physically or does she have a photo? And what was he like as a person?'

I paced in a circle round the flat while Steve typed. I racked my brains for answers, reasons why it couldn't be him. Why would he use a different name to have a baby with another woman, only last year, and where was that baby now? If true, it would mean he'd cheated on Brenda. But no, that was too awful to contemplate. These two men just happened to look similar, *surely*?

'She's replied.' Steve pressed his fingers to his forehead.

'That was quick.' I darted over to the screen.

'She says: "He was lanky without being really tall. Always immaculately dressed, wore V-neck jumpers, no shirt – trying to pull off that cool middle-aged look. Black hair and designer stubble. Like I said, they didn't want to keep in touch. Would have been too painful for me anyway. Clean break was easier. Pleasant bloke, could get moody. Sheila, was lovely and so grateful."'

'Sounds exactly like him, doesn't it?' My voice was almost a whimper. I pictured Malcolm wearing one of his usual V-neck jumpers, without his beard. I shuddered.

'Shit.'

'Ask her if they owe her any money, or if she was paid in full.'

We waited for her answer. Perhaps she'd gone offline. I held my throat, not wanting to give in to the urge to be sick. How could he have had a baby with another woman, for another woman? Where was Brenda in all this?

'Ask where they lived, if they've got an address?'

He typed it in.

'Here we go. She says they still owe her five grand. They lived in Leeds, but the address will be out of date now because they were moving to Sheffield. She doesn't know how to go about recovering the money they owe her, because she couldn't get in touch with them.'

I let out a breath and sat down. 'Do you think they ever lived in Leeds? I don't remember them mentioning it?'

'Maybe he has a second house, for this other family.'

'Oh god. If only Brenda would get back to me. This can't be right. It must be someone else.' I stood up again, my hand to my forehead.

'You want to be the one to ask Brenda about it? Don't be daft.'

'I'd have to tell her. But maybe she's already found out what he's been doing and that's why she's not been in touch.'

'Hun, I think we need to face the fact that she may be in on it, that they've both conned us.'

I shook my head, trying to take in his words. 'No! I'm telling you, it can't be them.'

'We need to keep searching and hope we hear from another surrogate.'

'They wouldn't do this to me!' I cried and threw myself on the bed. A slideshow of images played in my mind, the bruise on Brenda's wrist, the flash of anger in Malcolm's eyes, him having a baby with someone else and the twins abandoned somewhere, crying for their mummy.

Chapter Forty-Two

In the morning, I dropped Alice at Mum's and took a bus to the radio station at the edge of town. Lucy greeted me in the foyer in a yellow version of the same suit she was wearing last time.

'I'm about to go on air, but I'll see you in the studio in about fifteen minutes. I've made a list of questions, I thought you might like to look it over and think about your answers. I don't want to spring anything on you.' She gave me her practised smile.

'Thanks,' I said.

'Tilly will look after you until it's time.'

A woman in a smart jumpsuit stepped forward and showed me to a lounge area with a coffee vending machine.

'Help yourself,' she said.

I pressed a button for a black coffee and looked over the list. The questions seemed reasonable enough. I paced around the room, trying to calm my nerves. I checked my Twitter account. My tweet about being on the radio today to launch #ChangeUKLawOnSurrogacy had already received twenty likes and six retweets.

Five minutes before I was due to go on, Tilly took me through to the small bright studio and gave me a glass of water. I sat quietly on a stool opposite Lucy, who was wearing headphones and talking into a large mic surrounded by panels of buttons and flashing lights.

'Next up, we have Charlotte, a kind-hearted young woman who had a dream of being a surrogate for a childless couple. Unfortunately for her, it didn't all quite go to plan. Her experience is a cautionary tale for any one of you out there thinking of having a baby for someone else.'

Lucy pressed a button which I guessed was for an advert break. She pulled off her headphones.

'How are you feeling? Not too nervous I hope?' She drank a mouthful of tea.

'A bit. I'll be okay.' I sipped my water. My hand was shaking.

'Great. Try and relax.' She put her headphones back on. 'Welcome to you, Charlotte, thanks for coming in today to share your incredible story.'

'Thank you for asking me.' My stomach dropped into free fall. I tried not to think about the thousands of people listening, including Mum, who I told this morning. Instead I pictured Steve, cheering me on.

'Some of you may remember Charlotte from a few months ago, when I spoke to her during our mother and baby clinic special. Would you like to recap for us, Charlotte?'

'Er, yes, I was about seven months pregnant then, with twins, which I was having for a couple in their late forties. We met on a surrogacy website. The wife had suffered many miscarriages. I already have a daughter of my own and wanted to help them.'

Lucy leaned into the mic. 'Did you choose them or did they choose you?'

'They approached me, answering my post on a forum saying I'd like to be a surrogate for a couple who couldn't have a baby of their own. It's illegal to advertise yourself as a surrogate, so it's something people tend to drop in casual conversation. The woman then messaged me privately and we got chatting. My partner and I met up with them and we got along straight away. She immediately reminded me of my mum and all the pain she'd been through. We really clicked.'

'Did it take you long to get pregnant?'

'Yes it did. Not until the third try. I wasn't expecting that.'

'But that pregnancy didn't last?'

'That's right. I miscarried at about six weeks.'

'But you wanted to try again? I take my hat off to you, Charlotte!'

'I didn't at first. I wasn't sure I could go through it. I'd had terrible morning sickness and, worse than that, it was churning up all my emotions about my mum's losses.'

'But you did try again and this time you found out you were expecting twins. How did the new parents react to the news?'

'They were delighted. I was a bit worried they might not want two babies. We'd not discussed multiple births, I suppose because it was unlikely to happen.'

'So what made you want to become a surrogate in the first place?'

I hesitated. Mum was listening to this. 'I'm the firstborn but my mum had several stillbirths after she had me. At the end of it all, my parents split up.'

'That's quite a traumatic experience for anyone. How old were you?'

'I was five when she had her third and fourteen the final time. Dad left when I was sixteen.' I twisted the edge of my top around my index finger.

'That's very young. How do you think the experience affected you?'

'My nan looked after me a lot back then because Mum wasn't around much. She cried a lot, shut herself away. I missed her a lot. Each time it was quite far along, seven, eight months, so it was traumatic to lose them at such a late stage. I promised myself that one day I would have a baby for a woman like her. I saw a programme about surrogacy on TV. The intended mother's joy when she was given her new baby really stuck with me. I wished someone could have done that for Mum. When I was expecting my daughter, I met a surrogate at prenatal class. After talking to her, I knew I really wanted to do it.' I coughed, my throat had gone dry. I drank some water. I hadn't intended to give anywhere so much personal detail.

'And how does your mum feel about you doing this amazing thing for a childless couple, in her name, so to speak?'

I hesitated. 'She's not keen to be honest.'

'Ah that's a shame. Has she said why?'

'She sees it as me giving away her grandchildren.'

'Oh dear, that's a tricky one, isn't it? Because you are the biological mother of the twins, aren't you?'

'Yes.'

'So can you tell us briefly how that works?'

I sighed, I really didn't want to go into this. 'I used the sperm from the intended father to impregnate myself artificially.'

'And is that still the most common method?'

'I believe so.'

'So how was the pregnancy after I spoke to you?'

'It was much more difficult than I thought it would be. I breezed through my pregnancy with my daughter, so it was quite a shock.' I told her briefly about the health problems I'd had.

'How about the birth?'

'It was all a bit of a rush in the end because I developed pre-eclampsia. My blood pressure went sky-high so the twins had to be born by caesarean.'

'That must have been a scary time for you and your partner. I understand that pre-eclampsia can threaten the life of the mother and baby. How did he cope with the thought of possibly losing you, especially as the babies aren't his?'

Ouch, that was a bit low. She wasn't sticking to the list any more.

I frowned at her, but her face didn't change and she left another gap I was expected to fill.

'It was difficult for all of us. My priority was to bring the babies safely into the world.'

'And you certainly did that. A boy and a girl.' Lucy smiled. Was she still on my side?

'Yes. I had to stay in hospital with them for a week.' I sat back in my stool and crossed my arms. My experience, as she called it, was a juicy story for her.

'That must have been hard for you, spending time with the babies you had promised to give away.'

'It was, I won't lie.'

'Isn't it more usual for a baby to be handed straight over to its new parents?'

'Yes it is, but this couple wanted it to be private, so we didn't tell the hospital. I was lucky to spend those first days with the twins.'

'But wasn't there a danger that you'd bond with them? Did you consider changing your mind about giving them up?' She was not going to let up. Should I cut and run?

I leaned closer to the mic, staring directly at Lucy. 'No. I knew the deal from day one.'

'And it was a good deal, wasn't it, Charlotte? The intended parents paid you thousands of pounds, much more than a surrogate would normally get for expenses.'

'It was a generous amount of money.' I should have known we'd get on to this.

'Some might say you sold your babies, Charlotte.' She picked up a pencil from the desk and leaned back in her stool, a smug look on her face. 'What would you say to those people?' She pointed the pencil at me.

Was that really what the audience thought too? I frowned at her, speechless. 'I... I'd say they're wrong. I didn't sell them, because that's illegal in the UK. We were paid a fair amount for expenses. We haven't received the final payment, which is partly why I'm here, to warn people about the risks of becoming a surrogate.'

'Can you tell us how much money you *have* received?'

'Fifteen thousand pounds,' I lied.

Lucy gave a low whistle. She tucked the pencil behind her ear. 'That's a fair whack, as my old dad would say. And what's the average amount?'

'Between about eight and fifteen.'

'So, in hindsight, do you think it's all been worth it?'

'Yes and no.' Any minute now I was going to grab that pencil and stab her in the arm. If only people knew how much I'd wrestled with that question in the last few weeks. The fact was, we had been promised a lot more money than we needed for expenses, so we'd sold our twins, hadn't we? If anything bad happened to them, I wasn't sure I would be able to forgive myself.

'No because the couple you had the babies for have cut you out of their lives?'

'They said we could stay in touch, it was part of our agreement. This is one of the things I came to talk about.' I jabbed her list with my finger.

'Go on.'

'When a surrogate makes an agreement with the intended parents, it's not actually legally binding. I think people should know that if they're thinking of becoming a surrogate or are looking for one.'

'I see, but you've signed a parental order, giving the new parents full rights to the twins?'

'Yes, and that *is* legally binding, but what I'm saying is that any other arrangements about contact with the child, or money agreed for expenses, doesn't matter in the eyes of the law.' I carried on before she could stop me, 'I've launched a campaign on Twitter this morning to get the law updated. It's not changed since it first came in, in 1985. Just search for the hashtag, Change UK Law on Surrogacy, all one word.'

'And therein lies the cautionary tale, dear listener.' Lucy waved her hand in a circle, trying to wind things up. But I hadn't finished what I had come to say.

'Do your research. Check who the intended parents are and take time getting to know them. Be prepared for them to go back on any agreement, such as the expenses amount they agreed, or if they promised you could continue to see the baby.'

'You sound upset, Charlotte. Do you feel these people have let you down, betrayed you even?'

I nodded. 'I do. I was as careful about everything as I could be. I grew close to the intended mother. I believed we were friends, that we understood each other. I'm still hoping they'll get in touch.' I linked my fingers.

'But as you've given up your parental rights in the eyes of the law, surely it's the new parents' prerogative not to want further contact with the birth mother?'

'Yes, of course, but I'm upset because they specifically agreed to keep in contact. Now I'm never going to see the twins grow up.' I rubbed the side of my throbbing head.

'Well, thank you, Charlotte, it's been enlightening.' Lucy pressed a button and took off her headphones.

'You didn't stick to half these questions.' I chucked her list across the table.

'I wanted to engage the listeners, give them a bit of background and once we started I didn't want to interrupt the momentum.'

'Bullshit.' I stood up.

'Would you like to appeal to the new parents to come forward if they or someone they know is listening?'

Sly cow. 'I suppose so.' I sat back down.

-

When I left the studio, I stopped outside to steady myself against the door. Making a sensational story out of my desperate situation. What about the babies? The innocents in all this. I didn't even know if they were being properly looked after. I made the mistake of checking Twitter. Amongst many supportive tweets, the trolls were out in force:

> @LUVya4evva
> She sold her soul for less

> @MyMilkShakes
> Selling babies is NOT smart, law or no law

> @dreamzy89
> People like you make me sick, pretending it's about helping someone, when it's actually about you making fast cash from innocent babies

I switched my phone off, my fingers trembling.

On the way home, I called in at Mum's to pick Alice up.

'I suppose you heard it all,' I said, following her down the hallway to the living room.

'You know my views.' She picked up a thriller facing down on the sofa and dog-eared a page before closing it.

'Hello sweetheart.' I wiped apple and banana from Alice's mouth, then lifted her out of the high chair, kissing her pink cheeks.

'I think you should go to the police.' Mum turned down the TV.

'What can they do?'

'You need to find out where the twins are.'

'But we're not the legal parents any more.'

'These people owe you a lot of money. They've cheated you, Charlotte. How can they be trusted with children? What if something terrible has happened to them?'

I did not need my mother trying to prove she was right all along, especially after the experience I'd just had.

'I said there was something funny about them, didn't I?'

'Leave it, Mum.'

'Especially the man, Malcolm wasn't it? I can spot a roving eye a mile off.'

'What?' I could hardly believe what I was hearing. I stuffed Alice's chubby hand in the arm of her coat.

'Giving me the eye he was.' She planted her knuckles on her hips.

'I really have to go, Mum.' I pulled the coat around Alice's shoulders and did up the top button, not bothering to put her other arm in. I noticed a few chocolatey fingermarks on the beige leather sofa and hoped they'd wipe off or I'd be in trouble. 'Thanks for having Alice, Mum, got to dash.'

In the car I laid my head on the wheel. Mum was right, anything could have happened to the twins, and it was all my fault.

Chapter Forty-Three

When I reached home, Steve was already sitting in front of his laptop. The aroma of vinegar and salty chips filled the room.

'You're back early,' I said, putting Alice down on her play mat.

His eyes didn't leave the screen. A takeaway bag sat on the kitchen counter unopened.

'Everything okay?' I moved closer, not wanting to know what he was reading, but at the same time desperate for answers.

His shoulders slumped. 'Not really.' He swung round and took my hands, examining them for a second before snagging my eyes with his. 'We've had another reply.'

'That's good, isn't it?'

He shook his head and let go of my hands. 'She's not the only one.'

I frowned at him and squinted at the screen, blinking so much the words moved.

'Two other women say they recognise Malcolm as the intended father of their babies.' He turned back to the screen.

'What? Are they weirdos copying each other?'

'No. They've messaged separately.'

'That's insane.' I shivered.

'They all know him with different names and different wives.'

I'd never seen Steve look so shocked, his face ashen.

'Do you believe them?'

He nodded.

'It would explain how he got Brenda's name wrong and why she took it so badly.' I pulled up a chair next to him. 'What do they say?'

He clicked on a name and it opened half a page of text. 'Same sort of thing. This one here says the intended mother had red hair. She managed to take a sneaky photo of them too. It's a bit blurry, but it looks like Malcolm, doesn't it?'

I peered at the image, trying to latch on to something familiar. There they were, the bright white teeth, black hair. 'Definitely not Brenda though, she's a much slimmer build. What does this actually mean? Do you think Brenda knows about these other women?' I tried to swallow down the lump in my throat.

'Who knows. Could be some sort of cult.'

'Really? But why the different names?'

He shook his head. 'Both mentioned seeing a woman following them. I think we should go to the police.'

'And say what, we signed our twins over to their new parents but they're not answering the phone? And we think a random woman is following us? They'll have a good laugh at that. I haven't seen her since we handed over Rose and Robert.'

'OK, so what about the money they owe us and these other babies with different mothers?'

'We can't prove anything. I think the only way we'll find out the truth is if we drive to Orkney and confront them.'

He sighed. 'You know how far it is, don't you?'

I took two plates out of the cupboard and dished up the fish and chips. 'Can we do it so close to Christmas?'

'Probably.'

'We must try and find the twins. I won't wait around any longer.'

I passed him his dinner. We ate in silence, the pair of us reflected in the grey TV screen. Me chewing a piece of fish, Steve dipping chips in tomato ketchup. Looking at us like this, no one would have a clue what we were going through. If this were happening on TV, in a soap, we'd have been screaming at each other by now.

'I heard you on the radio. She was a bit rough on you.' Steve wiped his plate clean with the last couple of chips and stuffed them in his mouth.

'I suppose a lot of people will think we did it for the money.'

'But we're not the ones who've been conning people.' He sank back into the sofa. 'Whatever you think, Brenda must have been in on it too.'

'But she was genuinely upset when I miscarried.' I handed Alice a couple of chips and a piece of cod. 'Did these other women say they were paid well too?'

'Seems so, until the last payment bounced. Shit. We're never going to get that last fifteen grand are we?'

'We've still got money from the second cheque, although I planned to save that for Alice. Have any of them reported him?'

'One of them has, but the police pretty much ignored it.'

'What did I say?'

'At least it'll be on record.' He shoved his plate on the table.

'If this really is Malcolm, he needs to be stopped.' Why had I been so trusting? If only Brenda would call and tell me what was going on. I kept thinking back to the day we handed the babies to them, how off she was with me, suddenly like a stranger. Could she have known that Malcolm didn't intend to keep in touch with us? Perhaps Steve was right, she was as bad as Malcolm. But I kept coming back to the bruises. The times she'd seemed scared of him.

'What about these other babies?' Steve said. 'That's what, at least five he's fathered?'

'What does he want all these children for?' I'd seen grotesque news stories passed round Facebook, of drug cartels kidnapping children in south America, harvesting their organs to sell to wealthy foreigners, and another of children being trafficked and sold as sexual or domestic slaves, some while still babies. I held my throat, willing myself not to be sick.

Chapter Forty-Four

We set off on Saturday morning after scraping the ice off the car. I brought sandwiches and a flask of tea. Alice slept for the first three hours. But when she woke up, she wouldn't stop crying and kicking the back of my seat. We pulled over at the services. Steve and I drank coffee and hot chocolate while I fed Alice a ham sandwich cut into soldiers. Maybe we were mad going all the way to Orkney. But I couldn't think of any other way to contact them.

When we were back on the road, my phone rang. My heart leapt. I fumbled in my bag, praying it was Brenda.

'Where are you?' Mum's spiky voice drilled in my ear. 'I thought you'd be here by now.'

I appealed with my eyes to Steve. He pulled a face.

'You've forgotten, haven't you?'

'Mum… I…'

'Garden centre?'

I'd been so consumed with contacting Malcolm and Brenda over the past couple of weeks, I'd completely forgotten we were taking Alice to Santa's Grotto.

'I'll go and see Santa myself then, shall I?' She sniffed.

'Oh Mu-um, I'm sorry, we can go next year.'

'I thought it'd be nice. So, where are you? You've not even phoned.'

'We're away for the weekend.' I clenched my teeth. I couldn't bring myself to tell her what we'd found out.

'So close to Christmas?'

This was the last journey I wanted to be making. 'We'll be back in time for Christmas day, I promise.'

'Where is it you're going to?'

'Um… Scotland.'

'Oh. What are you going up there for?'

'We just fancied it.' I blinked at Steve.

'Isn't that where those people live?'

'Sorry, Mum, got to go, the line is breaking up, speak soon.' How could I tell her the truth?

Steve and I sat in silence for the next hour. I tried to work it all out in my head. There had to be an explanation for all of this, why Brenda wasn't answering my calls, why Malcolm seemed to have had children with other women, but my brain was all over the place, I couldn't make any sense of it.

'It's obvious they don't want contact with us any more,' Steve said.

'Doesn't explain the cheque though.'

'If it really is him that's had those other babies, I'm guessing he never intended to pay it, same as the other surrogates. They knew we'd have no comeback, that's why they've scarpered.'

'But they've been so generous up till now.'

'I bet that was part of getting us to trust them.' He clenched his jaw and gripped the wheel tighter. 'Don't you see? We've been well and truly scammed.' He banged his fist on the car horn at a lorry swerving into our lane.

'But we've become friends with them. They've paid us a lot of money. It doesn't make sense for them to suddenly duck out of it.' I daren't even contemplate them cheating us because it made me worry even more about the twins.

'What about Malcolm being weird when I took their photo?'

'They wanted to keep their privacy. I respected that.'

'They didn't want us to have any evidence, more like.'

'Maybe not.'

'What if they heard you on the radio – twice – and they're thoroughly pissed with us?'

'Does that even matter after what the other surrogates have told us?'

We carried on for another hour. Neither of us brought up what we would do if we didn't find them in Orkney, but the question hovered in the air between us.

I dozed off and dreamt we pulled up to their big house just as Malcolm was unloading their suitcases from the Jag. Brenda was already indoors, putting the twins to bed in their fairy-tale cots. Julia and Joseph were so beautiful and smiled when they saw me. Brenda was beside herself with guilt that she'd switched her phone off and we'd had to make this frantic journey to find them. We stayed the night in one of their luxurious bedrooms and the next day, Malcolm handed me fifteen thousand pounds in crisp fifty-pound notes. They invited us to stay with them at their holiday home next summer, so we could spend three glorious weeks with the twins.

I woke up as Steve stopped the car in Blackpool. The Tower and famous Golden Mile of Christmas lights were welcome beacons in the darkness and rain. We ate kebab and chips in the car, fed Alice and used the public toilets. Then we carried on through the evening to Glasgow, where I'd booked us into a B&B.

I slept heavily that night. It was the first good sleep in days, from pure emotional exhaustion.

After breakfast the next morning, we checked the forum. I read out a message from yet another woman who said she recognised Malcolm as Peter Finch, living miles away in Cornwall. She had their baby boy six months ago. Again, the last cheque had bounced. They'd tried to find him but it had backfired.

'What do you think she means?' I said.

'Ask her, we need to know everything.'

I typed a reply but nothing came back.

Steve started the car and we set off again. The icy wind picked up, driving rain at us like the edge of a knife. I thought we'd never reach Kirkwall, but we managed to catch the ferry from Aberdeen. We arrived at the remote B&B at 11.30 p.m.

The woman let us in and fed us home-made soup full of indistinguishable chunks of meat and thick rye bread. Our room right up in the loft could only be accessed by a narrow staircase. Steve carried a sleeping Alice into the dimly lit space with a slanted low ceiling. He laid her in a cot decorated with painted daisies.

I woke at first light and stood at the small leaded window, looking out at the barren landscape. It didn't seem like the sort of place Malcolm and Brenda would choose to live for their jet-setting lifestyle.

After breakfast, we headed towards their address. My stomach turned over. What if they weren't there? What would we say to them if they were? We parked on the street. It was an imposing property, even more stunning than in the photos. An old E-type Jaguar was parked outside the garage. We walked up the drive, Steve carried Alice, who pointed at our feet crunching through the tiny stones. I banged on the door with a lion-head knocker. After a few minutes, the door was opened by an elderly man wearing beige trousers and shirt.

'Can I help you?' He sounded like royalty.

'We're here to see Malcolm and Brenda Stewart, are they in?'

'Who's that?' He tipped his ear, touching a hearing aid with his finger. Perhaps this was Malcolm's father.

I repeated their names more slowly.

He shook his head, appearing to be completely baffled.

'Who is it, Dad?' a woman called to him from the other end of the hall. He turned back to tell her, but she was behind him in a moment. 'Can we help you?' she said, taking off a pair of worn-out gardening gloves.

We repeated our question.

'I'm sorry, we don't know these people, have you got the correct address?'

I showed her the court papers.

'Oh, it's very odd. That's clearly our address, but I've never heard of them. Who are they exactly?'

I explained what had happened.

'I think you need to report them to the police. This is not where they live, I can assure you. This is my parents' home and has been for the last thirty years.'

For a second, I was too stunned to speak, my head spinning.

'We're sorry, but can you show us proof?' Steve asked, moving Alice onto his other hip.

The woman's dark eyes bored into us. Her skin flushed pink from her neck up. In one swift move, she turned to the hall table behind her, grabbed a utility letter from a gilt tray and held the envelope up for us. *Mr and Mrs J. Hutton* and their address behind the little plastic window. I stared at it, my pulse rocketing.

'Thank you, we're sorry to have bothered you,' Steve said.

The woman nodded and shut the door.

'Shit. What do we do now?' He ran his hand through his hair. 'We've been properly mugged off. Not the only ones either.'

We trudged back to the car.

'How will we ever track them down if he's using different names, different addresses and having babies all over the country? Where can the twins be? What have they done with them?' My voice became shrill. 'What if he's a paedophile?' I stumbled onto my knees and vomited in the grass by the fence.

Chapter Forty-Five

The line between the murky sky and sea blurred together. I gave Alice a bottle of juice and hugged her to my side on the back seat. Could Brenda have betrayed me? Apart from the last time we saw them, she'd always been so thoughtful and kind. I'd tried again for her after the miscarriage, because she was so desperate. She'd made me feel like I was her final hope. What was I supposed to think now? Did they want to go it alone as parents and pretend they never used a surrogate? Maybe they wanted to make out to their friends that Brenda had given birth to the twins herself. But why make up their address? What about the other women and babies?

'If the address on the court order is false, how can the transfer be legal?'

'I don't know, maybe it isn't.' Steve checked the forum on his phone. 'No more messages, not even from that last woman.'

We drove to the local police station and asked to speak to an officer in private. I'd already decided before we got there that I didn't want to tell them at the counter window, because you never knew who was earwigging. One of Nan's favourite words. After a few minutes, we were shown into a room not much bigger than a cupboard. I explained our situation to the female officer who came to talk to us. She invited us to sit at a table. She sat opposite with a notepad and pen. I parked the pushchair next to us and handed Alice a picture book.

'So, you see, we believe the new parents of our baby twins have given a false address on the parental order.' I placed the document on the table while Steve explained that we'd gone to the address.

'And the people living there confirm this is their address, and that these people aren't residents, and are not known to them in any other way?'

'That's right. And we can't get hold of them on the phone or online. It was our last resort coming all the way up here to try and speak to them face-to-face.' Steve sighed deeply.

'If something has genuinely happened to Malcolm and Brenda so they can't respond to our messages… it makes me worry about the welfare of the twins. But it doesn't explain the false address,' I added.

'I understand your concern, but there may be a perfectly reasonable explanation for this. I'll take a copy of the parental order and check out its authenticity. If it is proven to be a false address, the document will be invalid.'

'And what would that mean for us?' I asked.

'I imagine parental responsibility would revert to you.'

'But we don't have a clue where else to look for them.'

'If this couple are found to have deliberately given you a false address, they would be deemed to have kidnapped your children.'

'Oh god.' I blinked black dots in front of my eyes. Steve took my hand.

'There's also a woman who's been following us. We took a photo of her in Brighton. We're not sure if it has anything to do with all this, but it's the same woman who we've seen outside our work and home.' Steve leaned his elbow on the table and showed her the picture on his phone.

'I'll take a copy from you, but if you see her again and are still concerned, do report it to your local police.'

We left in a daze as we made our way back to the car. It was hard to take in that we'd got to the point of having to report it.

'I honestly don't know what we should do next,' Steve said, unlocking the car. He strapped Alice in and we shut the doors just as the first few spots in the air turned into heavy grey sheets of rain.

'I just wish Brenda would contact me to explain herself.'

'Face it, hun, it's not going to happen. And if the police do find out the papers are false, how are we going to find our twins then?'

'I don't know.' I peered out of the window but couldn't see anything beyond it. We were trapped inside this tiny prison. The noise of the rain grew so loud, I had to raise my voice. 'I'm really glad you're calling them *ours.* If we do get them back, are you okay that they're not biologically yours?'

'Yeah, pretty much.'

'You said ages ago that you'd put one up for adoption if they didn't want it.'

'That was before all this. Anyway, I saw them coming into the world, didn't I? I held them, fed and cared for them, almost as much as you did.' His face crumpled as he turned to the window.

'I know and I'm pleased. I needed to check, that's all.' I rested my head on his arm while we waited for the rain to ease off.

–

All the way back to Aberdeen on the overnight ferry, my brain would not switch off, even though my eyes were scratchy and half closed with exhaustion. Steve checked the forum before he went to sleep, but there were no new messages.

Reasons why Malcolm and Brenda had lied to us swirled around my mind. A growing dread trickled through my veins. Why so many babies? What if they'd planned to traffic them abroad all along?

Stop! I shook my head, trying to scramble these thoughts, telling myself they were alive and well. I longed to see my babies so much my arms ached to hold them. I *had* to believe they were being well looked after or I'd drive myself insane.

I checked the time. It was three in the morning. I logged onto the forum one last time before I tried to sleep. There was one new message. I clicked on it, but there was no name, only a line of words and symbols. STAY SAFE!!! STOP SEARCHING!!! I blinked at the letters all in capitals – shouting at me. Could this be Brenda? WHO IS THIS? I messaged back. When there was no reply. I typed, CALL ME, PLEASE!!

I switched my phone on, but the battery was running low. In my rush, I'd packed the wrong charger. I fell asleep holding the phone to my ear so as not to miss a ring or a text, but by the morning, the battery was dead.

Chapter Forty-Six

Alice cried half the journey down to Edinburgh, leaving my nerves brittle, ready to shatter at any moment. At times I wished I could cry along with her. I needed to sleep and not wake up until this was over. I told Steve about the anonymous message. It couldn't have been Brenda, she would have tried Steve's number too, wouldn't she?

We stopped at Stirling Services on the M9 for a coffee and to check the forum on Steve's phone. The early mist was beginning to clear but small wisps still hung in the air like lost spirits.

'There's one message,' he said, when I came back from changing Alice's nappy.

'Who's it from?' I slotted a coffee for us to share in the cup holder on the dashboard. Steve kissed Alice's face and chatted to her as he strapped her back in her seat.

'It's from the woman that contacted us before, the last one that said she knew Malcolm as Peter. She's warning us not to look for him.'

'Why?' I poured two tubes of sugar into the cup. I didn't usually sweeten my drinks, but I needed the extra energy boost. 'What does she say?'

'Are you sure you want to hear this?' He sat back in the driver's seat and turned the heater fan down.

'Of course I do. Did she send that warning to me last night as well?'

'I don't think so. She says, "*I don't advise searching for this man. My husband went looking for him four months ago, hoping to get the money owed to us. He's been missing ever since.*"'

'Shit. Poor woman. She must be out of her mind with worry. I wonder what's happened to him.'

'Whoever sent you that text last night thinks we're in danger as well.'

'I hope she's reported it to the police. Ask her where he was looking.'

'Why?'

'Because we need to go there.'

'Are you serious?' Steve frowned. When I didn't frown back, he raised his eyebrows and typed a reply. 'There, done. Happy?'

'It's our first genuine lead.' I took the phone from him and immediately checked for a reply.

'Except we don't know anything yet. Ask her if the police have searched for him,' Steve said.

The sugar shot through my veins. What could have happened to her husband? Were we really in danger too?

The ping of a reply gave us both a start.

> *Peter was living in Sheffield at the time. That was one of the places my husband went to look for him. The police searched but by that time there was no sign of him (Peter/Malcolm).*

'Didn't one of the other surrogates mention him moving to Sheffield?'

'Yeah, from Leeds.' We were actually getting somewhere.

'Could Malcolm have gone back there?'

'Worth a try.'

I asked her for the address. Her answer came straight back. I drank a mouthful of coffee and scanned her reply.

I really don't want to give it to you, then you disappear too!

PLEASE! I messaged back *YOU'RE OUR ONLY HOPE!* I balled my hands into fists.

Steve leant against the window.

Five long minutes later, she messaged the address to us. I burst into tears.

Chapter Forty-Seven

We drove to Sheffield and arrived in Hillsborough at almost 9 p.m. It was a quiet, leafy road. The guest house was a double-fronted property surrounded by a low neat hedge. The old couple that answered the door wore green matching fleeces. They introduced themselves as Sarah and Paul. We followed them into their vast farmhouse-style kitchen. Rows of different-coloured teapots were lined up on a Welsh dresser.

'Good journey?' Sarah smiled, peering over her glasses as she shook our hands.

'Not bad, thanks.'

'What's the little one's name?'

'This is Alice,' Steve said, holding her tight.

'She's just fallen asleep.' I held her favourite blanket.

'Bless her. Paul will show you straight up so you can get her settled in.' She unhooked a key from a selection in a small cupboard. 'Then come and have some hot chocolate and supper, when you're ready.'

'Have you come far?' Paul asked, striding up the stairs, two steps at a time.

'Been on the road from Aberdeen since about seven thirty this morning.'

'Driven some miles today then.' He waited for us at the top.

'Clocked over four hundred in all.' Steve carried Alice up and I followed with our rucksack.

Paul opened the heavy wooden door to our room and handed us the key. He pointed out an en suite with a sliding door in the corner. The double bed sat in the middle, with plenty of room to walk around it. A travel cot stood right next to the bed with a side table behind it. The room had a homely feel. They'd left a few toys in a box and an extra blanket on the end of the bed.

As soon as we'd changed and settled Alice, we went back down to the kitchen, lured by the aroma of grilling bacon.

'Are you passing through or stopping in Sheffield for a while?' Sarah asked, putting the milk away. The fridge door was covered from top to bottom with postcards from around the world, held there with souvenir magnets. She brought our sweet-smelling hot chocolate drinks to the table on a tray. Steve opened his mouth to speak, but I shoved his leg under the table and spoke first.

'We've come to search for someone.'

Steve and I exchanged a look. I didn't want either of us saying too much about our reasons for being there.

'We have an old address for them in Sheffield so thought the new people might remember him.' I glanced at Steve, passing the baton of our story.

'We're on our way back from Orkney.'

'Been searching up there too? That's a hell of a hike with a little one.' Sarah buttered our bread and placed three rashers of bacon in each sandwich before chopping them in half and handing them to us on blue and white striped plates. If she'd taken a moment longer, I would have started drooling. I hadn't realised how hungry and tired I was.

'Is it a relative of yours?' Paul asked me.

'No, we're not exactly related.' I looked at Steve to help.

'He owes us money,' Steve said.

I pinched his leg under the table.

'Oh dear, that doesn't sound too good.' Paul sat at the other side of the table filling his pipe.

I pressed my lips tightly and smiled. 'Who are all these lovely postcards from?'

'Colourful aren't they? They're from some of the children we've looked after over the years. All grown up now with their own families.' Paul's smile brightened his whole face, making him appear younger. He beckoned us into the sitting room and pointed above a piano. Scores of framed photos of various aged children filled the wall.

'We couldn't have our own, so we decided to foster,' Sarah said from the doorway, 'it's been the greatest joy of our lives.'

'A life's work.' Paul nodded, gazing over each little face. 'We remember all their names, don't we, pet?'

Sarah gave a long satisfied nod, her broad smile clearly lit from within.

'Goodness, what a wonderful thing to do.' My throat choked up. If only we could have helped a couple like this.

'Over a hundred in all.' Paul linked his hands behind his back and puffed out his chest.

'We only stopped a couple of years ago,' Sarah said, turning back to the kitchen.

'Decided we needed to slow down after my heart attack,' Paul said.

'Sorry to hear that. Are you better now?'

'Yes, I've made a good recovery, thank you. I go for a walk twice a day and I've cut out red meat.'

We gathered back in the kitchen and finished our drinks and sandwiches.

'I don't suppose you have a phone charger I could borrow please?' I'd spotted that Sarah's mobile was the same make as mine.

'Yes of course. Take it up with you.'

'Don't go running off with it though,' Paul said.

Everyone laughed except me. We'd been too trusting of people we hardly knew, and they'd run off with something much more precious than a phone charger – my babies.

We said good night and went upstairs. Alice didn't stir. I plugged the charger in next to the bed and lay back on the soft candlewick cover, just like the one Nan used to have, only pink not yellow. As soon as my phone came to life, three missed calls pinged onto the screen.

'Steve, look at this.' I held it up. 'But hang on, I don't recognise this number.'

He took the phone from me and pressed return call, but there was no ring tone. 'Whoever it is has blocked your number.'

'What if it's Brenda?' I snatched it off him.

'You don't know that.'

'Who else would it be? She must have seen my message on the forum begging her to call me. What if Malcolm saw it first and took her other phone away to stop her contacting me? And now he's blocked me from this one.'

'Maybe the police will be able to trace the number so we can find them.'

'Do you think she's all right?' I clasped my hands together.

He shook his head. 'I've no idea.'

'She was trying to tell me something once, when we Skyped. It was about the only time I spoke to her without him there. I'm sure he caused her bruises otherwise why else would she hide them? I keep going over it in my head. I'm sure she'd contact me if she could. My gut is telling me there's no way she would deliberately do anything to hurt me or the twins.'

'Keep your phone switched on then. If it was her, maybe she'll try again.'

But it stayed silent.

Chapter Forty-Eight

The next morning, we thanked Sarah and Paul for their hospitality and drove to the address the woman from the forum had given us. As far as she knew, Malcolm had lived in the terraced house on the steep road in Middlewood, two years ago. Now it was full of university students. A boy with scruffy hair answered the door. It looked like we'd woken him up. He said they'd only been lodging there since September and hadn't heard of Malcolm under any of the names we gave him. It didn't seem to me the sort of place that would appeal to someone like Malcolm, with his expensive tastes.

The disappointment sapped our strength. All the way home, I kept my phone practically strapped to my hip. But there were no more calls. I tried calling the number back again, but the line was definitely dead. Steve said it couldn't have been Brenda. If it was her, why would she give up so easily? My thought that Malcolm had discovered her trying to contact me and had forbidden her to reply was only strengthened. I prayed she was being more assertive when it came to protecting the twins. But a voice in my head whispered back at me: *stop kidding yourself.*

-

We arrived home at lunchtime. All I wanted to do was sleep. What a wasted journey we couldn't afford. I didn't know how we were going to find them.

I collected the post from the box. Steve sang 'Hickory Dickory Dock' with Alice while he strapped her into the high chair. She swayed from side to side, palms up, singing, tick tock, tick tock, long after the end.

I sifted through the junk mail and found my letter to Brenda marked, *Return to Sender*. I showed Steve, then chucked it in the bin.

I cooked Alice toast soldiers and cut up cubes of cheese. Steve and I sat in front of the TV with a Cornish pasty from the garage and a bag of crisps each.

He switched over to the news. I went to the bathroom. As I washed my hands, I stared at my pale face in the mirror. Part of me was missing, gone forever. We were back to square one and I'd given away my two beautiful babies. What killed me most of all was not knowing how they were or where they could be. I couldn't imagine this deep longing for them would ever go. Why hadn't I listened to Mum?

Steve was standing behind the sofa when I went back in. He'd paused the news, staring at the screen.

'You need to watch this.' His voice broke in several places. He reached out to the sofa to steady himself, his hand trembling as he pressed play.

'The body of a woman has been found at the foot of a cliff at West Bay in Dorset at five past six this morning. Her identity has been confirmed as Paula Bennett from Sheffield. Her next of kin has been told.'

'How awful,' I said.

Steve put a finger to his lips and pointed at the TV. A photo of a ginger-haired Brenda filled the screen.

'Oh my god.' A shiver ran through me.

'In a statement, Paula's husband confirmed that she had gone missing from the family home over a year ago. She leaves two teenage

sons, aged sixteen and nineteen. Her death is not being treated as suspicious.'

'What the actual fuck?' I shouted, planting my hands on my head.

Steve stared at the TV in a trance.

'Did they say anything about the twins?'

He shook his head, hands cupping his nose and mouth as though trying to stop himself throwing up.

'Why would she do that, I mean really?' Tears fell from my eyes. 'It doesn't make any sense. Why was she on a cliff in Dorset?' I wiped my eyes.

'I can't believe how much she lied to us.' Steve rewound the programme and we watched it again, sitting on the edge of the sofa, eyes fixed to the paused image of Brenda.

I grabbed the laptop and searched for the story. 'Says here, Paula's husband came home from work one day and his wife was missing, along with a few personal possessions. He'd suspected her of having an affair for some time and guessed she'd left him, but there was no note from her. He only became worried when she hadn't contacted him or their boys after about a week. She'd been registered as a missing person ever since. So, she must have gone off with Malcolm and changed her name. Except this is only fifteen months ago. They told us they'd been together twenty years and we bought every word of it.'

'Hang on, hang on, don't you see?' Steve said, 'Brenda – the woman we know, who we *think* we know – doesn't even exist.' He flung his palms open as if it was obvious and we were the biggest idiots for believing them.

'She existed to me,' I cried, staring at him, while everything wound down to slow motion. His dry lips cracked open as he spoke. A tiny bead of blood burst out. He licked it away with his tongue.

'But don't you see? She was pretending to be this poor childless woman when she was already an experienced mum of teenagers. She lied to us every step of the fucking way. She lied to you, Charlotte, completely took you in.' He slapped his hand on his forehead.

'If Brenda's dead, who's looking after the twins?' My words dragged into a slur. I covered my face with my arms.

'We have to think this through.' He knelt next to me. 'We're absolutely certain this woman is Brenda, right?' We paused at the photo in the news story, made it as big as possible on the laptop screen. We nodded at each other. Even though it was taken a few years ago, there was no doubt it was the woman we knew as Brenda. 'So where's Malcolm? Is that even his real name?'

'Her husband's called Nathan, I think.' I scrolled up the news story. 'Yes, Nathan Bennett. Could he actually be Malcolm?'

'I thought he was the lover she ran off with? Are there any photos of him?'

'We don't know that for sure. I can't find any,' I said, scrolling up and down. I did a general search for his name but nothing came up.

'We need to get back to the women on the forum. Get them to prove they really knew Malcolm.'

I passed the laptop to Steve and he messaged all of them, asking them to provide some proof. Within the hour, the first woman emailed a photo of her cheque. 'She says she wanted a reminder of receiving that much money. Ironic isn't it? See the name, L. Brown.'

'That's definitely him then.'

'One of the other women has come back with a scan of the parental order.'

'We'll have to go to the police.' Steve squeezed my arm. 'These babies could be in real danger.' He caught me with a look of fear in his eyes I'd never seen before.

My body gave an involuntary shiver. I couldn't bear to admit it had crossed my mind more than once.

'We have to go right now.' He transferred the photo of Malcolm and Brenda from his phone onto his laptop as well as the one from my phone, so they could be blown up bigger.

'We have to go for another ride, sweetheart.' I gathered Alice in my arms. Steve carried his laptop out to the car.

As we drove off, everything that had been said, everything that had happened flooded my mind. Somehow, I had to hold it together.

Chapter Forty-Nine

At the police station we told the duty officer that we had information relating to the death of the woman at West Bay. He told us to wait while he went off to speak to a colleague.

We were led through an electronic locking door into an incident room, an empty space except for a solid metal desk and four plastic chairs on one side. Above it was a double tape machine housed in an industrial-strength casing, jutting out of the painted brick wall.

Steve held his laptop under his arm and stood staring out of the tiny barred window. I hugged Alice tight, trying to hide my trembling body. After a few moments, Police Inspector Johnson came in and introduced himself. He invited us to sit down. We explained our story, how we knew Brenda, about the money owed to us and the women online who'd recognised Malcolm by different names.

'So, let me get this clear, you know the dead woman under the name of Brenda Stewart?'

'Yes, it's here on the parental order.' I passed him the piece of paper.

'But do you have any evidence that this is the same person as Paula Bennett?' He dragged his hand across his bald head as though rearranging a full head of hair.

'I have a photo of them on my laptop I downloaded from my phone,' Steve said.

'Okay, let's see it.'

Steve opened up the photo. 'I took it at the twelve-week baby scan. Malcolm got really upset, insisted I delete it.'

'But you didn't.' The officer peered at the image. 'Can you make it any bigger?'

'I thought he was being out of order so I copied and pasted it, told him it was gone.' Steve grinned at his ingenuity.

'All the time we knew Brenda, her hair was dyed blonde, but I noticed ginger roots coming through once,' I said, rocking Alice in my arms.

'It's not quite clear enough, do you have any other photos?'

'The only other one is from Charlotte's phone, we took it at the hotel when we handed the twins over about two months ago.' He showed it to him.

'Yes, I can see now that it's the same woman.'

'She had an American accent but it often slipped. She said she lived in New York when she was young, but now I'm not sure if anything she said is true.'

He wrote it down.

'Do you know who the man is?' I asked. 'I mean, it's not Paula Bennett's real husband, is it?'

'I'll need to speak to Dorset police. I suspect it's the man Mr Bennett thinks Paula ran off with.' He wrote in his notepad.

'They told us they got married twenty years ago and had gone through several miscarriages.' Saying their lies aloud made the truth hit me. I rearranged Alice on my lap, trying not to cry. If I told him about Brenda's bruises he'd think I was a terrible mother for handing over the babies when I already had doubts about them.

'Can I see the photo on your phone so I can check the date it was taken?'

I handed Alice to Steve and took my phone from my back pocket.

'I'll need to take a copy of this for evidence.'

'I hope it helps. I'm really worried about the twins. We showed the parental order to the police in Orkney, because the new parents lied about living at this address, but they never got back to us.'

'I'll pass this information straight on to the investigating team in Dorset. They may already be looking for this Malcolm character. Then I'll check their address on the parental order with my colleagues in Orkney.'

I nodded and squeezed my hands together. The inspector left the room.

'I can't believe we've been so dumb.' Steve scratched his head.

'Or that she had two teenage sons. I completely fell for their story. No wonder she seemed so natural with babies.' I pressed my fingers to my forehead, trying to force it all to sink in. She'd lied to us and now she was dead, and we had no idea what had happened to the twins.

Twenty minutes later, the inspector came back.

'It's definitely her. This information has been enormously helpful to the investigating team. They believe your first photo was taken about five months after Paula went missing from her family home.'

Steve passed Alice back to me. I gazed at her smooth perfect skin, the pure innocence, relying on us to care for her and feed her. I pictured the twins, and the three of them together fixed in my mind.

'Leave it with us. I'll take your laptop for now. And I'll need to check your medical records, Charlotte, to corroborate everything you've said about having twins for these people.'

I sighed. 'Please let me know if you find out anything at all about the babies, because they don't have their mummy now and we haven't a clue where Malcolm is.'

One of his colleagues came and took the laptop away.

'Will you be speaking to the other women who are saying Malcolm fathered their babies too?'

'Yes, we'll look into it, find out more about the woman whose husband went missing. There's clearly more to this story than a suspected suicide.'

'What could he want all these babies for?' I asked even though my brain couldn't process it.

'Do you think he could be trafficking them?' Steve asked, grimacing.

I shuddered and held Alice closer to me. Her eyes were almost shut.

'I wouldn't want to speculate at this early stage.'

The inspector's colleague knocked on the door and called him out of the room. Steve strapped Alice in her pushchair and I gently rocked it back and forth. I couldn't stop shivering. It couldn't be real. We must have got it wrong. Part of me still expected Brenda to text me, say everything was fine. I couldn't take in that she was dead. Steve put his arm around my shoulders. And where the hell was Malcolm? I'd heard about babies being trafficked all over the world, but wasn't that in places like Malaysia, India or China? It couldn't happen here, in England, could it?

Steve took his jacket off and draped it round my shoulders. Alice had dozed off. I pulled the blanket up to her chin.

The inspector blustered back in, worry lines carved deep in his face. He probably wasn't anywhere near as old as he looked.

'Sorry to keep you waiting. We've had news of a significant development from Dorset police. A local resident has come forward saying she saw a man running away from the scene. Another claims that Paula was not alone on the cliff. She may have been pushed. This case is now being treated as a suspected murder enquiry.'

Steve and I collapsed into each other's arms.

Chapter Fifty

'In light of this, I need to ask you more questions about this Malcolm character,' Inspector Johnson said. 'I'll be recording the interview. I want you to go back to the beginning and tell me everything you can.'

Steve held me together, his arm around my shoulders. Going through every meeting, phone and Skype call took longer than I expected. It was gone midnight when we were finally coming to the end. I could barely keep my eyes open, yet pinpricks of adrenaline kept startling me awake, reminding me Brenda was dead and we didn't know where the twins were.

'There is something else about our surrogacy arrangement I need to tell you.' Steve stared at me as he spoke. He squeezed my hand to reassure me. We both knew we had to tell the police everything. 'I hope we're not going to get in trouble over it.'

I patted Steve's leg. Alice was still asleep, her little mouth slightly open.

'And what is that?' Inspector Johnson looked as tired as we did but he kept reminding us that the first few hours of an investigation were often the most crucial.

'We chose to have babies for this particular couple partly because they were offering to pay a lot more than anyone else. To be honest, it was my decision. I persuaded Charlotte that they were our best bet. My business partner got cancer and I needed to bail him out while he went through chemo. And I've been hoping to move us to a bigger flat. Basically, we needed the extra cash. Charlotte clicking with Brenda was a bonus. I saw the extra money as generous, truly taking into account how difficult it is for the surrogate.'

'I see, so how much are we talking here?'

Oh god, now we were going to get in trouble too.

'They agreed to pay thirty-five thousand pounds in total, but we didn't receive the final fifteen because the cheque bounced, and you know the rest. Malcolm increased it from twenty-five thousand when we found out Charlotte was expecting twins.'

'I don't believe it's an offence to receive more than the average amount for expenses.'

'There was a chance I might have had to give up work because of a number of health problems during the pregnancy, so the money would have covered loss of earnings,' I said.

'We also needed childcare for our own daughter, especially when Charlotte was ill.'

The inspector nodded. 'Well, like I said, I don't think it's a problem and it's certainly not our priority at this moment in time. So that's all for now. You can go home and we'll keep you updated.'

'Hang on, you haven't told them about that woman,' Steve said, stroking my hair, knowing that all I wanted to do was go home to bed.

'What's this?' The muscle in the inspector's cheek started hammering.

'But you told me I was imagining things,' I said to Steve and yawned.

'Yeah, but now I'm not so sure. A couple of the other surrogates mentioned it too. It could be important.'

'He's right, please tell me any tiny piece of information, even if you think it's not linked.'

'Well, since the first pregnancy, the one that I miscarried, a woman has been following me. I didn't see her face very well, but she had black curly hair and wore a trouser suit. She even turned up in Brighton when we went there for a weekend. Steve managed to take a photo of her.'

'She could certainly be linked. I'll take a copy of it if you have it there?'

Steve showed it to him, then handed over his phone.

'Now, is there anything else?'

'I don't think so,' Steve said.

'Hang on, what about the missed calls on my phone?' I showed them to the inspector. 'It was on our way back from Orkney, my battery had died so I didn't realise until we stayed over in Sheffield. We didn't recognise the number, but I tried to call it back, thinking it might be Brenda contacting me at last. But the line was dead. There'd been an anonymous message on the forum the night before, warning me to stop searching for Malcolm. I'd replied asking her to call me.'

'I'll hang on to this for now if you don't mind?' The inspector took my phone. 'See if we can trace the owner. Now, if something else occurs to you, please ask to speak to me directly.' He took the photo of the woman from Steve's phone and handed it back to him. 'Right, I'll get back to you as soon as I have some information.'

On the way home, my stomach tumbled into knots. Alice stayed blissfully asleep, even when Steve moved her from the buggy to her car seat.

'The twins are out there somewhere,' I said into the black steamed-up window. I shivered at the windscreen wiper's squeak, like the sound of a small injured animal.

'Why have children with lots of different women though?' Steve pulled a face of disgust.

'Do you think Brenda knew about the others? Perhaps that's why she acted so strangely sometimes, putting on an American accent. They said on the news she was born and bred in Sheffield.' I stroked my stomach as though the babies were still there, safe and sound. 'I don't understand how she could leave her sons without saying anything to them?'

'That gets me too. All that sob story we fell for about them being desperate for a baby. I swear she was as bad as him.'

'It's so hard to take in that she's dead.' My voice sounded croaky, worn out from talking so much. 'How could she betray me?'

We fell into silence.

'We have to find Malcolm,' I said as we stopped at traffic lights. 'Do you think it was him on the cliff? I mean, if it was, if he's capable of killing Brenda, god knows what he plans to do…' I watched the muscle pulsing in his cheek as the light turned to amber then green. 'We have to go back to the forum. That woman must have more details about where her husband went looking for Malcolm.'

'I thought you wanted the police to find him?'

'I do, but I can't sit by and do nothing.'

Steve pulled up outside our flat. 'I'm worried too, but I think we should leave it to the police.'

'We have to try and do something. What about going back to Sheffield, contacting Sarah and Paul? If that's where Brenda was brought up, someone must remember her, especially now it's splashed all over the news. It might give us a lead as to where Malcolm is.'

We sat for a few moments, trying to take in what was happening to us. The car made little sounds like a ticking bomb as it cooled down. I pushed open the door. The wind had dropped to a gentle rustling of leaves. Somewhere in the shadows came the long mournful howl of a cat, so easily mistaken for a crying baby.

Chapter Fifty-One

I gathered a sleeping Alice up in a blanket. Once inside, I stripped her coat off and laid her in her cot. Steve poured us each a shot of whisky. I knocked mine back in one go. Rough as anything, it burnt my throat, but I didn't care, I already felt numb, my eyes sore from exhaustion. The constant prick of tears I'd mostly managed to keep at bay for the last few hours suddenly came flooding out. I fell into Steve's arms, sobbing into his T-shirt.

I lay awake most of the night, going over each of our conversations with the inspector. I shut my eyes and tried to block it all out, but my thoughts kept coming back to the twins. I had so many questions for Brenda and I tried to imagine what her answers would have been. I had to admit that I hadn't known her at all. The person I was so sure I'd had a close connection to, didn't exist. She was someone completely different with a separate life. All of it had been an elaborate lie to trick us.

-

We both woke up early the next day. I'd barely slept at all, yet I felt wide awake. I started to sit up, but the full force of everything that had happened yesterday pushed me down. I groaned.

'We need to go back to Sheffield.' I stared at the ceiling, half expecting it to fall on me. 'There must be an old friend or neighbour of Brenda's we can talk to. She might have confided in someone about meeting Malcolm and planning to go off with him. They might know where they were living, give us a clue where he is now and, more importantly, where the twins are. I don't care about the missed payment, all that matters to me is knowing they're both safe.'

'Let me check how busy we are at the garage today, see if the guys can manage on their own.' Steve grabbed his phone and jumped out of bed. 'I want to nail that bastard.'

I was so grateful that Steve was treating the twins as his own – as *our* children – he didn't care that they were biologically Malcolm's.

A few minutes later, the doorbell rang. Steve pulled his jeans on and went to answer it. I was putting my dressing gown on just as Mum came in.

'What are you doing here?'

'What do you think? I saw the news. It was her, wasn't it?'

I nodded, dumbly.

'Where are my grandchildren?' Mum's voice came out as a wail. 'We need to find them. Is there anything I can do?' Mum put a hand out to me.

I shook my head, batting her away.

'Let me look after Alice for you, at least.'

'I don't think we want her out of our sight to be honest.' Steve put his arm around me.

'I understand, I really do. You know I'm here for you, Charlotte.'

'Are you? Even though you've not supported me through any of this?' I raised my voice, burying my hand in my hair.

'Because I was scared something might go wrong, or that you wouldn't be able to part with your babies.'

I shook my head.

'After all the babies I've lost, now my grandchildren have gone too,' she cried, 'something terrible could have happened to them. They were having a debate on London radio, some expert talking about gangs abducting babies and children in different countries, then trafficking them all over the world to become domestic slaves, sex workers or to organised gangs of paedophiles. They even put children in special compounds to harvest their organs,' she sobbed.

'I don't want to hear any of this,' I screamed, trying not to let the images of everything she'd said crowd in on me. 'I think it's best you go, Mum,' I shouted. Any moment I'd say something I'd regret.

She didn't move. Steve held me closer.

'Mum, please go! I can't deal with this right now.'

'It's all right, I'm going. I'm sorry, Charlotte. I'm sorry you ever felt you had to do this because of me.' Mum paused at the door. 'It's the last thing I wanted.'

How had things gone so wrong between us when it was Mum's experiences that had spurred me on to help another woman? She was the one I thought would understand. Here we both were, hurting over the same thing and yet we'd never been so far apart.

Chapter Fifty-Two

By 9.30 a.m. we'd collected my mobile from the police station and were on the road. I rested my head against the window, closing my eyes for a second as the ice-pinched trees along the A1 flashed past. I wondered if the twins were wrapped up warm and being fed. What if Malcolm had left them somewhere and they were cold and starving? How long could they survive in this weather?

I sat up. If anything happened to them… My breathing accelerated, heart pulsing. I held the door handle tight, trying to concentrate on calming my breathing. I gulped every breath, barely taking enough oxygen in. What if they were dead too? Silver spikes darted in and out of my vision. I forced my eyes wide.

'Hey, what's up?' Steve glanced at me and rested his hand on my arm. 'Are you okay?'

I nodded, counting in a deep breath. I blew it out slowly until the spikes faded.

'That's it. They'll be all right, I promise.' He patted my arm.

I nodded, slowly calming. 'It's so hard not to worry about them. I hope Malcolm is looking after them.'

'Bloody better be. It's weird though, paying surrogates for all these babies. How many more have there been?'

'I don't know, but I've got this sick feeling in the pit of my stomach, in my bones, like part of me is missing. We have to find them as soon as possible.'

I flicked on my phone. The Twitter campaign account already had over two hundred followers. I answered people's comments and thanked everyone for their support, then blocked all the trolls. I typed Nathan Bennett into the search engine. A list of news stories came up.

'Hey, there's an interview here on Radio Oxford with Brenda's real husband.' I turned the speaker up.

'*When Paula first went missing, I suspected she'd met someone else and was deciding whether to go off with him or not. She'd been acting a bit strangely for a couple of weeks, but I didn't realise the signs until she'd gone. I never saw her again.*'

'He seems as confused as we are,' Steve said.

'Poor bloke. And how awful for their sons.'

'Why don't you call Sarah and Paul, see if they can help us?'

I dialled their number and Sarah answered straight away. I explained why we were coming up again so soon. Sarah said they'd lived in Sheffield all their lives, so they may well be able to help us. She suggested I have a look at their local newspaper online. I thanked her and as soon as I'd finished the call, I pulled up the page for the *Sheffield Star* on my phone. Brenda's face was all over it. *LOCAL WOMAN FOUND DEAD. DOUBLE-PAGE SPREAD INSIDE* A chill ran through me. What had Brenda been trying to tell me that day over Skype?

'It says Brenda went to Hillsborough primary school. There's a quote from a woman who was in her class. Zoe Barton. Still lives in the area.'

'Doesn't mean they were friends though, does it?'

'She could know who was or where she lived. Hey, I wonder if Paula Bennett has a Facebook page.'

'Good one. Not sure how you're going to know which are her real friends though, unless this Zoe Barton can tell us.

She might know if there's a private group for ex-pupils.' Steve opened his window. A gust of icy wind blew in.

'We're stuffed if Brenda didn't confide in anyone about meeting Malcolm or her plans to leave her husband.'

'Does seem a spur-of-the-moment decision.' He closed the window again.

'I doubt that. It must have been hard for her to leave her sons. It might have taken weeks or months to decide. Why don't we try and speak to Nathan? See what he can tell us.' We had so many questions but right now there were no answers.

–

We arrived in Sheffield at lunchtime. Sarah and Paul hugged us as though we'd been friends for years. They welcomed us into their warm kitchen. The smell of fresh cake filled the air.

'Dreadful business,' Sarah said, switching the kettle on. She lifted a chocolate cake from the wire rack onto a plate. 'Stick BBC One on, Paul.'

'Have you seen the news?' He clicked on the TV in the corner.

'We've not really had a chance.' I took some crayons and a colouring book out of my bag for Alice and sat her on my lap.

'You might want to brace yourselves,' Paul said, lowering his bushy eyebrows.

A news reporter not much older than me was standing on Chesil Beach in West Bay, in front of the towering cliff made famous by a TV drama. She crunched her way across the pebbles, towards a white cottage called The Ship, to its small glass-framed sunroom jutting out on wooden stilts over the beach.

'*This is where Mrs Miller was sitting when she saw someone at the top of the cliff at about five twenty-five a.m.,' the reporter explained.*

'She picked up her binoculars when she saw two people at the top. A man and a woman appeared to be arguing. Or could he have been trying to persuade her not to jump? All we know is that at five thirty a.m., Paula Bennett fell to her death.'

The camera followed the reporter inside the cottage, where Mrs Miller, an elderly woman wearing a bright flowery cardigan, was standing in the sunroom, in exactly the same place close to the side window where she had a clear view of the scene.

'I assumed it was an accident or suicide. That's the usual, I told the police when I called them. I thought the other person up on the cliff would report it too and give more detail about what happened.'

The reporter came in close to the camera. '*But what seemed at first like a clear case of misadventure, or at worst suicide, has taken a more sinister turn.*' The reporter spoke as she trotted back outside to a tall woman wearing an anorak, with two springer spaniels jumping up and down. '*Mrs Kent, can you tell us what you saw early yesterday morning that gave you cause for alarm?*'

'I was walking the dogs along here as usual when we crossed the path of a man who seemed to be in a dreadful hurry. I'd seen him from quite a distance back. He was up on the cliff with someone, standing near the edge. A few moments later, one was falling and the other was scrabbling down the cliff at such a rate, I thought he must be coming to call for help. But, to my astonishment, he didn't rush to the aid of the person who had fallen at all, he ran off, straight past me. I called to ask if he was all right, but he just grunted and didn't stop. Both dogs were barking at him like crazy.'

'And is that when you saw Mrs Miller waving to you at the window?'

'That's right. We're both early risers so we give each other a little wave every morning. The man ran that way, down the side of the café. Mrs Miller opened her window and shouted out to me that someone

had fallen or jumped off the cliff. I told her I'd seen it too and to call the police and an ambulance immediately.' The camera panned over to the foot of the cliff, where a white tent had been set up and cordoned off by the police.

'Oh god. Poor, poor Brenda.' I clasped my hands together.

The reporter turned to a police inspector. '*How can the public help you with this case?*'

'*We're appealing for any information as to the whereabouts of the man seen running away from the scene, who we believe was posing as Paula Bennett's husband.*'

'*And what do you think his motive was for pretending to be married to her?*'

'*We now know that he posed with several different women as childless couples, with the purpose of producing babies with unsuspecting surrogate mothers.*'

Shivers ran up and down my body. I passed Alice to Sarah and stood nearer the TV, holding my tea.

'*What does he want these babies for?*' the reporter asked.

'*We're not sure at this time.*'

'*How many are we talking about? And where are they now?*' the reporter frowned.

'*We can't give any more details. It's an ongoing investigation. But, like I said, if any member of the public recognises this man, they should contact us as soon as possible. Do not approach him, he may be dangerous.*'

An artist's impression of the man seen by Mrs Kent filled the screen.

My cup of tea dropped from my fingers. I sank to my knees, hands gripping the soft rug.

'It's only fucking Malcolm,' Steve shouted.

Chapter Fifty-Three

Sarah made me another cup of tea and stirred a heaped teaspoon of sugar into it. I couldn't stop shaking. Paul draped a fleece blanket around my shoulders. I hugged Alice inside it with me, kissing her hair.

'I've spoken to my close circle of friends and one of them knows a woman who works at the same supermarket as this Zoe Barton. I don't think she knows her to talk to, but my friend Janet says she's going to have a word with her, let her know you're here hoping to speak to her.'

'Thank you.' I rocked Alice back and forth, her big blue eyes watching me as she chattered away to her doll.

'Do you think she will?' Steve asked, spinning his mobile in a circle on the table.

'I would certainly hope so.' Paul packed his pipe with tobacco and stood in the yard to smoke it, letting in a gust of cold air.

Steve reached over and laid his hand on my arm. 'All we want is our babies back safe and sound.'

I smiled at him for saying that.

Paul gave a nod and bluey grey smoke streamed out of his mouth. He closed the door.

Sarah patted Steve's shoulder.

'Shall we go upstairs and find some toys?' she said to Alice and offered her hand. Alice looked back at me.

'It's okay, darling. I'll be right here when you come down.' I guided her out of the blanket and Sarah took the tiny fingers gently in hers.

'That's it, give Mummy and Daddy a few minutes to themselves, shall we?' Sarah grabbed her mobile off the table.

'Thank you.' I sifted my mind for more words to say, but I couldn't catch hold of them.

Steve moved towards me and we tipped our heads together, foreheads touching. He kissed my trembling hands. I pictured the twins bound up in blankets, left out in the snow. I pushed the image away and tried to focus on a blank space of wall.

My phone rang. I stared at the screen. The reality that Brenda was dead kicked me in the chest all over again. I answered and put it on speaker.

'Inspector Johnson here. I take it you've seen the photofit of Malcolm on the news?' He paused, waiting for my reaction.

'Yes, it's a shock to see it's him, even though we guessed it might be.'

'I've been in touch with my colleagues in Orkney.'

'Oh, thank you. What did you find out?' I asked.

'Neither Malcolm nor Brenda are on the local register under any of the names you gave us and the address supplied to the court has been confirmed as false.' He paused. 'This means the parental order is null and void. They must have got someone to forge the court stamp and authority signature. I suspect it's the same for the other surrogates' parental orders.'

Steve and I looked at each other. I tried to take in what the inspector was saying. If only my head would clear. 'What does this mean for us?'

'The twins are officially still yours. We're now treating this as a child abduction case.'

I let out a whimper. My brain tried to process his words, but they floated away, out of reach.

'Over a hundred officers are out there right now searching for all the babies and, of course, Malcolm. I'll let you know of any further developments.'

I thanked him quietly and ended the call. I stared up at the clock. I expected it to have stopped, for the whole world to be holding its breath, but the second hand ticked relentlessly on, determined to take me further and further away from *my* babies.

My head thudded in pain as though I'd walked straight into a wall. Their faces swam in my mind's eye, the pair of them dressed as china dolls with cherry flushed cheeks.

'Our babies are missing, kidnapped.' I whispered the words, daring not to say them too loudly, hanging on to the belief that this couldn't be happening.

Chapter Fifty-Four

I wept, not caring that it was loud and messy. Steve passed me a handful of tissues and I wiped my eyes and nose. I wanted my babies back.

'They could be anywhere, with anyone. How will we find them?'

'I don't know.' Steve's eyes were wide and staring. 'We have to believe they're safe.'

Sarah came back downstairs with Alice, who was holding Paddington Bear. 'We had a great little hunt around, didn't we?'

'Show Mummy who you've got there,' I put my arms out and Alice pushed the teddy towards me. 'He's almost as big as you.'

'I couldn't help hearing your call,' Sarah said to us, 'I'm so sorry. Knowing they're still yours makes it even more imperative that you find this man and get your twins back.'

I nodded, searching through my mind for the right words to say.

'Janet's bringing Zoe over before she goes to Radio Sheffield for an interview. They should be here any minute.'

'That's brilliant, thank you.' I put my free arm out and Sarah reached down and hugged me and Alice. 'We can't thank you enough for being so kind, both of you.'

–

Ten minutes later, there was a knock at the door. Two women stood on the doorstep. Janet still had her work tabard and name tag on. She introduced Zoe, then said a taxi was coming to pick her back up in twenty minutes. We thanked her and Zoe came in. She looked a bit younger than Brenda. She was dressed casually in jeans, jumper and a smart jacket. We all sat round the kitchen table, Alice in my lap. Paul brought over a pot of tea and a plate of biscuits. Sarah opened a cupboard and took out a toy teapot and cups and set them up on a food trolley. She offered her hand to Alice as she toddled over to join her.

'Thanks, Sarah. Go on, sweetheart.' I helped Alice slide to the ground and let Sarah take her. 'Thanks so much for coming,' I said, turning to Zoe. 'As Sarah has probably told you, we're keen to find out more about Paula Bennett. We knew her as Brenda. I am – *was* – her surrogate and we're desperate to find our twins.'

'Can't imagine why she needed another baby with two strapping lads at home.' Zoe examined her neon-coloured false nails.

I wanted to scream at her that my babies were missing and that every second she wasted was another moment when their lives might be in danger. I swallowed hard. 'We believed… I mean they told us, they'd been trying for a baby for years.'

'She kept very much to herself, that was the trouble with Paula,' Zoe said, helping herself to a chocolate wafer. 'A few years ago she'd be like posting personal, family stuff every day on Facebook. I haven't seen her since the school reunion about eighteen months ago.'

'How did she seem? Did she speak much about her marriage?' I asked.

'A bit down in the mouth, to be honest. She didn't say, but I suspected there were problems at home. She hardly talked about

Nathan. There were fewer mentions of him and the boys on Facebook by then too.'

'Did she have any close friends in Sheffield or on Facebook, maybe on a school page?' I took a plastic cup from Alice and pretended to drink from it.

'Her closest friend died in a car crash up by the stadium three years ago.'

'That's awful.'

Alice took the cup from me.

'Yeah, hit her really bad. She got quite deep into believing in angels and fate, things happening for a reason.'

'Do you think it could have been a trigger for her hooking up with Malcolm?'

'Could well have been. She had this saying on her Facebook page after her friend died about grasping opportunities when they present themselves and the power of Yes.' She gave a sideways grin as if to say she would never be taken in by such crap.

'Do you know where she lived in Sheffield?' Steve asked, taking a cup from Alice. She giggled when Steve slurped loudly.

'Yeah, quite near the station. Nathan and the boys are still there.'

'You know him then?'

'No, my dad does.'

'Do you suppose Nathan would be willing to see us?'

'Don't know. I could find out.'

'That would be great. We would like to pay our respects.'

Zoe nodded, then continued, 'Paula's last post was about a year and a half ago. She said she was moving to Peterborough for a little while. That's in Cambridgeshire, isn't it? She didn't say "we", so I did wonder then if they'd split up.' She took another biscuit.

'I don't suppose you know an exact address in Peterborough, do you?' Steve asked.

'Sorry, she never said. Soon after that she deleted the post. In fact, quite a few of her posts and photos disappeared. Her account closed about a year ago.'

'Is there anyone else who might know?' I asked.

'I shouldn't think so. She didn't keep in close touch with any of us. To be honest, I think she looked down at anyone who didn't aspire to move away from here. I don't like to speak ill of the dead, but she'd always acted like she was a cut above the rest of us. Full of airs and graces, my mam always said.'

A taxi hooted outside. It was a few minutes early, thank god.

Zoe plucked another biscuit between her nails. 'Turns out she just vanished from home one afternoon with no warning. Nathan didn't have a clue about it, poor bloke.' She stood up.

What was this woman doing giving media interviews about someone she hardly knew? Was she trying to make herself sound important, benefit in some way from Brenda's death? 'Thank you. We're so grateful to you for coming to speak to us.' Steve stood up.

'Up, up.' Alice raised her hands to him.

Steve picked Alice up then, stepped forward and shook Zoe's hand. 'We're very grateful.'

'Do please let us know if Nathan is willing to see us.'

'Yeah I will. I'll get back to you later.'

Sarah showed her out.

'What now?' Steve bounced Alice up and down in his arms, making her giggle and say, again, again, except it sounded like, *gen, gen*.

'Shall we ask the surrogate on the forum if her husband ever went looking for Malcolm in Peterborough?'

'Good idea.' He lowered Alice down and tapped his phone.

'More tea anyone?' Sarah filled the kettle.

'A quick one, then we'd better get home, thanks.' I sat Alice back on my lap and played Pat-a-Cake.

'Why don't you stay the night if you're going to visit Nathan? Save you a trip back up here,' Paul said.

'Do you have a room available? What do you think, Steve? Don't you need to be at work tomorrow?'

'There's no one staying here at the moment, it's so close to Christmas. We're not going to charge you.' Sarah smiled, clearing away the plates.

'Are you sure?' I reached out and touched her arm. She nodded.

'The guys won't mind, it's not exactly been busy at the garage.'

'We will stay then, thank you so much.'

'Shepherd's pie all right for tea?' Sarah cleared the cups onto the tray.

'Ooh, yes please. That's your favourite isn't it, Alice?'

Alice grinned at us, showing her new teeth.

After we'd eaten, Zoe called to say Nathan had invited us to his house that night at 8 p.m.

Chapter Fifty-Five

We parked outside Nathan's house under the glow of yellow light from the street lamp. The rumble of a dustbin being dragged out to the pavement splintered the silence. In the distance, two dogs barked in conversation. I stood by the car and tried to imagine Brenda walking up the path as Paula Bennett. What kind of person was she really? The last time she walked away from here had she known she was going to pretend to be childless? Did she know she'd never come back?

Steve carried a sleepy Alice and rang the doorbell. Sarah had offered to babysit but I wanted Alice to stay close to us. The man who answered was tall, well built. His hair a mix of brown and grey. He seemed on edge, unwilling to open the door fully at first, peering into the darkness beyond us, as if he thought we were being followed.

'We're Charlotte and Steve,' I said.

He grunted something and looked right through us.

'Zoe arranged for us to be here at eight?'

'Yes, yes, you'd better come in.' He ushered us past him, checking up and down the street before shutting the door and bolting it.

The house stank of boiled chicken; a greasy, cloying smell that hit the back of my throat.

'Are you okay, mate?' Steve asked.

'They won't leave me alone.'

'Who?' I said.

'If I knew that, I could do something about it.' He stalked off into the living room.

A boy's face appeared in the darkness at the top of the stairs.

'Hello.' I held my hand up to the pale-faced boy. He blinked a few times and lowered his head. A stair creaked as he crept back up.

'So you're this… this surrogate then?' Nathan said, not looking at me. He didn't offer us a seat, so we stood by the fireplace with its mock art nouveau tile surround. Display cabinets lined one long wall, full of various collections of animals and Disney characters. Pink velvet curtains framed the French windows, a matching scalloped pelmet across the top. Piles of clothes took up two chairs. Everything seemed so dated and nothing like the taste of the woman I'd known.

'We knew Paula as Brenda. We believed her and Malcolm were a couple who couldn't have children.'

Nathan shook his head. 'What's this bloke like then, rich is he?'

'He seemed quite well off.'

'I didn't like him.' Steve moved Alice onto his other shoulder. 'Thought he was right about everything, didn't he?'

I nodded.

Nathan perched on the arm of the sofa. 'If only Paula had talked to me first, I'm sure we'd have worked things out.'

'Did she tell you anything?' I wanted to add: *about being unhappy, thinking about leaving.*

'She left so suddenly. I thought we were fine – you know, we quarrelled like any couple does.' He paused. A half-assembled Christmas tree stood in the corner, a twist of tinsel around its branches. 'And then, a few weeks later, the messages started coming.'

'Who from?'

'Paula to start with, saying she needed to be away from us, that she was happier in her new life and to leave her alone.'

'So you'd been texting her then?'

'I wanted to know where she was, when she was coming back. She didn't take much with her, so it took a while before I realised she'd actually left me. Left *us*. How was I supposed to explain it to the boys? I could just about forgive her for leaving me, but not contacting them? Walking out on their lives without a word? That's unforgivable.'

'What happened then?'

'I couldn't stop myself messaging her. I was desperate to see her, for her to explain to me face-to-face what was going on. Then I started getting anonymous texts from someone, threatening me if I didn't back off, saying all sorts about how Paula's life was better without me dragging her down. I guessed she'd left me for another bloke.'

'Did she say anything about Malcolm?'

'She didn't text or email again. It was only this other person. I blocked the number in the end but then notes were shoved through the door. On their own to start with, then with dog turds, razor blades, syringes. I mean it was sick. There are kids in the house. I called the police then, but they couldn't do anything. She'd left of her own accord and I had no way of finding out who was threatening me. I guessed it was the man she'd gone off with.'

'How do you know she went off with a bloke? She might have been kidnapped.'

'I went through her old emails. He'd been chatting her up. Over time it was clear she'd grown fond of him. He was offering her the world with knobs on.'

'What was his name?'

'Didn't use his name, only his initials. LB, I think. I don't remember any Malcolm.'

'He's been using various names,' Steve said.

'So that was it, the police wouldn't help you?'

'They called it a domestic. No crime had been committed. If I found out who was dropping rubbish through my letter box they could go and have a word, but that was it.'

'Do you think it was Malcolm?'

'I know it was now. Since Paula…' he blinked. 'They've taken her computer, traced emails to a phone in his name.'

I went to the window as a woman walked past with a Labrador. It was a quiet, normal street.

'I don't understand why she would lie about not having children,' Nathan said.

'Because it's a scam. Malcolm's up to something with those babies. I dread to think what.' Steve wiped his mouth with the back of his hand as if he'd just spat out something bad.

'What she's done it's… it's nothing like the woman I know… *knew*. That I loved. Paula was kind, thoughtful. She loved children and was a good mother. Those boys are broken without her.' His hollow eyes latched onto mine. 'Do you think she loved this man, is that what it's all about?'

'I couldn't say. Sometimes they seemed to be easy in each other's company and other times…' I brushed my hand on Steve's fingers, 'sometimes she seemed scared of him.'

'Go on.' His eyes grew wild-looking as though he hadn't slept for days.

'A couple of times, I had the feeling she was trying to tell me something, but Malcolm was always there watching her, and then this one time,' I swallowed hard, 'there were bruises on her wrist. I thought at first I'd imagined it.'

'You think he was forcing her to stay? Maybe she had wanted to come home.' He sat up straight, his eyes a little brighter. 'I'd have forgiven her just about anything. Why didn't she come home?' He covered his eyes with his hand.

'She had the twins to look after, remember?' I said gently.

Steve's phone buzzed. 'Here, we've had a message from yet another woman on the forum.' He flashed the screen at me.

'Saying what?'

'"This man is the intended father of my baby too. I'm booked in for a caesarean on Thursday."'

'Shit, get her number, we have to tell the police. They might be able to use her to catch him.'

Chapter Fifty-Six

We left Sarah and Paul's in the morning, thanking them again for all their help, and arrived home at lunchtime. The phone rang as soon as we got in the door.

'Charlotte, it's Lucy from Bedford Radio.'

'What do you want?' I was tempted to put the phone down.

'I heard the news, I'm so desperately sorry.'

'Are you?'

Steve switched on the TV. I waved at him to turn it down.

'Of course, we all are. We'd like to show you our support by doing a follow-up interview.'

'You are joking?'

'I know it'll be incredibly hard for you, but we're willing to pay generously, and I'm sure the publicity will go a long way to help your Twitter crusade.'

At that moment, a photo of me and Steve came up on the news.

'Hang on, Lucy.' I covered the mouthpiece.

'*The surrogate, Charlotte Morgan, and her husband, Steven Morgan, are the legal parents of the missing twins.*'

The photo of the twins at the hospital, taken by the photographer the day after they were born, flashed up on the screen.

'*The babies were last seen alive on the fifth of December.*'

I dropped the phone. *Last seen alive.* The words shook me. Steve told Lucy to call back later.

'Charlotte Morgan acted in good faith, handing the newborn twins over to a couple she believed had struggled over many years to have a baby of their own.

'Paula Bennett went missing from her family home fifteen months ago. Police are appealing for the man known by several names including Malcolm Stewart, Ian Turner and Peter Finch, to come forward. Members of the public are advised not to approach him. It is believed he has fathered several other babies with women he met on an unregulated surrogacy forum. This case throws a spotlight on the inadequate surrogacy law in the UK. Charlotte has started her own campaign on social media and is fast gaining support from an array of well-known faces and members of the public.

'Police ask for anyone who has information about the missing baby boy and baby girl to please get in touch with Bedfordshire police. The number is on the screen. Anonymous calls can be made to the National Crime hotline.'

I hugged Alice, kissing each of her fingers and toes, rocking backwards and forwards. 'We have to pray for your half-brother and -sister, little one.'

The photo of Brenda with her real husband and their teenage sons had become permanently imprinted on my brain. Why pretend to be childless? Why say she'd had all those miscarriages? So many lies. They'd played on my sympathy, preyed on my kindness, used my body. The tight knot in my stomach wouldn't shift. There was something so sick about what they'd done. They'd seemed genuinely pleased when I became pregnant. But I fell for it. Would they have cared if I'd died? Had any part of their relationship been real or had that been fake too? The Brenda I thought I knew wouldn't have been capable of hurting the babies, but how well had I really known her? Could she have hurt them and Malcolm killed her because of it? Not according to Nathan. His Paula was a kind, loving wife. But he hadn't guessed she'd do this to him.

A loud banging on the front door gave me a start. Steve looked through the spyhole and pointed to the right, which meant it was Dan and Carly, back from their holiday in Spain.

'Oh my god, you poor things.' Carly rushed in and gave me a hug. I breathed in her Parma violet scent. There was something so comforting about it, I didn't want to let her go. Her newly dyed blue hair made me smile, if only for a second.

'I don't know what to say, mate,' Dan slapped Steve's arm and they half body hugged. 'There's a shedload of reporters outside.'

'Shit.' Steve shut the kitchenette window and pulled the blind down.

They sat with us round the TV while we watched the same two reports over again.

'There must be something we can do to help,' Carly said when the adverts came on.

'Could do with some food if you don't mind going to the shop?'

'Yeah, course.'

I wrote a short list and gave them some cash. While they were out, I returned Lucy's call and agreed to the interview if she came to the house. I had to do something. Getting my story out there might help someone. She said she'd come over the next morning.

Steve searched all the news feeds online, hoping for an update. We thought we might have heard back from the police by now.

Dan and Carly returned with the shopping and hot burgers and chips. The aroma made me feel hungry, for the first time in days.

'One of the reporters wants to do a story on you for their weekend magazine.' Dan handed me a piece of paper with a name and a mobile number. I stared at the scribble, wondering how my life had come to this.

–

In the morning, I took Alice up to Jean's flat. She welcomed me with a warm hug.

'How are you doing?' she asked, taking Alice's hand.

'I'm overwhelmed with everything that's happened, but I thought talking to Lucy again would help someone else.'

'You're being so brave. I'll be listening. And don't worry, Alice will be fine. We're going to stay indoors and play, aren't we, poppet?'

Alice nodded.

'Thank you.' I hugged Jean again, then knelt down and kissed Alice's hands. 'Bye bye, sweetheart, see you in an hour or so.'

Lucy arrived at 10 a.m.

'How are you?' Lucy asked, handing me a bunch of yellow roses. It seemed a strange thing for her to do. I invited her in.

'I'm… all right. As long as I keep busy.' I rushed over to the sofa to straighten up the cushions. 'Many out there today?'

'Loads of paps and reporters. They saw the radio signage on my car, I'm afraid.'

'They're going to hear this anyway, aren't they?'

Lucy nodded. Where was all her usual pomp and drama? A part of me wanted it back, so we could act this out, pretend it wasn't real.

'Are you okay, you look a bit pale,' I said, looking at her properly.

Lucy's smile twisted into a strange shape. She dug deep in her bag, sniffing all the while and pulled out a packet of tissues. Was she crying?

'I… I'm actually pregnant myself, only twelve weeks, but everything is making me cry, especially to do with babies. And this story. Your twins…'

'Oh, Lucy, I'm really pleased for you. I was the same, it's hard not to get emotional about everything. Let me get you a cup of tea.'

I switched on the kettle and allowed myself a little smile. She wasn't so bad after all.

I brought our drinks over. She took out her notes and wired up a mic to her recorder. After a little intro, she asked me to update the listeners on the situation since Brenda's death.

I told her I couldn't talk about the ongoing investigation, but I said we'd driven to Sheffield to meet the old school friend, Zoe, and then Brenda's real husband, Nathan. I didn't mention the surrogate who was about to hand over her baby. I expected the police had been in touch with her by now.

'And I see your campaign is going strong on Twitter. What are your next plans?'

'I'd like other surrogates to come forward and tell their stories. Why they believe they need more protection in law. Sheila Day's high-profile case hit the headlines only last year, but has anything changed? No. What are the government waiting for? A death? A trafficking ring to be uncovered?'

'And remind us about the Day case, for listeners who aren't familiar with it.'

'Sheila gave her baby to the intended parents, but they didn't keep in touch with her. She decided to pay them a visit to see how they were getting on and found they were living in squalor. The baby was undernourished, dirty and in a babygro so small, its toes were buckled.' Images of Rose and Robert in this neglected state flooded my mind. My eyes welled up. I swallowed hard.

'Did she report it to the authorities?'

'Yes, of course, and all credit to them, they acted quickly and took the baby into care. The parental rights were stripped from the new parents. They were convicted of negligence, but the court wouldn't let Sheila have the baby back. He was put up for adoption.'

'What a tragic case. I understand she plans to appeal?'

'I believe so.'

'Do you have any theories as to why Malcolm was having babies with so many women?'

'I can't really comment. I don't want to jeopardise the investigation.'

'I understand, but there has been speculation in the press about a possible trafficking ring acquiring these infants.'

'I can't talk about what might or might not be the reason. The thought of any of it makes me sick to the stomach. These are innocent babies we're talking about.'

'I completely understand.' Lucy blinked, her eyes watering again. 'So, what are the main changes you'd like to see to the law on surrogacy in the UK?'

'Well, the law hasn't changed for over thirty years, since the first UK surrogate, Kim Cotton, in 1985. Surrogacy grew slowly until the internet took off and celebrities started being honest about using surrogates. Now it's opened up to single people looking for someone to co-parent a child with, as well as more same-sex couples having families. Anyone can go on a forum right now and hook up with a stranger, agree to have a baby together, whether that is co-parenting, sperm donation or surrogacy, but neither side in a surrogacy transaction is protected by law. I thought I'd transferred my parenting rights to the intended parents. Fortunately for me, the document was fake, but usually that's the only part of it that is legally binding. Couples come up with agreements which are sometimes pages long, but none of it holds any water in a UK court of law.'

'Thank you, Charlotte. I'm sure, like me, our listeners feel more informed. I know from the comments we've been receiving that many of them remember the first surrogate story over thirty years ago. The law often takes a while to catch up with changing times. We wish you all the best in the search for your twins.'

'Thank you for having me back on, Lucy.'

–

Dan and Carly came over in the evening, and we listened to the interview. I could hardly keep up with the tweets and retweets on Twitter. I noticed that an MP had reposted my tweet, saying how important it was to consider whether the existing law was enough to protect children from being trafficked. She'd even started following me. Perhaps I really could make difference. But there were even more tweets from trolls. I couldn't help reading a few before blocking them.

> **@sweatyboy**
> You should be strung up selling your kids for loadsa cash #kidsforcash

> **@Monkfishpout**
> No way do you deserve those babies back! They should lock you up

@muthaf**ker

Your kids would be better off in care than with you #worstmuthaintheworld

I switched my phone to silent. These people didn't understand.

'Hey, look at this,' Steve said, stooped over his phone. 'There's a reply from that woman on the forum. She's admitted that her husband did go to a house in Peterborough. She's given us the address. Says he followed Malcolm there. Decided to wait outside the tall gates because there were a couple of heavies with Malcolm. He didn't want to risk confronting him on his own. He phoned her, she told him to come home but he wouldn't. So she asked him for the address, told him to wait and see if her brother and his mates could come and help him. But she couldn't get hold of her brother and when she tried to call her husband back, there was no answer. She never heard from him again.'

'Really? Shit. Right, give it here.' I took it from him. 'We're going there first thing in the morning.'

'Are you sure?' Steve sat forward in his seat.

'Yes.'

'I'll come with you.' Dan finished another can of beer.

'Carly, would you be able to mind Alice for us?' I asked.

'Course. You sure it's a good idea though? That man is dangerous.'

'It's a risk I'm willing to take.'

Chapter Fifty-Seven

At 5.30 a.m. Carly tapped on our door as arranged. She came and sat with a sleeping Alice, while we crept out before any reporters turned up. Steve and I jumped in the front of Dan's work van. I typed the Peterborough address into my phone. Forty minutes.

'It's got high gates, according to Streetmap. Hopefully we won't need to climb over.' Steve gave a nervous laugh.

'I've got a ladder in the back. Is the gate likely to be alarmed?'

'Probably.'

'Let's stick to the plan of making out we're delivering something,' I said.

As we grew closer, I left a message for Inspector Johnson, telling him the address we'd been given and that we were on our way there now.

When we pulled up a short distance from the house, it was still dark outside. Dan dipped the headlights. There were no street lamps down this end of the private cul-de-sac. All the houses were set back from the tree-lined road. Mostly oversized detached properties with large front gardens, double and triple garages. Dan leaned over the back of his seat and grabbed three caps and fleeces. They all had a red logo stitched on, *Parcels To You*, and mini go-fast stripes in yellow.

An early-morning commuter drove past, giving us a start.

'The boxes full of packing foam are ready in the back. We'll carry two each to the door. You both need to keep your heads down, make sure you're hidden so when he opens the door he only sees me.' Dan blew out a breath.

He wasn't the only nervous one. My chest tightened. I pictured Carly back at the flat. What if Alice woke up early and wouldn't stop crying for me? I took a deep breath and tried to focus on what we had to do.

'Right, as soon as I get in, I'm going straight upstairs to look for the twins. You two need to keep whoever is downstairs distracted. Good luck.' I high-fived each of them. My heart sped up to full throttle.

'Let's get him,' Steve said.

Dan drove slowly up to the mock-Georgian-style house. The whole property was surrounded by an eight-foot wall with electronic gates to the front. There were no cars on the drive, but there was a triple garage to the right. Two lights were on downstairs. Was Malcolm working this early? If the babies were here, surely he'd need help looking after them.

Dan pressed the intercom buzzer. No answer. He pressed again, firmer this time.

'Yes?' A woman's voice. Or was it a child? Foreign, maybe Chinese. Oh god, had we got the wrong house?

'Delivery.' Dan kept it businesslike, as though he was expected. We heard a click and the gates slid open.

We all looked at each other in surprise.

'That was a bit too easy.' Steve frowned.

'Don't worry about that, let's just do this, stick to the plan.' I squeezed Steve's hand and didn't let go.

Dan drove in. The gates closed behind us. We were trapped here. Dan backed the van up on the left-hand side of the drive, in theory so we could drive straight out again, although I wasn't sure how. We all jumped out. The cold air pinched my face. My breath billowed out in small white clouds. We took two boxes each from the back.

The front door was already open. A maid the size of a child stood aside for us to go in.

'Shall we take them to the kitchen for you?' Steve asked.

The maid nodded but didn't move. Had she understood? My heart was pounding into my throat.

Steve pointed down the corridor behind her, making out the boxes were heavy and we'd be doing her a favour. Finally she turned inside and we followed her. I held back until she was out of sight with Dan and Steve trailing behind her. I put my boxes down behind the front door and ran up the sweeping staircase, two steps at a time in my silent trainers.

At the top was a closed door and at least three more down a corridor to the right and three to my left. I could hear a baby crying. My legs were shaking. I carefully turned the handle nearest to me and eased the door open. My hand shot to my mouth. Three metal cots stood in the centre of the vast room. The kind they had in children's hospital wards. White chipped paint, deep barred sides, almost like cages. An old rocking chair and changing table stood in one corner and a wardrobe and chest of drawers in the other. The smell of milk lingered in the air. I crept forward. Three tiny babies were fast asleep. Above each of them was taped a piece of scrap paper scrawled with: *Boy, 6 weeks, (mother red hair); Girl, 7 days, (mother dark brown hair); Girl, 7 weeks, (mother blonde hair)*. Jesus. What were they here for? Were any of them mine? I peered closer. My stomach twisted. They looked too young. Sudden, silent tears shook my body. Hold it together. Call the police. Search the other rooms. I dialled 999 on my mobile and reported that I'd found three babies at Malcolm Stewart's home.

I pushed open door after door to more and more cots. My mouth dropped open, aghast. Which were mine? I peered at each in turn, frantically trying to recognise Rose and Robert. I thought I'd memorised their faces, but they changed so quickly.

Were these all surrogate babies? Did any of the surrogate mothers wonder what had happened to them after they gave them away, or did they just presume they were being looked after?

In three rooms on the right were five more sleeping babies. I stood looking at them, but none were familiar. One started to shift around, so I quickly came out. I peeped round the door of the first room on the left. A waft of dirty nappy hit my nostrils. A nanny was feeding a baby rocking gently in a chair, facing the window. The baby seemed older the way she was holding it, maybe two months, but I couldn't get a closer look without the nanny seeing me. In the last room were three more cots, but they were all empty. I touched the edge of one and set off the crude rocking motion. Three mournful notes burst out of the broken sheep mobile clamped to the side. I grabbed at the soft animal shape, fumbling to make it stop. I held it still, half expecting a nanny to burst in.

After a moment, I picked up a cotton blanket and pressed it to my nose. I'd told myself I'd recognise the smell of Rose or Robert, but there was nothing familiar to latch onto, nothing to link them here.

Downstairs, a car door slammed, making me jump. I ran out to the landing.

'Who's that parked on the drive?' a man shouted.

I froze at the familiar voice. The front door flew open and Malcolm strode in carrying a baby in a car seat. Its cries sent chills right through me. He dumped it on the floor with a clonk. A nanny trotted up, hands together as though praying for forgiveness. She unstrapped the baby and whisked it away into a downstairs room, shutting the door behind her.

Malcolm wasn't wearing his usual smart trousers and trademark V-neck jumper. Instead he had a tracksuit and trainers on and looked like he hadn't showered.

'Oi you scum!' Steve bowled across the hall from the direction of the corridor, followed by Dan and a nanny holding a baby's bottle like a grenade.

'What the hell are you doing here?' But before Malcolm could say anything else, Steve had landed a punch in his face. Dan stood back, arms crossed, nodding his approval. The nanny ran up and down the hall, crying for help, hands and bottle waving by her ears.

'That's for what you did to Brenda. Want some more?' Steve bared his teeth as he lunged at Malcolm's stomach, toppling him over.

'Where are my twins?' I screamed, running down the stairs.

'And where's our money?' Steve growled, standing over him.

Even with blood dripping from his mouth, Malcolm still managed a sly grin. 'You people only care about the money, don't you? Haggling with me, always wanting more.' He rolled on his side and spat blood onto the shiny white tiles. 'Look at you both. What kind of parents are you, giving your babies away for a wad of cash?'

'What have you done with our twins!' I shouted, standing in the middle of Steve and Dan.

'Oh dear, couldn't you find them?' he said in a mock-whiny voice. 'He's not even their father. I am, remember? They're *our* children, Charlotte.' Malcolm gave a gurgling laugh and spat blood on the floor again.

'You're a sick bastard.' Steve kicked his leg.

'What kind of sad little life would they have in that tiny flat of yours? They're better off with parents who really love them and can give them anything and everything they want.'

'What are you talking about? Where *are* they? Tell me – please – I'm begging you – where are my babies!' I screamed at him.

At last, police sirens filled the air. I thumped the button by the front door to open the gates. Malcolm made a run for it through the house into the back garden. I ran after Steve and Dan who rugby-tackled him. Malcolm landed face down on the lawn.

At last we'd found Malcolm, but we were no closer to finding the twins.

–

Steve linked his arm through mine as two officers escorted Malcolm from the house in handcuffs. Inspector Johnson arrived with an armed police unit.

'You should have left it to us, you could have been hurt,' the inspector said.

'What will happen to all the babies upstairs? When will I know if any are Rose or Robert?' I asked.

'They'll all go into temporary care for now. We'll let you know as soon as we can.'

'Can't I go back up and find them?'

'Sorry, this is a crime scene now. We'll be taking DNA samples from all the babies to be certain of who belongs to whom.'

A girl not much older than me got out of the back of the police car. She told us she was the surrogate from the forum, the last one due to meet Malcolm.

'Thanks for helping me,' she said. We hugged.

'What will happen to your baby now?'

'I'm thinking of putting him up for adoption.'

We both looked up. Malcolm grinned at us from the back of the squad car as it sped off.

Chapter Fifty-Eight

'The police arrested a forty-nine-year-old man, who has been using the alias Malcolm Stewart, during a raid at a property in Peterborough early this morning. He has been charged with the murder of Paula Bennett and the abduction of nine babies, found at the premises. Three Filipina nannies, also at the house at the time of the arrest, have been taken in for questioning.'

I switched off the radio and stared into space, my mind blank. I hadn't even been to bed. The kitchen clock told me it was 9 a.m., but for me time had stopped. I pictured the twins tucked into their cot in the hospital, a few hours old. I'd overridden my instinct to protect them. I'd failed them. Given them away to a criminal. Stupid, stupid girl. Why hadn't I listened to Mum instead of pushing her away, assuming she was being selfish? I'd acted like a rebellious child.

A car pulled up outside. Two doors slammed shut. I jumped up and peered out of the kitchenette window.

'All clean.' Steve came out of the bathroom, holding Alice. She repeated his words.

'It's the police.' My voice sounded alarmed, as though we were the ones who had reason to hide. Part of me dreaded the truth, but the agony of not knowing if the twins were among those found safe in that house paralysed me.

Steve squeezed my hand before letting them in.

Inspector Johnson's face was solemn. He seemed to have aged since yesterday. An older policewoman with a kind smile followed him in. My eyes darted around our messy room: the unmade bed, toys strewn across the floor, the faint sour smell of Alice's nappy. I pulled clothes off two chairs for them to sit down. They didn't seem fazed by any of it. We both sat on the bed, Alice at our feet playing with a jigsaw. Steve held me tightly round the shoulders; his skin as cold as marble on my bare arm.

'Have you found them?' My voice was barely a whisper.

'I'm afraid we're not certain yet,' the policewoman said, 'we have to do DNA tests on all the babies.'

'Because the parental orders are fake, no tests were done at the time, which would have been the normal procedure,' Inspector Johnson said. His face softened. Perhaps he was more hopeful than he was giving away.

'If I could test you now, we'll find out as soon as we can if any of them are a match.' The policewoman pulled a long-handled swab out of a packet.

I nodded and shut my tear-filled eyes. She gently swiped around the inside of my mouth and dropped the sample inside a clear plastic tube.

'All the babies found have been taken into care. Social services will carry out a welfare enquiry,' Inspector Johnson said. 'We'll make them aware that you're the biological mother if any prove to be yours.'

'Thank you.'

'The nannies are being questioned, but none of them speak much English so we've had to call in translators. We doubt they've been told much about the set-up, but I'm sure we'll glean some information from Mr Brown.'

So that was his real name. I tried to shake the dark thoughts pressing heavily on my mind. I daren't contemplate what I'd do if the twins weren't among those at the house.

'I know you can't say much, but off the record, do you really think Malcolm fathered all those babies?' Steve grimaced.

'It seems entirely possible from what we know so far,' Inspector Johnson said.

'What did he intend to do with them?'

'That we're not sure of yet.'

Steve tipped his head back and blew air from his mouth.

The inspector's reply was enough to send chills through me. When would I wake up from this nightmare? If the twins weren't there, where the hell could they be, and who were they with?

Chapter Fifty-Nine

After the police had gone, I pinned up a Santa stocking for Alice. I wished I had one for Rose and Robert too, their first Christmas. The not knowing pressed on my thoughts. I'd almost forgotten to buy presents or food because I couldn't focus on anything else. I only had a few things for Alice, a light-up push-along car, a chunky set of story books and a new T-shirt with *Santa's favourite helper* embroidered on the front.

I kissed Alice and sat her in the buggy still in her pyjamas and tucked her in with a blanket.

'Where are you going?' Steve stood across the doorway.

'I need to clear my head.'

'I'll come with you.' He grabbed his jacket.

'No. Let me go, I need to be alone.' I wouldn't look at him.

'You're blaming me aren't you, for all of this?' His swung his arms out.

'Why do you say that?'

'Because I made you do it, didn't I? I wanted the money.'

'Let me get out, I can't even breathe.' I pushed past him with the buggy to the hallway and out of the main door. I didn't blame him, I blamed myself. I was the twins' mother and I should have protected them.

The air weighed heavily after the earlier downpour, leaving the streets deserted except for the occasional car splashing past, spraying water over the pavement. I kept my head down and marched on, hoping I'd come to the edge of the world and fall into oblivion.

I reached the park on the other side of town and stopped under an oak tree. Distant thunder rumbled across the sky. I told Alice it was a lion snoring. I pushed on, letting the rain wash away my tears. When I reached the main road, I glanced both ways, certain it was clear, but as I stepped out, screeching brakes pierced my ears, my head. But something pulled me back just as a car whizzed past, hooting its horn at me.

'Jesus, Charlotte, what are you trying to do?' Steve let go of my coat.

'It was clear a second ago.' I tried to get my breath back.

'Getting killed is not going to help anyone. How could you be so careless, putting Alice in danger? She should be your priority.' He took the pushchair from me and started walking back. I ran to catch up with him.

'What were you doing following me anyway?' I asked.

'Your mum called. She wants to know if we're still going over for Christmas dinner tomorrow.'

'Do we have to?' I stopped in the middle of the pavement.

'She's worried about you. You need to give her a chance.'

I saw my younger self then, standing on the other side of the street, just as the fortune teller had described – a lost child, playing on my own, outside my mother's bedroom door, praying for her to stop crying. When she did eventually come out, she'd step over me, curled up on the floor like an embryo and accuse me of trying to trip her up. I spent hours longing for Daddy to come home, but as soon as he arrived, he'd lock himself away in the shed, the radio crackling out tunes that filled the gaps around the door, making sure there was no way in.

'Let's go home,' I said, realising that Steve was waiting for me. 'There's going to be another downpour in a minute.'

–

We woke early on Christmas Day and exchanged a small present each. I gave Steve the new Paul Weller CD and he bought me a diary and pen. Neither of us was in the mood for Christmas. We would have quite happily gone back to bed, but we played along for Alice, helping her to open her gifts from us and Santa.

We set off for Mum's mid-morning, grateful that I didn't have to cook and knowing we could leave at any time.

Mum answered the door with a flushed face and wet hands.

'Come in, come in.' She pecked each of us on the cheek. 'I'm in the middle of checking the turkey.' She rushed back to the kitchen, her fluffy slippers slapping against her bare feet. We took off our coats and Steve followed her in holding Alice, while I went up to the bathroom. On the radio, a choir of young children were singing 'Little Donkey' followed by 'Silent Night'.

I remembered holding baby Jesus in one of my school nativities, in a freezing-cold church with all the angels around me in their silver tinsel halos. I'd stared as hard as I could into the doll's eyes, tipping it backwards and forwards to make the eyelids close and open again, willing it to come alive, praying for a Christmas miracle, so I could take home a real baby for Mum. She'd sat in the front row, tears running down her pale waxy face, eyes fixed on the statue of the Virgin Mary behind me.

When I came back from the bathroom, the radio had been turned down low. Mum and Steve exchanged a glance. All of a sudden Mum rushed forward, arms out wide. I flinched but made myself stand still to let her hug me.

'I heard the news. I'm so pleased he's been caught and those babies are all right.'

'They don't know if that's all of them yet.' I fought the urge not to shake her off. I counted the seconds in my head until she released me. Steve handed me a glass of white wine. I sloshed it down my throat like medicine; a dose of alcohol to steep my brain in.

'Were the twins there?'

'We don't know yet.' I tugged at my hair, my T-shirt and the baggy flesh underneath. My body remembered them. Their roots were within me.

Mum's arms wrapped around me again and this time I gave in and clung to her, my legs buckled but she held me up as I sobbed.

When I finally pulled away, Steve lifted Alice up to me. I grabbed some kitchen roll and cleaned my face up. I kissed her cheeks and smiled as she said, 'Mummy.' He poured me another glass of wine and quietly took Alice into the living room. I drank a mouthful, more slowly this time.

'When do you think they'll know?' Mum asked, stroking my back. She'd been crying too. This was hurting her as much me. I'd been so selfish pushing her away.

I shook my head.

'We just have to hope.' Mum checked the turkey while I sipped my drink. She shoved the hot shelf back in and kicked the oven door shut, but as usual it bounced open. We both smiled at how ridiculous it was. She'd been saying for years she needed to get a new one. I bent down, turned the handle and pushed it firmly closed.

'It can stay there now until it's ready to eat.' Mum opened the window, her back to me. A tendril of dried-up wisteria reached in. She washed her hands and wiped them over and over on the towel, not once looking up.

'Mum?'

'I… I want to say sorry.' She folded the towel into a neat square and smoothed it over.

'What for?'

'Having a go at you the other night. Not realising how badly you'd been affected by what happened to me.'

'Maybe I was too young to understand the full picture.'

'Even so.'

'I… I thought I'd done something wrong, that I wasn't enough for you… because you wanted another baby, then another.'

'I'm sorry. I can see that now.' Her fingers brushed her lips.

'It hurt that you barely acknowledged me when you were grieving for them – I loved them too.' I didn't mean for the words to snap so sharply from my mouth. I sounded like a child.

'I know and I'm truly sorry.' She bowed her head. 'I should have acknowledged that and known when to stop trying, to appreciate what I already had. You *and* your dad. I can see now that I messed things up for both of you, all of us.'

'Oh Mum.' I took a step towards her, my hand outstretched. 'I know how much it hurt you. I tried so hard to be a good girl, so you'd love me and stop torturing yourself. All I ever wanted was for us to be happy again.'

Mum took my hand, her eyes wet with tears. 'If I'd stopped sooner, you'd never have thought to be a surrogate and we wouldn't be in this terrible situation.'

'What's happened now is not your fault. I wanted to do this. I think it was my way of trying to fix the past. Despite everything, it's helped me to come to terms with what happened to you.'

Mum nodded, unable to speak. I put my arms around her and wondered why we hadn't been able to be this honest a long time ago.

'I have something for you.' She broke away from me and reached out to the counter for a small gift she pressed into my hand. I unpeeled the tape and took off the silver wrapping paper. Inside the box was a pendant with three small gold rings on a chain.

'One for each of your children,' Mum said, wiping her tears away.

'It's beautiful, Mum, thank you.' I hugged her.

Steve brought Mum's presents in. She unwrapped a framed photo of Alice and another of Rose and Robert, the one originally meant for Brenda.

'They're just perfect, thank you.'

Steve helped me fasten the chain around my neck. I kissed each gold ring, saying all their names, silently praying for the twins' safe return.

We ate Christmas dinner and watched the Queen's speech, followed by the news, but there were no updates.

'Will you let me know as soon as you hear something?' Mum asked as we cleared the pudding bowls.

'Yes, of course.' My stomach went into a spin. I tried my hardest to believe the twins were among the ones found safe in that house. By the sound of it, those babies were healthy and well looked after. But a tiny itch of doubt kept scratching the back of my mind. Were they just the lucky ones?

–

On the drive home, Steve reached for my arm and gave it a gentle tap. 'I'm so glad you had a chat with your mum.'

'So am I. It's the first time I've had the courage to tell her how I really feel.' I lifted the pendant she'd given me, the three gold rings. 'I still remember feeling hopeful every time she got pregnant that this was going to be *the one*. But the inevitable would happen and by the last one, I'd lost her for good. It was as though each loss broke her in pieces, and she never quite fit back together. She'd be cold and silent for days after, sometimes weeks, as though she'd forgotten that she already had a living, breathing daughter right there, one that loved her and longed for her cuddles. She'd turned to stone, forgotten how to show love. And then I think of her before it all, as this young vivacious woman, blonde hair sweeping back and forth as we danced round the kitchen to David Bowie on the radio, me barely up to her waist then, swinging our arms from side to side. It felt like my mummy had been stolen from me.'

Steve rested his hand in mine and we sat in silence for several minutes.

'I hope you can both put it behind you.'

'Do you know, the more I think about it, the more I realise I've been trying to turn the past into something positive to help myself.'

'I'm so proud of you.'

'Thank you.'

–

It was the day after Boxing Day when the police came back with the DNA results.

'I thought you'd tell us over the phone,' I said, letting Inspector Johnson in. His nose and cheeks were ruddy, probably from too much Christmas cheer.

'Not with this kind of news.' He sat in a chair opposite us on the sofa. I tried to swallow but my throat closed up.

'One of the babies matches your DNA,' he said.

'Only one?' I cried.

'I'm afraid so. Your baby girl.' He allowed himself a brief smile.

'When will I get her back?' I laced my fingers, bending them back and forth. I would never let my babies out of my sight again.

'We hope to reunite you with your daughter soon. You'll need to make an emergency application to the court as soon as possible. Once social services have visited you, and both they and the judge are satisfied that you were misled, we can bring her home.'

'Where's our boy?' Steve asked.

The inspector sighed. 'We're not sure where he is at the moment. Several of the babies are missing.'

What did that even mean? Where could he be and who was he with? The momentary spark of joy at the news that Rose was safe and well, had been whipped out from under our feet.

'How many surrogates did he use?' Steve pulled a face.

'At least twelve that we know of.'

'He's sick.' I pushed my fist to my mouth.

'There is one more thing we found out. The missed calls you received were from a mobile phone registered to Paula Bennett – Brenda. We think you were right in your assumption that she tried to warn you not to find them. Unfortunately, she paid for it with her life.'

'Oh Brenda. It must have been her messaging me on the forum too. I asked her to call me. There I was thinking she'd betrayed me. I should have asked her more questions about how Malcolm was treating her.' I blinked at Steve as the enormity of our part in it hit me. I swallowed before I could speak. 'We might have been able to save her.'

Chapter Sixty

We woke to the news the next day that Malcolm had been hiding out in a smaller property in Peterborough, where they believed he kept several women against their will, who he used as intended mothers; women he blackmailed to carry out his sick plan, using a different name and a different woman each time. He went back to the big house to take the newest baby there. The police had followed him after the handover from the surrogate on the forum. My call had confirmed the address.

'All that time they were looking for him, he was right under their noses.' Steve pointed at the TV with his razor, then ducked back into the bathroom.

'They've also found the missing husband of the surrogate that helped us – found dead in the grounds – not the only one either. God, she must be in pieces. They think the other bodies could be intended mothers who tried to escape.'

'Shit, you're joking me?' Steve peeped round the door, shaving foam covering half his face.

I stirred half a Weetabix into warm milk and tested how hot it was on my tongue. I handed Alice the plastic spoon. She dug down into the milky mixture and shovelled it into her mouth. What if Steve had gone searching for Malcolm on his own? That could have been his body found at the house. Goosebumps rose on my arms.

'Guess what Malcolm's real name is?' I called.

'Go on?'

'Leslie Brown.'

'Wasn't Brown the name on the cheques?'

'Yep.' I couldn't take my eyes off the TV.

'What did they just say? Turn it up,' Steve shouted.

I rewound the news.

'He was living in the loft of a three-bedroom detached with one of the intended mothers. She was abducted from her family six months ago.'

Steve came in dabbing his face on a towel.

'They've filmed inside the house we went to.'

I pressed play. The camera panned round the front of the property. Inside the entrance hall, the reporter, a man in a suit, walked around the ground floor until he reached the massive kitchen and glass-roofed annexe with sofa, opening up to the large garden and a wooded area beyond, where the bodies were found.

The reporter paused in the living room with the cream leather sofas, where Malcolm and Brenda had been sitting the first time they'd Skyped us. Then he strolled across to the stairs and spoke right into the camera. '*And who would have thought that up this swirling staircase, in this exquisite house on a private road in Peterborough, would be a secret that has not only shocked this quiet neighbourhood, but the whole nation.*'

When he reached the top of the stairs, he strolled along the landing, pushing open door after door to reveal the now-empty cots, in five of the eight bedrooms.

'*This is where nine newborn babies were found, some only days old, acquired by the self-proclaimed entrepreneur and businessman, Leslie Brown. Many, if not all of the babies, were fathered by him, with unsuspecting surrogate mothers, like Charlotte Morgan. Did Leslie Brown see himself as a god-like figure wanting to fill the world with his offspring? Or is there a more sinister reason as to why he wanted so many children, and why several of the babies are still missing?'* The camera panned in close to the reporter in his sharp suit and rolling banter. '*One theory is that these innocent babies have already been trafficked to the other side of the world, to be brought up as domestic slaves or, worse, as sex workers. What has happened to them is a mystery that may never be solved.*'

'They can't say that!' I shot out of my seat and screamed at the TV.

'How much worse can this fucking get?' Steve pulled on a shirt.

'Have they no idea what this is doing to us?' I threw a teddy at the screen.

Steve wrapped his arms around my shaking body.

'I don't know what to think any more.' I broke away from him and drew my hands down my face. I hadn't bothered wearing make-up in weeks.

Steve grabbed his coat off the back of the chair. 'Come on, let's do this.'

I wiped Alice's mouth and fumbled putting her new red shoes on.

'Are we ready?' Steve picked Alice up and kissed my forehead.

We dropped Alice at nursery and drove straight to the court. The clerk was expecting us. My head was throbbing. She ushered us into a small room, not unlike the one at the police station. She talked us through filling out an emergency application to the court to get our baby girl back, clearly stating that we were victims of a crime. Surely the fact that we'd been duped by a criminal would go in our favour?

Soon we were back in the daylight. I was surprised to see that the world still looked the same. We had no idea which way the decision would go. We stood on the steps facing each other. Steve took my hands in his as though we were standing at the altar. He looked down at his feet then up at me with red-rimmed eyes.

'I promise you, I'll do everything in my power to get our baby girl back.' We held each other tight, both silently more determined than ever, hoping Rose would come back to us soon. Today could decide the rest of our lives.

Chapter Sixty-One

Steve went back to work the next day. Mum came over and helped me clean the flat from top to bottom. We went to a garden centre afterwards. I wandered around following Mum, not taking anything in. We sat in the café drinking coffee, but everywhere I looked there were mothers with their babies. I didn't know whether to cry or scream.

'What time did you say she's coming?' Mum asked in a soft voice.

'Three.' I checked my phone. 'Steve should be on his way home soon.'

'Do you have an idea what sort of thing she's going to ask?'

'The policewoman said they'll want to know about our circumstances, see where we live, what kind of people we are.' I shoved my cup away so it rattled in the saucer. 'See what kind of mother gives her babies away.' Maybe they'd take pity on us for being fools.

'Stop that now. Will they know if the council can rehouse you?'

'I suppose it depends how quickly they process our application and whether they think we deserve to get Rose back.'

'Surely it's about Rose deserving to be returned to her parents?'

To a mother who gave her baby girl away?

–

Steve was already at home with Alice when we arrived. He was wiping over the kitchen surfaces and cupboards while Alice played on her toy piano. I knelt down and smoothed her hair, kissed her soft cheek. She held her hand out to me and I blew on her palm, making her giggle.

'We've done all that.' Mum waved at Steve to stop.

'I know. I just wanted to do something.'

Steve and I hugged. I drew back first and for a long moment we stared at each other, then parted to opposite sides of the room. He hung the tea towel over the cooker door and lined up the coffee, tea and sugar jars so the names were at the front. I moved Alice's toy box against the back wall next to her cot, knocking her rag doll onto the carpet. The one I'd bought her when she was born. I picked it up. The rosy cheeks were faded. Its sequin eyes coming loose. I pictured Rose's little face and Robert next to her, grabbing her hand. In slow motion, my body folded as if the air had been punched from my lungs. Steve reached out and helped me to the sofa. He held me until my throat was too raw to cry any more.

'There's no way they're going to give Rose back to us, is there?' I said eventually in a croaky voice.

'They will, I promise you,' Steve cupped my face and looked deep in my eyes, 'and if they don't, we'll fight to get our children back. You've got a whole army of supporters on social media too, they'll help us.'

I nodded and wiped my nose. He stroked my hair.

'I've already spoken to Dan about helping him out with deliveries, at weekends and early mornings.'

'Have you?' I pulled back and held his hands.

'We'll have another mouth to feed, hopefully two.'

I kissed his palms. 'A women's magazine has asked to interview me about surrogacy and my campaign. They're offering to pay me. I'd like to do more if I can, spread the word.'

Alice came and sat with us, dragging a large picture book onto her knees.

'You know it's almost three?' Mum held her hand out to me. I took it and stood up. She hugged me without saying a word. When she pulled away, she was crying too.

'Look at the pair of us. What's the social worker going to think?' I said.

'Steve's right though, Charlotte, we have to fight this all the way. We'll do everything in our power to get your twins back.'

Chapter Sixty-Two

The woman from social services turned up in a Mini Cooper, umbrella in one hand and our lives in the other, tucked inside a soft leather briefcase. When I let her in the main door, she shook rain from her coat across the tiled floor.

I cleared my throat. 'I'm Charlotte.'

'Lorna Drake.'

As we shook hands, I tried to find her behind the straight fringe and orange-rimmed glasses. Beady black eyes blinked back at me, not giving anything away.

I silently let out a deep sigh and led her into our flat. Mum leapt forward, introducing herself. Steve stood behind holding Alice, who was sucking her thumb.

'Please, come and sit down.' Mum swept her arm out to show the odd array of seats, then fussed around, asking if she'd come far, if she wanted tea or coffee. No, she didn't like anything with caffeine. Orange squash.

Lorna gave a brief smile and sat at one end of the sofa bed, knees pointed together. There were splashes of rain and grit up her skin-coloured tights. She hauled her case off the floor and took a clipboard and unicorn pencil case out.

'Let's start, shall we? How many rooms do you have here?' Her pen was poised above a tick box.

'Erm... this is it, except the bathroom just here and the kitchenette over there. I extended my arms in both directions like cabin crew.

She shook her head. 'You'll need a bigger house for starters.'

I dropped into the wicker chair. How could I feel defeated already?

'Can we apply for one now?' Steve asked. He opened a book for Alice and sat on the floor with her on his knee.

'You'll have to contact the council and they'll email the forms to you.'

'Can't they come and live in my house temporarily, it's three bedrooms?' Mum gave her the glass of squash. Lorna drank it in one go and handed it straight back.

'I can come and assess its suitability, yes.' She tapped her pen on the paper. 'I'd need you to fill out a police check form too, please.'

'Yes, whatever you need,' Mum said.

I threw a glance at Steve. His eyes flicked up and down.

Lorna asked me why I'd wanted to become a surrogate, how we met Malcolm and Brenda, what sort of checks we did to find out about them.

'What do you mean checks?' I asked.

'Well, for instance, to see if they really were married, did own a legitimate business, lived at the address they gave you. I understand you didn't go to their house at all?' Her eyebrows shot up as she flicked through a few of her papers and pointed to something. 'Not even once?'

'They said they lived in Orkney. It was too far for us, so we met them at a hotel in Peterborough most times.' It sounded ridiculous now, not visiting their home, but it didn't seem important at the time. We'd met them in real life, seen their house on Skype calls. They were grateful for what I was doing for them. We'd had no reason not to trust them.

'Right on their doorstep as it turns out. Handy for them.'

'How were we meant to know that?'

Lorna's black eyes were on me again. I thought she'd never look away.

'We had no reason not to believe them.' I realised how naïve we'd been. My head throbbed.

'We met them one time in London before we decided to have their baby,' Steve added.

'They seemed a genuinely nice couple.' I looked over at Mum standing in the kitchenette, her expression stern.

'You gave the twins to them not knowing who they really were.' Lorna rested her hands on the piece of paper full of notes, no doubt all about how unfit we were. Oh god, she'd already made up her mind.

'We did all the checks we possibly could. Their website and business looked… real,' I said.

'They conned us. Even Brenda, I mean, Paula Bennett was conned too. He bloody killed her!' Steve shifted Alice onto my lap and stood next to me. 'Haven't you seen the news?' He stepped forward.

'Steve,' I said through clenched teeth.

Lorna carried on, unflinching. 'But one thing you did know about them is that they were willing to pay you more expenses money than anyone else.'

'That was my fault. I persuaded Charlotte we could do with the extra cash.' Steve touched his forehead.

'Oh dear, one bad decision after another.'

'But why not be paid more when she was basically giving them the use of her body, her womb? She had all sorts of complications during the pregnancy and ended up having an emergency caesarean because of pre-eclampsia. She nearly died.'

Lorna stared at him for several moments, then wrote something down.

'You can't put a price on what she did for them, that's all I'm saying.'

'And who is going to look after these babies? You both work, don't you?'

'I don't have a job at the moment, but I'm starting at college part-time soon, to train to be a teacher. And Alice is at nursery now.'

'Do you think you can cope with three children?' She squinted at me.

'Yes, we believe we can and we've got Mum to help us.'

'Why are you asking us about both twins? Robert's not been found yet.'

I tried to give Steve a warning look. He was going to mess things up if he wasn't careful.

'Because we like to keep twins together if we can.'

'So, we'll get both back or neither of them?' I asked.

'Let's not speculate at this stage. The welfare of the twins is paramount and, of course, growing up together would be the best outcome for them.' Lorna gave a brief smile.

'Have you any idea what this is doing to us?' Steve asked, raising his voice. 'Got kids of your own, have you?'

Lorna actually shut right up. Her hand sprung to the silver heart hanging from her neck. When she let go, I could see it was one of those handprint pendants. Shell had one made when her first baby was born sleeping. I elbowed Steve. Lorna caught me gawping at her. We both looked away.

'I'm sorry, Charlotte,' Mum came and stood the other side of me, 'I know you didn't want me to say anything, but I really feel that I have to.' She wiped a tear away from her eye. 'You see, Lorna, I know this is my daughter, and you'll think this is easy for me to say, but you really won't find a more loving person to be a mother to those twins. She wanted to be a surrogate primarily because of my stillbirths. I regret trying so many times because it took me away from her and broke our family apart. When Charlotte met Brenda, all she wanted was to help her experience the joy of holding her own baby. Money didn't come into it for her. Whenever I questioned her – and believe you me I asked her all the questions you're asking and many, many more, because don't forget, these are my grandchildren we're talking about here. When I questioned her, it always came back to her needing to help someone like me. She couldn't let Brenda down. And maybe you think it's a flaw and she's been naïve, but Charlotte believes in the good in people, and I think that's rather wonderful,' Mum's voice wavered at the end.

'Thanks Mum.' I reached for her hand. Steve put his arm across my shoulders. The three of us linked together in front of this woman who had the power to make or break our future.

Lorna took a form out and handed it to Mum. She put her clipboard and pen away and stood up. 'I think I have everything I need for now. You'll hear something in the next couple of days.' Her tone was rigid, frosty. We'd blown it.

I showed her out. As we shook hands, face-to-face, I caught the tiniest glimmer in her eyes.

Back inside, I threw my arms around Mum and Steve.

'You were incredible, Mum. Thank you so much.'

'It's the least I could do.'

'Did you mean it about us moving in with you?'

'Of course I did.'

'Dare we even hope that we got through to her?'

'I don't know, I think I mucked it up.' Steve sat hunched on the sofa, head down.

I'd thought our nightmare was ending, but our fate lay in the hands of that stern woman. I had to prepare myself for the worst, for the powers-that-be deciding that Rose and Robert's future shouldn't be with us.

I slumped next to Steve as though I was a puppet who'd had my strings cut. He put his arm round me and I pressed my face to his side. It would be the hardest most painful decision to accept, but if I was sure the twins were safe, being cared for by a couple who genuinely loved them as much as we did, maybe it would be easier to live with.

Chapter Sixty-Three

The next three days were the longest of my life. It was impossible to sleep at night and when I did drop off, I had vivid disturbing nightmares about the twins being ripped away from me at birth. We tried to keep to a normal routine, but I couldn't settle to anything. Lorna Drake assessed Mum's house once the police check had been completed. Another magazine emailed about interviewing me as soon as we found out if Rose was coming back to us. On the third day, Inspector Johnson called, his voice unusually chirpy.

'Good news. The court confirms that you are still the legal parents of Rose and, following the welfare report, they accept that you were misled by Leslie Brown and therefore Rose should be returned to you as soon as possible.'

'Really? She can come home?' Instant tears filled my eyes. 'Is she okay?'

'She's in excellent condition. If you're able to move into your mum's temporarily until the council have found a house for you, Social Services can bring baby Rose home to you tomorrow.'

'That's incredible news. We can move in straight away, it's all arranged.' Mum's two spare rooms were permanently ready for guests, so it was only a matter of moving our things. I'd never have dreamed of living back with Mum, but over the last few weeks we'd grown so much closer.

'We'll be coming over tomorrow as well, to update you. I'd like Steve to be with you please.'

'I'll make sure he's here. Any news about Robert?'

'We're still gleaning information from Brown and the other woman who'd been living at the second house. I'm hoping to be able to tell you more tomorrow.'

'Thank you so much.'

My baby daughter was coming home. But not having Robert back too was like a knife in my side. I called Steve. He promised to come home after lunch. He'd see if Dan would help us move our stuff in his van.

Next, I phoned Mum. 'It's good news,' I said quickly before she could worry, 'they're bringing Rose home tomorrow, which means we can move in this afternoon.' My smile was the biggest in far too long. I stroked Alice's hair. She was going to have a little sister after all.

'That's wonderful, Charlotte. I can't wait to see her. I'll have two granddaughters.'

'I'm sure I won't sleep tonight.'

'Do you want me to come and help you pack?'

'Yes please.'

'Any news on Robert?'

'Nothing yet. I'm not sure if I can face it, Mum. What if the stories about trafficking are true?' My voice trembled. 'I can't stop worrying what's happened to him. What they might have *done* to him. I'd never be able to forgive myself.'

–

Mum arrived with a boot full of old newspapers and cardboard boxes she'd picked up at the supermarket.

'What time are they bringing Rose?' She took all our mismatched plates out of the cupboard and started wrapping them one by one in newspaper.

'Lorna said it would be at ten.' I took a pile of second-hand paperbacks off the shelf and dropped them in a box.

'She'll need her mummy's cuddles.' Mum stacked each of the wrapped plates.

'I know and I try not to think about whether she was left to cry.'

Mum nodded. 'Is there anything you need for her that I can get?'

'I don't think so. You're doing so much for us already, Mum.'

'I want to do everything I can to help you get them both back,'

I touched the three gold rings hanging around my neck and made a silent wish that I'd have them all back together.

By the time Steve came home from work, we'd almost finished. Dan helped him load the boxes into his van.

'Gonna miss you,' Carly said, giving me a hug. Her blue hair smelled of Parma violets.

'You too. We're not going far though, come and visit any time.'

'I was counting on you for a bit of help and advice.' She looked down at her boots.

'I'm still here for you… Carly? Oh my god, stop that, you don't mean?'

Carly grinned and patted her flat tummy.

'When are you due?' I squealed.

'September.'

'I'm so happy for you both.' I hugged her. 'Did you hear that, Steve?'

'Yeah, good isn't it?' He and Dan came in for the next boxes.

'And you're feeling OK? No sickness?'

'Not once and I'm fourteen weeks already.'

'Oh, you lucky thing.'

'I'm really pleased for you, Carly,' Mum said.

'Good news about Jack too,' Steve said, 'he's finished his chemo. It's gone really well.'

'That's brilliant,' I said.

Carly helped me pack my clothes while Mum finished up in the kitchenette.

When everything was in the van, Steve and I took one last look around the empty flat. I thought about the day we'd brought Alice home for the first time and then the twins. It had been so hard saying goodbye to them. This was the fresh start we needed, but I'd still miss the old place.

Mum took Alice in her car and we met them at her house. Steve and Dan unloaded the boxes while I carried Alice in.

'You'll have to share a room with your sister Rose and hopefully your brother Robert too.' I put her down and she ran around, twirling in circles, giggling.

I caught her hands. We would never be completely happy again until all our little family was back together.

Chapter Sixty-Four

Early the next morning, a car pulled up outside Mum's house. I ran out to greet them. Steve followed behind, carrying Alice. Lorna Drake smiled widely while her colleague unstrapped Rose from her seat and handed her to me, loosely wrapped in a soft white blanket.

'Hello, my sweetheart, look at you, welcome home.' I cradled Rose in my arms and kissed her cheeks and her tiny paper-thin nails. 'Look at her, she's perfect.' Her eyes shone at me, now a clear topaz blue. She'd grown so much, almost four months old already.

Steve kissed her forehead and put his arm around me. He leaned Alice forward so she could see her new sister. Mum stroked Rose's hair.

'Thank you for all your help,' I said to Lorna. She smiled and patted my arm.

As the social workers were leaving, Inspector Johnson and WPC Reed arrived.

'Shall we go in?' Steve led the way. He offered them seats on Mum's sofa.

I sat on the two-seater, holding Rose out on my knees in front of me, my eyes locked on hers, rocking gently, backwards and forwards. 'My little baby Rose, I've missed you more than you'll ever know. Mummy and Daddy love you so much. We'll never ever let you go again.' Tears misted my eyes. I felt Mum's hand on my shoulder. Steve knelt down by my side with Alice, who pointed at Rose and said, *baby*, in a delighted and surprised voice that made me smile even more.

'That's right, this is your baby sister.' I raised Rose's hand and kissed her palm. Steve did the same. Alice copied us and we all laughed.

'Let's get the kettle on,' Mum said, passing me a tissue, then wiping her own eyes too. 'What can I get everyone?'

'Two teas please,' Inspector Johnson said.

'One sugar for me, thanks,' WPC Reed added.

'Tea for us too please, Gloria,' Steve said. I smiled, the stress and tension momentarily lifting from my shoulders. But I'd never relax completely until I knew Robert was safe too.

'Do you have any updates for us?' Steve asked.

'We do. We have more information about why there were so many babies in the house, what they were there for,' Inspector Johnson said.

The smile slid off my face. I sat up straighter. Steve let Alice down onto the rug and she toddled off to her toy box. He sat next to me on the sofa. I couldn't stop staring at Rose's perfect little face, the long eyelashes and creamy skin. Where was Robert at that very moment? Who was holding him, feeding him? When Mum had finished giving out the tea, I passed Rose into her arms. Mum's smile shone in her eyes and softened her face, reminding me of when she was younger. Steve reached for my hand and kissed it.

'We have found evidence in the second house Brown was hiding in that the babies were being sold on to wealthy families around the world, for substantial sums of money.'

'What?' I stroked Rose's downy hair.

'Jesus.' Steve frowned. 'How much for exactly?'

'Up to £120,000 for a boy, £80,000 for a girl.'

No wonder Malcolm was so keen on wanting boys.

Steve smacked his hand to his forehead. Mum tutted.

'Unfortunately, we believe your son has already been sold,' WPC Reed said.

'No, no, please don't say that,' I whispered.

'Shit!' Steve sat up straight. 'So, hang on, we willingly gave our son to a criminal and he sold him to a complete stranger?'

'We're doing all we can to trace Robert,' the policewoman said. 'We've recovered a lot of paperwork and we're confident we'll be able to find out where he's been taken to.'

'Do you think they're kind people?' My voice was barely audible.

'We can't know what sort of people they are at this stage. I'm sorry.' The policewoman glanced at the inspector. His Adam's apple moved up and down before he spoke.

'The woman we arrested at the property was pretending to be married to Brown, like Paula Bennett was. He used them to draw surrogates in. She's given us a wealth of information. We're not dealing with one man here. He's part of a highly organised international baby-selling ring.'

'Jesus! How were we to know that?' Steve stared at me.

'There's no way you could have known, except maybe if you'd got to know them better first. It's possible you may have suspected something, but not necessarily, because, as you said, they were very convincing. Paula was given scripts to learn, told what not to say. Even if you'd done a search for them on the internet, you may never have picked up on it. Brown deliberately selected young vulnerable women like you. Ones that could do with the extra cash, that wouldn't ask too many questions, or be picky about the paperwork. They had the fake parental orders all ready to go, which is why they didn't take long to process. And the regular trips abroad were to meet potential buyers for the babies they advertised on the internet.'

I shivered.

'Hang on, you mean they advertised our babies for sale?' Steve frowned.

'I'm afraid so. The client would visit a specifically set up website, browse through the surrogate mothers, pick the one that suited them according to height, colouring and due date. They targeted rich couples prepared to pay big money for a blonde-haired white British baby like yours.'

'There were pictures of me on their website?' I could hardly take it in.

'Yes, every time you sent them a photo update showing your bump, it was uploaded.'

My mind flicked through all the intimate photos I'd emailed them at various stages of my pregnancy. Some of me wearing only a long T-shirt or a cropped top and low-slung joggers. People I didn't know sizing me up like I was a golden goose.

'Who does that? Who buys a baby they've never seen from someone they barely know?' Steve opened his hands and snapped them shut again.

'He'd meet the couples who registered an interest on the site. They could be anywhere in the world. He'd often tell them the same story, that the original couple the baby was meant for had changed their minds, and now this poor little baby didn't have a family to go to. They'd fall for it, thinking they were doing a good thing, saving a child.'

'Playing with people's lives, with their feelings,' I said.

'We also found out that the woman following you is head of the European cell. Her job was to keep tabs on all their surrogates. It appears she bailed out of the country as soon as the news broke about Paula's death. Interpol are assisting us in our hunt for her. Brown was a middle man, running the South East UK cell.'

'This is big business then?' Steve said.

'It's huge, especially in Asia. Europe is a relatively new target. Sources tell us it's possible the root goes right back to a new branch of the Russian mafia, run by women.'

'By women?' Mum said.

'Why would any woman do that?' I took Rose back and kissed her nose. She blew a tiny bubble from her lips.

'They hire agents like Brown to find surrogates on these unregulated forums. They make sure the women are in low-paid jobs, young and healthy; blonde-haired, blue-eyed are first choice, graded down.'

'Like cattle,' I said, running a hand over my hair.

'They're paid a good price, more than the women could ever expect to receive in their normal working lives; more than a year's wages in many cases.'

'And we were sucked in.' I sighed. I wasn't sure how much more I could listen to.

'The agents, like Brown, would go and interview the potential parents, make sure they had the money to pay, and take a big deposit from them. Like I said before, babies are being sold all over the world for premium prices. He'd get a healthy cut, the European agent a bigger cut and the rest goes back to whoever is running this. Unfortunately, selling babies is a lucrative business.'

'And what about Brenda? She seemed such a lovely woman. I completely trusted her.'

'Brown groomed lonely women like Brenda, befriending them online, letting them believe they were in a relationship with him. He'd meet up with them, gain their confidence, then abduct them from their families, force them to pose as his wife, as part of a childless couple to lure surrogates like you. Being a couple made it more convincing. In the UK, parental orders in surrogacy cases can only be granted to couples. Brenda knew that if she didn't comply, the lives of Nathan and their sons were under threat from this criminal gang. Once she'd completed her role and the baby had successfully been handed over to Brown, the woman would be allowed to return to her family, but only on pain of death should she ever breathe a word about it or where she'd been to anyone. Obviously any delay, such as your miscarriage, would have made the process longer and more distressing for her. All she would have wanted was to go home to her family.'

'And because of me, she never got to do that.' I'd never forgive myself for not trying harder to help her.

'You can't blame yourself, Charlotte,' Mum said.

'Malcolm was controlling. He barely let Brenda out of his sight. But he seemed kind and sensitive too. I'd never have guessed this was behind it all,' I said.

'Nor me.' Steve reached for my hand and linked his fingers through mine.

'There is something else we need to tell you.' WPC Reed looked pensive, biting her lip. How could there be anything else left?

'We did a DNA test on Malcolm – Leslie Brown, to confirm that he is indeed the biological father of all the babies.'

'Sick bastard.' Steve spat the words out.

'That is, all except for Rose.' The policewoman fixed her eyes on mine, then Steve's.

'Really?' I frowned.

Steve dug his fingers into his hairline.

'We'd like you to do a DNA test, Steve.'

We stared at each other, and then I smiled. Mum patted my knee.

'Yeah, of course.' He laughed but looked like he might cry.

'Unless...' WPC Reed cocked her head and squinted at me.

'There couldn't ever be anyone else.' I squeezed Steve's hand. 'We had sex several days after the insemination, but I thought we'd left enough time.' He nodded at me, struggling to hold back his tears.

'You're saying Rose and Robert could be mine, right?' Steve asked.

'Almost certainly, yes,' the policewoman said. The inspector folded his arms and tipped back in his chair with a satisfied grin.

'That's the best thing I've heard all day.' I crumpled onto Steve's shoulder. He already treated Rose as his own daughter, but for them to be a match would be incredible. 'We'll need you both to give evidence in court when we've pieced everything together,' the policewoman said. She took Steve's DNA sample.

'Of course. We need to stop them doing this again.' Steve took Rose from me. 'Can we do anything to help you find our son?'

'Leave it to us,' the inspector said.

We all stood up and shook hands.

I glanced at Mum. All I could hear in my head was her saying I'd sold my own children, and it turned out to be true. I wished I'd listened to her. If we didn't get Robert back, I didn't know if I could live with that mistake for the rest of my life.

Chapter Sixty-Five

After lunch, Mum took Alice to the park while Rose slept. I tried to sleep too but I couldn't with Robert on my mind all the time. I held the stripy blue and white cotton hat he'd worn to come out of hospital. I'd heard from a few of the other surrogates used by Malcolm. Some were looking to get their babies back too. The rest of the babies found in the house had been put up for adoption.

We spent the next few days in limbo. Mum looked after us, cooking meals and helping out with Alice, while we spent time getting to know Rose. I continued to keep the Twitter campaign going. More and more people were realising how much the law needed to be tightened up. I called Dad, then Sarah and Paul in Sheffield to update them on everything that had happened. They promised to come down and visit us soon. I made an effort to play with Alice while Rose slept, but I was so distracted, wondering if our son was still in the UK, if he was safe. Was it even possible to have him returned to us when these people had paid so much money for him? Who were they? What kind of people bought babies? I hoped they'd looked after him well. Steve went to work and came home as usual, but he seemed lost in his own thoughts too.

The day Inspector Johnson came back, Steve had the morning off work and Mum took Alice to the library. As soon as we shook hands, I sensed he had good news.

'I can confirm that you are indeed the biological father of the twins, Steve,' he said, unable to contain his smile.

'Wow… that's incredible news.' Steve cupped his hand over his mouth.

'I can't believe they're completely ours.' I linked my arm through his.

'I also need to tell you that we've found your son.'

'Really? Is he OK?' I cried. 'Where is he?' I felt for Steve's hand and held it tight.

'Dublin. Sold to an Irish woman with an American husband. We have evidence to suggest they were planning to move to the US quite soon.'

'God, imagine that. We may never have tracked them down. Have they looked after him?' I asked.

'He's been very well cared for. He's being brought back to the UK under the Haig Convention, so he'll go into emergency foster care for now, but I'm sure your case is strong enough to have him returned to you, especially now that you have Rose and you've both been proven to be the biological parents.'

'Do you know how much they paid?' Steve squinted. I didn't want to know.

'A hundred thousand euros.'

'Bloody hell.'

'What happens about the money? Does it mean they can fight us to keep him?' I asked.

'The money they paid is irrelevant in law. The child's welfare is paramount. I doubt they'd have a chance. Your child has effectively been abducted from you. They may even face charges.'

'I actually feel sorry for them. They must have been pretty desperate to pay that much for a child,' Steve said.

'They maintain they had the best of intentions – to create the family they always wanted. I understand IVF failed several times for them and the man was too old to adopt.'

'That's so sad. Can you tell us their names?' Why couldn't we have found a genuine couple like them?

'Tom and Mary Sutton. Look, I know this probably isn't the right time for you to make any kind of decision, but they're desperate to get in touch with you, when all this is over. They're heartbroken at losing Robert. I'm sure you understand.'

Steve and I held hands and looked at each other. I nodded, unable to speak for a second.

'We're grateful he went to good people. I don't think we'd have a problem letting them know how he is,' Steve said. He squeezed my hand and I squeezed back.

'When can Robert come home?' My voice sounded strange but level, my heart jumping. 'Their paperwork from Malcolm must be fake too?'

'I'm sure that's the case. You'll still need to see a lawyer. It'll probably be a lengthier process than before. But, in all honesty, I can't imagine any judge is going to deny Robert the chance to come home to his birth parents and twin sister. It's the ideal outcome all round. I'm sure the court will see it that way.'

'I hope so too,' I said.

Epilogue

Mum had organised for us to visit a farm and play centre with outdoor rides, climbing frames and a picnic area in the woods. From the outside, we probably looked like any normal fun-loving family. But this was our first proper day out, all together.

It hadn't taken too long for Robert to come home, thanks to Inspector Johnson and Lorna Drake backing us up again. His return to the UK had made front-page news. Every time I was interviewed, I took the opportunity to talk about the inadequate surrogacy law in the UK. Now it was being debated everywhere, even on *Question Time* and in Parliament. I was proud of myself for speaking up. It was good that people were listening to someone like me.

Steve lay on the grass, his head in my lap, the twins parked next to us in their double buggy, having a sleep while Mum took Alice to see the rabbits.

'Dad emailed to say he's coming over to visit us next month.'

'Have you told your mum?'

'Not yet.'

He pulled a funny face.

'I had one from Tom and Mary too. They've been given the go-ahead to adopt a baby girl from China. Isn't that great news?'

'I'm pleased for them. We should all meet up before they move to America.'

'That would be lovely.'

'Can you believe these two are almost five months old?'

I kissed their tiny toes. Whenever I looked at them, time seemed to slow down. I marvelled at every smile and every special moment. I touched the three little rings hanging from my necklace.

I'd never forget how lucky I was.

A Letter From Ruby

Hello!

Thank you so much for taking the time to read my debut novel, *Someone Else's Baby*. It's both exciting and terrifying sending my first book out into the world.

Thank you for joining me on Charlotte's journey. If you enjoyed *Someone Else's Baby*, I would really appreciate it if you could leave a review.

The idea for *Someone Else's Baby* came from watching a TV programme, where a young surrogate gave birth to a baby for a couple who'd been struggling to conceive for years. I was transfixed by this kind young woman. But when she handed the baby over, she looked forlorn, slightly 'rabbit caught in headlights'. The pregnancy and birth hadn't been as easy as she'd expected.

In my writer head I began to wonder about all the things that could go wrong. What if the surrogate didn't really know the couple she was handing her baby to? What if the intended parents lied about who they really were? When I researched my ideas, I was shocked to find that many of the terrible things I imagined are going on somewhere in the world.

The whole subject of surrogacy has fascinated me for years, because I know I would find it hard to give a baby away. Surrogates are very special people – to be able to give such a gift is incredible.

I find I'm drawn to write about subjects and circumstances that scare me, and as a writer, putting myself in a character's predicament isn't always easy!

I love hearing from readers, so do get in touch via Twitter, Facebook, Goodreads or through my website.

Thank you very much for your support.

Ruby x

www.herabooks.com/authors/ruby-speechley/
@rubyspeechley
Rubyspeechley.com

Acknowledgments

Firstly, thank you for everything, Mum and Dad. You passed on your love of words to me even before I could read and nurtured my early devotion to writing.

I'm indebted to my tutors, mentors, writer friends and many other friends and family not in the writing world. Thank you all for your kindness and never giving up on me.

Special mention to my dear friend, Susan Elliot Wright, who is always the first writer I tell about a new idea. If she is excited about it, as she was with this one, then I know I'm onto something. Huge thanks to Sara Sarre, editor extraordinaire at the Blue Pencil Agency, for always going above and beyond, especially with this novel. To Richard Skinner, the kindest, most nurturing teacher there is, who believed in me when I needed it most. To Jill Dawson whose encouragement since the early years has bolstered and sustained me. To my kind and generous MA tutor, Lesley Glaister, for her patience in guiding me through writing my first novel. To Wendy Bough, founder of the Caledonia Novel Award, who has shown me extraordinary kindness. To my WoMentoring mentor, Vanessa Fox O'Loughlin, to Keith Jebb, Angela Clarke, Julia McCutchen and Edwina Biucchi, for showing me the way forward. Thanks too to and the organisers of the Festival of Writing in York and The Arvon Foundation.

Thanks to my early readers, Fiona Mitchell, Alison Marlow, Rose McGinty, Lucille Grant, Rebecca Williams, Isabel

Costello and Susan Elliot Wright. Each one of you has helped to make this a better book.

Thanks to my many writer friends on and offline, for always championing me, reading my work and giving me advice when I've needed it, in particular to: Jude Brown, Caroline Priestly, Louise Jensen, Vicky Newham, Louise Mangos, Jane Roberts, Amanda Saint, Debi Alper, Britta Jensen, Tina Death, Debra Brown, Amanda Reynolds and all my Faber Academy novel writing group: Emma Goode, Laura Church, Isaac Jay, Cleo Harrington, Emma Cook, Mia Roberts, Phil Cavanagh, Kate Poll, Nicola Bye, Claire Cowburn Baker and Louise Macqueron.

Huge thanks to my agent, Jo Bell at Bell Lomax Moreton, for her constant belief, enthusiasm and kindness. Thanks to my incredible editor, Keshini Naidoo, who immediately understood the real story I was trying to tell. And to her fellow publisher at Hera Books, Lindsey Mooney – I'm so proud to be published by this dynamic female-led independent publisher.

Connie Atkinson, International Surrogacy Lawyer, and Hayley Lloyd, Senior Practitioner Social Worker, both helped immensely with my endless questions. I researched and read many articles, surrogacy websites and personal accounts, too numerous to list. Any mistakes are entirely my own. I want to thank the surrogacy community for everything they do to make surrogacy a safe, positive and fulfilling experience.

Finally, special thanks to my eldest son, Charlie, for his unwavering encouragement and love. To my husband Richard, for his support in every possible way, and most of all, for never doubting me. And to my youngest son and daughter, Edward and Sophie, for reminding me every day that I'm loved.